GRAVE BIRDS

GRAVE BIRDS

DANA ELMENDORF

/ll MIRA

/IIMIRA™

ISBN-13: 978-0-7783-8747-3

Grave Birds

Mira
22 Adelaide St. West, 41st Floor
Toronto, Ontario M5H 4E3, Canada
MIRABooks.com

Printed in U.S.A.

To Luke Dalton, may you always forge your own path.
I am in awe of your talent and so very proud of you.
Love you kiddo, Mom

GRAVE
BIRDS

Hell is empty, and all the devils are here.

—The Tempest, William Shakespeare

PROLOGUE

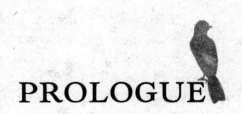

SOMETIMES THE DEAD have unfinished business.

"You see it, don't you, Hollis?" Mr. Royce Gentry's deep, rumbling voice stamped the air with white puffs. He squatted low next to my chair and nodded toward my grandaddy's grave where his coffin was being lowered into the ground. The men, Grandaddy's dearest friends, slowly filled in the dirt, one mournful shovelful at a time.

Cold frosted the morning dew into a thin white crust that covered the grass. There, off to the side, was a little bluebird, tethered to the earth by an invisible thread. It twittered a helpless, frantic sound as it desperately flapped, struggling to get loose. Delicate and transparent, it looked as if it was made of colored air. Muted, so the hues didn't quite punch through. It was a pitiful sight, the poor thing trying so hard to get back up in the sky.

A ghost bird, I had first thought when I saw it. Until I looked around and found there were many, many more in the cemetery.

It was a grave bird.

I swallowed hard and pretended I didn't know what Mr. Gentry was talking about. "No, sir. I don't see nothing," I said as I continued to stare at the phantom.

He gave me a scrutinizing look. He saw the lie in my eyes. But he let it go, for the now anyways.

I was only eleven; I didn't want to admit I was different. But I knew I was whether I liked it or not and would always be.

I had never so much as uttered a *hello* to Mr. Gentry until five days before. He's the one who pulled me from the freezing river and brought me back to life. Not by means of magic or a miracle, but with science: medical resuscitation for thirty-two minutes.

But a miracle happened all the same.

The adults stood around my grandaddy's grave, murmuring their condolences to my granny and my momma. It was that awkward moment after a funeral is finished where everyone seemed lost about what to do next, but we all knew we were going back to Granny's house to a slew of casseroles and desserts that would barely get eaten. Two of my distant cousins, bored from the bother of my grandfather dying, kicked around a fallen pine cone over an even more distant relative's nearby grave. Mrs. Yancey, our neighbor up the road, had just taken my twin brothers home since they were squalling something terrible, confused as to why we would trap Grandaddy in the ground. I watched as Mr. Gentry talked closely to Mrs. Belmont's son, who was visiting from New York City, but his flirting, normally an immersed habit, was on autopilot as he watched me watching the grave bird. Could Mr. Gentry see it, too?

Mr. Gentry was a Southern gentleman, who put a great deal of care into perfecting the standard. His suits were custom-made from a tailor in Charleston, who drove up just to measure him, then hand-delivered the pieces when they were finished. It didn't matter your standing in society, Mr. Gentry treated the most common among us as his equal.

He lived a lush lifestyle, filled with grand parties attended by foreign dignitaries, congressmen and anyone powerful he could gain favor with. Several times a year he traveled across Europe, something his job as a foreign consultant required of him. His friends, just as colorful as him, lived life to the fullest. A dedicated husband once, until his wife found interest in someone half her age. His two grown daughters, who didn't respect his choice in who to love, eventually wanted nothing to do with him. I think it left a big hole in his heart and what drew him to help our family out.

IN THE WEEKS after the funeral, Mr. Gentry began to fill the empty space in our lives where Grandaddy once stood. It started with an offer to cover the funeral costs, a gesture my granny refused at first, but it was money we didn't have and desperately needed. Then it was the crooked porch he insisted on fixing. Rolled up his starched white sleeves and did it himself, like hard labor was something he was used to doing. The henhouse fence got mended next. A tire on the tractor that hadn't run in a year was replaced. Then our bellies grew accustomed to feeling full on fine meals he swore were simply leftovers from his latest dinner party. They were going to be tossed, and we were doing him a favor by taking them off his hands. Beef Wellington, with its buttery crust and tender meat center, so savory I'd melt in my chair from the sheer bliss of a single bite. It felt sacrilegious to eat lobster bisque from Granny's cracked crockery, but that didn't stop me from slurping up every last creamy bite. And nothing yanked me out of the bed faster than the sweet buttermilk and vanilla scent of beignets. If a stomach could smile, I'm sure mine did. And often, whenever Mr. Gentry needed his fridge clear.

There's a bond that comes with somebody saving your life. Our friendship became something built on the purest of love. Where he had stepped into my life and filled the important role my grandaddy had once represented, I helped him heal the ache from being denied the chance to be a loving father.

A few months after my grandfather was put in the ground, Uncle Royce—who he eventually became—took me back out to the church's cemetery. He sat me down on the graveyard bench, a place you go when you want to sit a spell with the dead. The mound of dirt from my grandfather's grave had rounded from the heavy rain, slowly melting back into the earth.

He told me what I already knew, that I would be different now after the accident. He knew because the same thing had happened to him.

"You and I share something special," Uncle Royce started his story. We were two people who had been clinically dead then brought back to life. *Lazarus syndrome* he said they called it. Only months ago for me. Near forty years for him.

He had died for twelve minutes. Knocked plum out of his shoes when a car hit him at twenty-two years old. He says he stood over himself, barefoot, watching them work on his body. He thought he was going to ascend into the bright light but instead was sucked back into his body and woke up a few days later in the hospital.

A chill shivered up my spine: it was almost exactly what I had experienced.

I had felt myself float up and away from the river; I was no longer cold and wet. Sad or scared. An aura of peace enveloped me—or rather became me.

It had seemed like I hovered there forever in that state of infinite understanding. A warmth emanated from above, a light formed from all that came before me.

From the bright light my grandfather's voice reached out. His gentle words, simply known and not heard, urged me to go back. It wasn't my time yet. My place was still at home.

In a swooping rush, I was vacuumed back inside myself. I spat up a gush of water. My lungs burned. My body was freezing cold again. And Mr. Gentry was smiling down on me saying,

"That a girl. Get it all out." Far off down the road an ambulance cried that it was coming.

"You know what I think they are?" Uncle Royce said now, pointing to all the birds who were trapped, defeated, most of the color leached from their feathers. I didn't say anything, still not wanting to confirm that he was right, that I could see them. I just listened. "I think they're a kind of representation—a manifestation—of the dead's unresolved issues." I didn't know what he meant by that, but it sounded heavy and important, and that felt about right.

I could see it, in a way. Grandaddy had been mad at me before we went off the bridge. I'd stolen a gold-colored haircomb, complete with rhinestones across its curved top, as pretty as a peacock's feathers, from Roy's Drugstore. When Grandaddy found out, he had yanked me up by the arm, angry that the preacher's granddaughter would shame her family in such a manner.

He was scolding me on the truck ride home when I started crying about not having pretty things like the other girls at school.

He paused his lecture for a minute, and I could tell this bothered him; I could see the way it saddened his eyes. He was the preacher at a poor country church where shoes were often scuffed, clothes mended instead of replaced, and a good meal was something scarce. Family and Jesus were what was important. I found I felt small next to all the wealthy girls who attended the big, fancy church with their new shoes, their starched dresses, the silk ribbons in their hair. It made my poverty stand out, and I didn't like it.

Then Grandaddy said envy was one of the seven deadly sins, and I was setting myself up for a lifetime of grief by wanting others to love me for what I had instead of who I was. Shame welled over me, whether he intended it to or not.

I was crying something fierce, but I knew he was right. But hard lessons aren't easy to accept. Instead of apologizing or even letting him know I understood, I told him I hated him. Screamed it as loud as my young lungs could. Couldn't say who it shocked more, him or me. I wished those words back into my mouth as soon as they were out.

But it was too late.

A construction truck crossed the road on our right, not waiting long enough for other cars or paying enough attention. It smashed into the side of our truck and pushed us over the railing and off the bridge, down into the Greenie River.

"You should tell him you forgive him," Uncle Royce said, pointing to the mound of earth under which my grandaddy now lay.

"Forgive *him*?" Clearly, he didn't understand. I was the one who'd stolen something, who'd made my own grandaddy so ashamed, so disappointed. I was the one who'd spewed words of hate in our last moments together.

I had survived, and my grandaddy was dead.

If I hadn't have stolen that comb, he never would have come to town to fetch me.

He never would have died.

"He doesn't want you to think it's your fault. He feels bad he scolded you so severely over stealing that haircomb."

I turned my head slowly toward Uncle Royce. He couldn't have known about the comb: no one did.

"How do you know about that?" I said on whispered breath, almost too faint to hear.

He looked me straight in the eye. "Because his grave bird showed me."

CHAPTER ONE

BAD OMENS FALL in seventeens, according to Granny. Today is the seventeenth of May. It has rained nonstop for seventeen days, and this year marks the return of the seventeen-year cicadas. I didn't know hell was coming to Hawthorne, South Carolina. But sure enough, I'm sitting in the salon when the devil strolls down the middle of Main Street.

"Sweet Jesus," Miss Delilah mumbles as she quirks her tin-foiled head to peer out the salon's window. "Who is that tall drink of water?" Her old voice crispy, like tissue paper.

I feel the heat of him, even before I lay eyes on him.

As I turn my head and look out the window, the sun parts the rain clouds and shines its light on the man, an omen if I've ever seen one. Dressed in a sapphire-blue suit with a matching vest, he looks timeless and vintage all at once. His tie, dove-gray silk, hints to a vulgar wealth. A boutonniere made of game-bird feathers adorns his lapel. His face, as if carved from marble, is smooth and lean with a contoured jawline. It contrasts with his soft wavy hair. His long, assured strides eat up the ground, like a man with a purpose. He could have been born and bred from Hawthorne royalty with how he is dressed. None of us know him—though, we'll soon find out just who and what he is.

"Damn, I'm going to need a good whiskey to quench this thirst," Calista Franco, the salon's owner, says after getting a good look for herself. She guides Miss Delilah back to her chair, neither one of them taking their eyes off the man.

As he walks farther down the street, all the white dogwood blooms start to weep bloodred drops onto the sidewalk as he passes. The inky color diffuses onto the rain-soaked concrete into fat blurs, disappearing as quickly as it appears.

But it isn't the blood that scares me.

It's the grave bird perched on the man's shoulder. A fat little robin with a rusty-orange throat and a grayish-brown body, and it looks right at me.

"Oh shit," Calista says and jumps back from the window.

I startle, too, wondering if she saw the bird as well.

"He's coming this way," she says. Then she pats her rock star–teased hair and checks herself in the mirror before returning to me and the haircut she is supposed to be giving.

I look like a drowned rat with my hair sopping wet. Brown strands stick to my cheeks as the water runs down the smock and pools in my lap.

Nadine, even though she's freshly married, peers over the top of her *Southern Living* magazine, getting an eyeful. "False alarm." She slaps her magazine shut. "He's going into Boucher's next door." A premier real estate agency that specializes in grand estates.

There's a collective sigh of disappointment. Then the ladies break into a chatter of who he could be, where he's from, what he's doing here. Hope for him to be single lingers in the air. Calista's blow-dryer drowns out their voices as she styles my hair.

But my mind is still focused on the bird, filled with worry for what it means. It's been a few years since I've seen one: they're easily avoidable if you don't go to cemeteries. And I've rarely seen one outside a graveyard. And never attached to a live person.

"Hollis." Calista squeezes my shoulders, pulling me out of my daze. "What do you think?" She fluffs up my new shag cut as she eyes her work. Huge improvement. My long straight hair has served me well through college, but Calista declared a change was long overdue. "You look like you belong in the Pentecostal Church," she'd said an hour ago with a hand on her hip, determination in her eyes, and scissors at the ready.

As one of my two best friends, she says she's allowed to insult me, as long as it's for my own good, and it would seem my own good requires a hefty dose from time to time.

Looking in the mirror, I turn my head to soak in the new cut from all angles: I don't look like myself anymore. I like it. Nor am I used to these bangs, but I love them.

"Leave it." Calista swats my hand away when I go to play with my hair. "You want to look good for your appointment with the bank, don't you?" I nod. "Then, don't fuck up my masterpiece." Her lips curl into a crooked smile, like one side got snagged on a fishing hook. It matches her style. Her curled, short-in-the-front, long-in-the-back hair. T-shirts always black, featuring some obscure band. Jeans are edgy and something she finds at thrift stores. She looks like old-school punk merged with British fashion.

Women drive all the way from Charleston and Savannah and pay ridiculous amounts of money to get a haircut by the Calista Franco from New York. (Her dad's a restaurant owner from Upstate New York who's rumored to cater to Mafia clientele.) Lucky for me, I can still get the friends and family discount because I live on the edge of broke and starving.

As Calista pulls free the cape draped over me, chunks of my brown hair fall to the floor. I stand, shaking out my new do, marveling at the magic Calista can manage with a pair of scissors.

Maybe now I'll look closer to my age, or older if I'm lucky. Most banks aren't known for giving loans out to twenty-six-year-olds with sketchy credit history and inconsistent sources of income, even if they are trying to start their own company.

"Nadine?" Calista says. The way she stresses Nadine's name—from the tone alone—I know what she's getting at.

"What's wrong with my outfit?" I picked out a sensible white blouse and black skirt for this meeting.

Nadine Honeycutt, best friend number two, could have been Donna Summer's granddaughter. Just like the infamous disco queen, her fashion style is luxurious and dazzling, never mundane. Her father is one of the wealthiest Black men in the state, owning several of the most prominent funeral homes throughout the Carolinas. But that's not the first takeaway from meeting him or her. Nadine is a sweet, gentle soul, with a heart full of kindness. She spends most of her time volunteering at the local Veterans Association, seeing as how her father served in the Gulf War: she knows what those men suffered through.

Nadine turns in the chair she's been sitting in next to me, flicking through a magazine, her mind temporarily occupied by the latest celebrity gossip. She takes one look at my outfit and pinches the bridge of her nose. "Are you trying to get a job as the school's lunch lady? Because you're hired."

"Do they still have lunch ladies at schools?" I ask and am thoroughly ignored.

"Give me those." Nadine points to Calista's black pumps, which she dutifully kicks off—thankfully we wear the same size. Calista reluctantly accepts my dull tan flats in exchange. Nadine hikes my black skirt up high on my waist, shortening the length to above my knees. She pops the collar of my white blouse then untucks it, tying a knot in the front. She then orders me to swap earrings—my dinky silver hoops for her gold diamond studs. And finally, she ties the designer handkerchief from her purse (Hermès, I'm sure) around my wrist like a colorful cuff.

"Better," she declares, stepping back to assess her work.

I look back to the mirror. It isn't so much that I looked like a slump before, but Nadine has kicked me up a notch, that's for sure.

"Wait." Nadine steps back in and loosely cuffs my short sleeves so they hood over my shoulders. "Done."

"Classic eighties chic. Nice." Calista knuckle-bumps Nadine. "Now, go get that loan."

I glance at the clock on the wall: twenty minutes until my appointment. Plenty of time to arrive early and take a few minutes to look over my paperwork in the lobby.

"Right. Here I go!" I say as I back out of there with their *good lucks* and *goodbyes*.

As I turn around, I smack into someone and immediately flail backward, losing my step. An arm swiftly wraps around my waist to catch me.

Trying to right myself, my hands instinctually grab ahold of the lapels of his blue suit directly in front of me. I glance up and into a pair of dark, malevolent eyes. There's a pause where I seem to be caught in midair, fully absorbed in the man's gaze, the din of the salon having faded away.

"Oh" is all I manage to say before the grave bird on his shoulder tweets.

We both yank our attention to the tiny bird. I watch as it hops off the man's shoulder and onto mine.

And then—my body is pulled backward out of the present, like I'm falling somewhere into the past.

A day. A decade. A century.

I can't be sure.

The heady smell of rich earth grounds me as I run through the lush green palms. The sweet taste of banana lingers on my tongue. Bright sunlight flickers through the tree canopy high above, reminding me of the punctured tin lantern that fractures candlelight against my bedroom walls as it spins.

Playful foreign words from the woman chasing me enliven my steps. Joy fills my belly with giddy bursts of laughter, and I run faster. Large fern fronds tickle my legs as I rush through them.

Until I fall off the edge of nothing and into the burning smoke.

I land on a pile of giant silkworm cocoons, larger than my little body. They wiggle and writhe underneath. I, too, am a mummy, wrapped in white muslin sheets, squirming to get free. Their chrysalides split open, and out pops a bird from each one. Hundreds of them. Of every color and kind.

Their tiny wings flap with might, and yet the ground will not set them free. They push me up, lift me higher than the flames, giving me my own wings. Chirping I must go. To hurry, hurry and fly away home.

Eventually I do.

Let the earth rattle from the devil's arrival. And the skies darken when death rains its wings upon them. When the flames descend from the sky, they shall know their end is near. Their seed will be laid bare for they are not worthy of their name. The heavens will disappear with a roar. Into the lake of fire the guilty will be cast.

Vengeance will be mine.

"Hey, dickhead!" I hear Calista yell. "*Excuse me* is the polite thing to say," she hollers after the man as he hurries off down the sidewalk—the bird no longer on his shoulder and now no longer in sight.

Nadine rushes out. "Are you okay, Hollis?" she asks, helping me pick up my papers off the ground.

"Oh dear," Miss Delilah says, as she watches from the doorway. Over me falling or Calista's colorful language, I'm not sure.

My head whirs from the moment in time the grave bird wanted me to see. So visceral I felt as if I was there. Breathing the smoky air. Hearing the sounds. Feeling the fear. A walk through the dead's past. When and where I have no idea.

But it wasn't all the past, was it? It seemed as if something dark stepped in, there at the end, with a warning. Almost bib-lical in nature. How is that possible?

"You sure you're okay?" Calista asks, pulling me to my feet, tugging me from my spiraling thoughts. "You look a little peaked."

I only realize now that I'd fallen over, that he must have let go of me. I feel swimmy, like I've been on a boat all day, and now that I'm back on land I have sea legs. How did that man pick up someone's grave bird? He had to have seen it, too. He must have.

I shake my head, shrugging off the million questions I have—about the man, about the bird, about the vision.

About the devil coming to Hawthorne.

I look the direction where he disappeared.

I knead a cold ache cramping my right shoulder. "Yeah. Just dazed is all." I take from her the last of my paperwork. Miss Delilah asks if I take meds for low blood sugar. "No, ma'am. I'm not diabetic." Then I catch a glimpse of the time on my cell phone. "Shit, I'm going to be late."

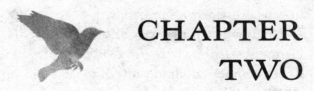

CHAPTER TWO

FIRST SOUTH BANK has sat in the same spot since it was built in the seventies, a stone's throw from the courthouse. Hints of its dated past sneak through, showing its age. The brass chandelier's patina has dulled to a brownish green, its glass globe ribboned with a harvest-gold band of flowers. Original knotty-pine wood paneling bleeds through the cream paint slapped on after the last makeover two decades ago. Even a scalloped magnolia wallpaper border running along the top of the wall screams of an era long since passed.

Three years I've worked to build my event planning business. It started with helping the local schools with their fundraisers, then it grew to include children's birthday parties and baby showers. Until I've finally impressed the upper echelon of Hawthorne enough, they're seeking me out to plan their anniversaries and holiday parties and even their weddings. This loan is what will take me to the next level.

Through the office windows I watch as my loan officer, Lizzy Biggins, talks with the bank manager about my file. This is the third time this month I've had to come in to sign the loan documents, as one small issue after another has held up everything being finalized. I'm starting to think we have another Grady Owens situation on our hands.

Grady was a cantankerous old man. He lived at the end of Hennessey Lane where the road disappeared into a dirt path. About another hundred yards or so later and you'd find Grady's place. A rickety shack that stood on stilts high above an old marsh that had long since dried up when they put in the levee so they could build the new subdivision.

Grady didn't like children. Or the government. Or people in general. But there was one thing he did love: his land. Selling it was not an option.

Some say Grady got his money during moonshine days. Others believe he had family up in Southern Illinois who owned oil wells, and he collected a fat check every month. He never had children. Or none that we knew of. I don't think he was ever married. The only friends he had were the animals that lived on his land. Some fifteen acres at the edge of Hawthorne where the town grew around him over time. He refused to sell one stitch of his property, not even to allow an access road through. He lived out there all by himself and preferred it that way.

So when he died, no one had a clue.

Except me.

For years, kids in Hawthorne would dare each other to trespass into the woods on Grady's land. For anyone able to bring back a piece of his crumbling house, you got endless bragging rights. Since I had died once before, everyone assumed I was extra brave. I was not. But I was extra curious.

Curiosity more than anything led me out and into the woods that day, traipsing through the trees and the former marshland, listening for animals or any other sign of life. Grady's shack wasn't a straight shot from the end of the lane. You could get lost if you didn't know how to read the moss and the sun. My nerves just about got the best of me and almost made me to turn back, but then I came upon the house at last. The old wood frame, with its rusty tin walls, had buckled to its knees as those stilt legs had snapped on one side. Unless he liked walking uphill to get to the other end of his house, I doubted very seriously anyone lived there anymore.

I quickly found out I was right.

A small fluttering caught my eye as a little bird jumped from the ground, only to be pulled back down the second it tried to get away. A grave bird. A fat gray-brown wren. Out in the middle of the woods, no cemetery around. It kept trying to get my attention.

My head told me to turn around and go back to the other kids empty-handed and forget about bragging rights.

But another part of me was saying it was my duty to set the bird free. Now I wasn't certain until I got right up on him, but the grave wasn't a traditional grave at all. Just scattered bones and tattered scraps of faded blue-jean fabric, probably from the overalls Grady was known for wearing. The hollowed eyes of his skull tufted with grass. It's where old Grady must have dropped dead, with his unfinished business and the grave bird manifested not long after.

It wasn't the first time I connected with the dead, but it was the first time the dead was aboveground. I would have run at the sight of his bones, but fear locked up my knees and glued me into place. Somewhere inside of me the obligation of what I could do, how I could help, nudged me forward.

I swallowed hard before I knelt down in the rotted leaves, close enough I could hold out my shaky hand for the little bird to perch. I don't know if birds can smile, but it felt like this one did. He took my invitation then and jumped right on my finger.

I felt myself fall backward, through the years.

Into the past.

She stands there next to a hundred-year-old oak tree in her butter-yellow dress, fitting snug across her bulging waist. She watches as the sun rises over Gunther Hill, the first place we ever kissed. The Queen Anne's lace itches the palm of my hand; the bouquet doesn't seem fitting for someone as refined as her. A no-nothing country boy like me doesn't deserve her love, but God bless it, she gave it to me anyway.

I'm so jittery it feels like agitated bees swarming in my belly. I wasn't gonna let the start of our new life begin without asking her to marry me first.

"Charlotte," I say as I kneel, holding up the bunch of flowers and the thinned silver ring my momma used to wear. When she turns, with the sun shining across her face, it takes my breath away. My heart beats so fast I'm certain I'll never catch it.

Her smile doesn't reach her eyes, though. Tears stain her cheeks. The whole world around me slows. Even the sun fears what's to come and shrinks behind a lone, dark cloud.

She doesn't have to say it because I already know. I'm sorry *are the last two words I ever hear from my only love's sweet lips.*

I never got my bragging rights. Nor did I go to the authorities to report I had found Grady's bones. The way I figured it, it was Grady's land, and he ought to hold on to it for as long as he could. It took about another two years before some business-man, looking to build more houses, went out there hoping to get the old man to sell. Then another two years for his property to be fought over, since no heir could be found.

Eventually, after going to court, the Hawthornes and their missionary church won the land in a city auction for much cheaper than it was worth—I mean, who's going to bid against God's missionaries? Those woods were chopped down, and they built forty houses in its place. Squeezed them together tighter than ticks on a dog. The Hawthornes got fat and wealthier.

That wasn't my first encounter with a grave bird, going back into the past, into a memory. Nor would it be my last.

Uncle Royce showed me how to listen to the grave birds over the years. Most of the time, just letting them take you on a walk into the past is enough to release the dead's guilt over any unfinished business they had left in this world and will set them free. Other times, the dead will hold on to their misery, unwilling to ever let go. Trapped to the grave forever. The rarest of times, they won't leave this world—or me—until I've finished their business for them.

From time to time I catch sight of Grady's small wren, watching me from the trees, following me around now that we've formally met. It's waiting for me to figure out how to fix what Grady couldn't while he was alive before it's fully free. There has to be at least a million Charlottes in South Carolina. Too many to find just the one. If she even was from South Carolina to begin with. But that fat little wren is patient, persistent.

I sit up taller as Lizzy Biggins returns to her office with my loan file in her hand.

Lizzy's long dark brown hair, with its polished shine, hangs down her back. Her nonprescription glasses lend her an authoritative, if impostor-like, quality. The Be Kind motto plaque on her desk is almost insulting coming from Lizzy: she's bad-mouthed and gossiped about more people than any other person in town. As her former friend, I should know.

The haughty air with which she takes her seat on the other side of her desk doesn't bode well for me.

"So, Hollis. Where is the detailed budget sheet for the Honeycutts' wedding?" Lizzy asks.

When Nadine married Jackson Honeycutt, the mayor's son, it was one of the grandest affairs held in Hawthorne in a long time. And one of the most coveted invitations. Papers from the neighboring counties wrote stories for weeks about how extravagant the reception was. Nadine says my innovative concepts and transformation of the venue made it spectacular. Her excellent taste and shrewd decision-making is what made the wedding perfect.

I'm no dummy. Lizzy wants the line-item details to Nadine's wedding so she can tell everyone she knows how much was spent and on what. Then she'll try to smear Nadine's good name, finding some flaw in how she spent her wedding money. There's no way I'm giving her the satisfaction. I haven't spent all my time and energy building an event planning business from scratch only to tarnish my reputation here at the goal line.

"My company's contract prohibits me from sharing my clients' personal finances." Then I lean in and whisper, "It's a common courtesy I'm sure even you can appreciate." Her face turns sour as mine grows smug.

"And yet I'm supposed to trust these numbers are accurate? We're supposed to just take your word that you have enough work lined up to pay the loan back on time? When we can't even see the projected personal revenue from said work? The bulk of your *income*," she emphasizes with air quotes, "is a small inheritance by a deceased nonfamily member, and if we're being honest . . . an unsavory member of the—"

I grit my teeth. "Royce Gentry was his name. And the details of this particular transaction aren't really relevant to my income. I have enough to cover the loan deposit the bank is asking for."

It has been a little over eleven months since Uncle Royce passed. He left me a hundred thousand dollars, with a proviso I'd do something spectacular with it. Using it to buy his house—or, rather, mansion—and turn it into Hawthorne's premiere event venue seems a fitting decision for the inheritance and my event planning business. His two daughters, who never had any interest in learning who their father truly was, only showed up to collect what he left them. Which ended up being a chunk of change substantially more than what he left me. They also got the contents of the house—minus an ornery butterscotch cat named Sampson and a sassy, swearing cockatiel named Louisa.

In regards to who would get the house, there was one stipulation: his godniece, Hollis Wade Sutherland, would get first rights to purchase the house at fair market value within one year.

I'm coming in by the skin of my teeth with only eighteen days left to make an offer.

God knows it's taken me the better part of the year to pull together the means to buy this place. No matter what the legalese says, I know the second we pass the one-year mark those daughters of Royce will sell his place in a heartbeat to someone else, like the developers who bought Grady's former property, guaranteeing more cookie-cutter homes packed into too-small neighborhoods that further drive the locals of Hawthorne out. A simple country girl like me would never have a chance against that. I'll feel a hell of a lot better once I sign these loan documents.

"Well, I'm not sure how many more rich benefactors you have left in your life, but the bank needs proof you're actually capable of successfully running a business and generating enough revenue to pay back the loan," she says, getting persnickety. I bite my tongue. For a business transaction, she's making this awfully personal.

I take a measured breath before I speak.

"All the bank needs is proof that I have sufficient income to carry the mortgage and twenty percent down. My last three tax returns, banks statements, and my credit report prove I'm capable."

"Yes," she says, dragging the word out painfully. "About that." She frowns at my credit report like it's a pitiful child begging for money. "This credit card debt is higher than First South Bank is comfortable with."

"Lizzy," I say, dropping her name rather frankly. "We already cleared this up in the beginning. You know very well my mother fraudulently opened a credit card in my name and ran up the bill then stopped paying it. Judge Michaels ordered for her paycheck—which runs through this bank, mind you—to be garnished until it's paid in full."

She quirks her head, staring at me with a blank, emotionless face.

She blinks once.

Twice.

"Hollis," she says, mocking my exasperated tone, "bank policy exclusively prohibits me from sharing a client's personal finances." Then she leans in to whisper. "It's a common courtesy I'm sure even you can appreciate."

I'm pretty sure I crack a tooth, biting down so hard.

"So." She happily claps my file shut. "Get a letter from Judge Michaels explaining what you're claiming, and we *might* be able to approve you for a loan." She stamps a big red PENDING on the manila folder and tosses it into a slush pile of other hopefuls.

I grip the handles of my satchel tightly. My eye feels twitchy. I'm scared if I unclench my teeth, I'll bite her head off. It's Friday, and I'll have to wait until Monday to get a letter from the judge—if she's not too busy with her court cases.

I have eighteen days left on my one year, three more won't matter, I tell myself.

"Thank you," I force myself to say. "I'll see you on Monday." I stand. A cold ache runs over my shoulder, the same place the grave bird had perched earlier. I shrug to work out the tightness. But an icy heat burns all the way to the bone.

"Monday it is." Lizzy's mouth forms a straight line: she can't even fake a smile. Then she sits up attentively, looking past me and into the lobby.

"Excuse me." She quickly rises, smoothing her hair and then checking herself in the window's reflection as she passes it. A huge smile pushes up her chubby cheeks, her eyes bright and hopeful.

I turn to leave her office and watch as the bank manager eagerly introduces her to the mysterious man in the blue suit.

"Lizzy," the manager says, "meet Cain Landry, one of our newest VIP clients."

I can't help but stare as I push past the now-forming crowd of employees all eager to assist Mr. Landry, but now that I see him closer there's an artistic quality to his features. A face that could have been painted by Michelangelo. The ceiling of the Sistine Chapel: an outstretched hand from God giving life to the first man. I can understand the crowd now.

"So nice to finally meet you." Lizzy stretches out her hand.

Cain has a pinched smile on his face as he shakes her hand, like he's unimpressed by her.

Huh. I huff a laugh. *I feel ya, buddy.*

Cain's eyes flit over to me. Sharp and keen. I feel a sudden jolt, like I've been run through.

A rattly crack of items begin to jitter on the bank clerk's counter. The vibration pulses across the floor, causing the whole room to shake.

"Is this an earthquake?" I hear Patrice Jackson ask as she braces herself in her office doorway. The other employees pause, some dart under their desks in anticipation of more shock waves.

I look up and watch the brass chandeliers swing back and forth. A bank patron darts out the front door. The manager calls out for everyone to stay calm, but my feet can't carry me fast enough. The giant faux-flower arrangement on the entrance table dances all the way to the edge and then crashes on the floor behind me as I pass.

That pain from my shoulder licks a flame across my back as I step out the bank's front door. A hot flash rips through me, and I respond with an unexpected hitch in my breath.

Outside, the world rights itself as if nothing is happening at all. I flap the front of my shirt to cool myself down, wondering if I'm losing my mind. I can't tell if my nerves are rattled or if my body is responding to the wicked warmth purring through me. I shudder, shaking off the last of those tingles.

What in the hell? I dare a glance through the bank's front window and watch as the three of them disappear into Lizzy's office.

Let the earth rattle from the devil's arrival.

Hell indeed.

CHAPTER THREE

"THAT BITCH," CALISTA MUMBLES. Wine bottle in hand, she sits crisscross on the chaise lounge on Nadine's balcony and pours herself another glass.

I shrug. "What can I do? Lizzy runs the loan department. I'm at her mercy." I dip a slice of French bread in the melted brie–honey medley Nadine made.

Nadine sighs. "What do you expect from a woman who spent our entire senior year reporting to the authorities every party she wasn't invited to?"

"Kick her ass is what we can do," Calista sneers, then takes a surly swig of her wine.

Nadine and I exchange amused looks.

From Nadine's third-story balcony, just beyond the thin line of forest, a sea of suburban rooftops chisel away at the landscape where Grady Owens's woods once stood. Streetlamps and porch lights riddle the carpet of darkness with twinkling orbs. From up here it's like a perch as if we're reigning over all of Hawthorne.

Past the outstretching fingers of the Italian cypress trees, lining Nadine's back lawn, Uncle Royce's house. Silhouetted by the backdrop of the full moon. The swooping slopes of the green copper roof peek out between the two towering oaks, over a hundred years old I suspect. Three years ago he retrofitted the greenhouse to be my studio apartment. It made it easier to take care of him while he was sick with prostate cancer. I would have happily moved in with him, but he said a young woman shouldn't be trapped in a home with a dying old man. I think he just didn't want me to witness him suffering as much as he did.

I sigh, staring at the only home that matters to me.

My house. Almost.

Jackson, Nadine's sweet husband, orders us an Italian smorgasbord of pasta dishes from Zamillio's, which of course calls for more wine. That's how it goes for the next few hours, our typical Friday night: drinking wine and stuffing ourselves full of fabulous food, unloading the woes of our week, and talking more shit about Lizzy Biggins—petty but satisfying.

But my every other thought flits back to Cain Landry.

Nadine is detailing her and Jackson's trip to Greece next summer.

Cain Landry.

Calista says she is looking to hire another stylist.

Cain Landry.

Hawthorne's Baptist missionary church is getting a new preacher.

Cain Landry.

My brain's been infected by this man. It's like I haven't ever seen a handsome face before. But it's something more than that. I'm unnerved by him and that damn grave bird. I catch myself glancing to the trees, half expecting it to be waiting on me to figure out . . . what? I don't know. How does one make sense of human silkworm cocoons roasting in a fiery pile?

"Are you worried about winning the contract for the Hawthorne gala?" Nadine asks, knocking me out of my Cain thoughts. She reaches for the wine bottle and then groans when she finds it empty.

"A little," I sigh, sipping the last of my wine.

Upper society tends to not want to work with people whose family has a . . . reputation. Every year, on the day of my grandfather's passing, Granny dumps bloodred dye into the town's fountain that surrounds a bronze statue of Saint Constantine Hawthorne, a missionary and our town's namesake. Granny blames the Hawthorne family for building a *vulgarity of a church* that led me to steal and Grandaddy to die. She stands at the fountain and curses every single Hawthorne ever born—by name—from Saint Constantine himself to his grandson, Jedidiah Hawthorne, all the way down to Noah's grandbaby, Elijah Hawthorne. Being kin to someone who publicly curses babies isn't the best way to win over clients.

I spent so much time blaming myself, I never saw the Hawthornes at fault. Granny, on the other hand, she's hell-bent on reminding them of her loss anytime their paths cross.

"The Richardsons' Eventique company has a bid in, too," I say. "And they have an exclusive venue rights contract with the Serendipity Country Club."

"That place is a dump." Calista picks at the last breadstick.

"Don't worry," Nadine tries to reassure me. "You'll get Royce's place and fix it up real nice. I love your design plans, retro Southern belle with a modern avant-garde twist. Those black glass chandeliers you have are to *die* for. And Royce would most definitely approve."

A smile touches my lips. He would love it, for sure.

I shouldn't worry like I am. The contractor is lined up, ready to go as soon as I get this loan. I'm robbing Peter to pay Paul to cover the cost for the renovations. All the favors I'm calling in from my best vendors is the only way I can afford it.

Maybe I have a better chance than I think. Wealthy locals around here are itching for a new event planner. The Richardsons have cornered the market since the eighties, having planned every birthday, baby shower, wedding, country-club dinner, and Christmas party in a thirty-mile radius.

But they're losing their flair and uniqueness. All the events seem to run together with their sameness. Same caterers. Same florists. Same tired venue, a run-down old country club. Locals are bored with their own parties—and that's a sacrilegious thing since Hawthornians are known for their epic celebrations.

People still talk about the Oz Masquerade Ball, where guests were given cryptic invitations that told them to dress in emerald green and meet in an empty meadow. When they arrived, they were whisked away in hot-air balloons to the mansion to celebrate the host's fiftieth birthday—a surprising event, since the handsome, glittering gentleman didn't look a day over eighteen.

If I can turn Uncle Royce's house into *the* premiere venue, I'll land all the Hawthornians' biggest events.

I check my phone, blinking through the wine blur to read the time. It's almost midnight. "I should probably go. My gala presentation is at ten tomorrow morning."

When I stand the whole world sways. "Ooof, I might have overdone it on the wine."

"Impossible," Calista says, blowing me a kiss good-night.

"You're going to kill it tomorrow." Nadine hugs me goodbye.

"Until later, ladies." I throw Calista a kiss back.

Barefoot and tipsy, I stagger out across her back lawn to the rear gate she had installed to cut the distance between our houses in half.

Even this late, the night is alive. Cicadas hiss from the trees above. Cricket chirps bounce in the night air. Some lazy jazz music hums out the window of Bren Dawson's place two houses down—I wonder what lucky woman she's entertaining so late in the evening.

My flats dangle from my hand as I cross the street. A long, purring meow greets me from the neighbor's urn planters. Sampson, Uncle Royce's butterscotch cat, stretches himself awake, like he's been waiting for me all night.

"How's it going, stranger?" He jumps from his perch at the sound of my voice, threading himself through my legs, as if it was I who hasn't been home the last three days. "Ms. Greene is going to murder you if she finds you bedding in her ferns again," I say as I scratch the top of his head. He murmurs a clipped purr and saunters off into the symphonic night.

Hanging low in the sky, a fat full moon casts a hallowed glow over everything. I peer up at it, swaying slightly. Stars dust the midnight sky like grains of sparkling glitter. They feel close, like you could reach up and pluck one out and keep it for yourself.

I do just that. Closing one eye, I pinch my fingers and steal one for a wish.

"To a bright future," I whisper in my palm and then blow it into the night.

My greenhouse studio is hidden in the back of Uncle Royce's house in the unruly rear gardens. I love the greenhouse's nineteenth-century architecture: scrolling green ironwork, the ornate copper-paneled base, Gothic arches that support the glass roof. The side gate yawns from being woken up so late. A brisk wind blows down the narrow path as I make my way down the side of the house, an odd chill for May.

Thank goodness the oaks are overgrown or it would be murder under the morning sun.

I reach for the levered door handle when a light pattering of feet causes me to freeze.

A shift in the darkness catches my attention down the stone pathway toward the reflecting pool.

"Hello?" I call out. The night swallows up my voice. The air is electrified from the sudden stark silence. I'm about to write it off as Sampson slinking through the gardens when I catch the glimmer of wet footprints stamped on the pavers.

Small footprints, as though from a child.

Instinct tells me to get my ass inside, but that curious streak draws me out farther.

"This is private property, you know," I say loud and assured, letting my voice be braver than my nerve.

Come find me, whispers a voice deep in the darkness. An innocent giggle cuts through the silence. My pounding heart stuffs itself in my throat.

"You know your mommy and daddy are going to be worried when they find you're not in your bed." Every lick of confidence I had has slipped loose. I move slowly through the overgrown garden toward the rear of the yard where I rarely venture—near the reflecting pool.

There on the ground is a small red feather. I bend down to pick it up. A shrieking yowl causes me to jump as two small figures dart across the darkness of the pathway in front of me.

"Damn it, Sampson," I curse the cat. "That better not be a new girlfriend." The slur in my words trips up my tongue. Then I realize I'm scolding a cat that doesn't listen to me anyways. "Great."

The warmth and chattering of the night returns. But my nerves aren't quite ready to let the moment go. Maybe my drunken ears only thought I heard giggling? Or it was the neighbor's wind chimes—yes, that's what I tell myself anyway and write it off to a head muddled from wine.

I stumble into the dark of the greenhouse, waking poor Louisa in her cage.

"Goddamn it, Hollis!" the cockatiel shrieks.

"Sorry, girl." I pat the cage with a sloppy hand, pulling down her cover once I find it.

"Goddamn it, Hollis," she mutters again, this time with less grievance.

"I know. I know. Sorry," I coo to her, dropping the found feather in one of the many jars on my bookshelf. Only two shelves high, but it rims the bottom of the room around three walls. Cluttered with knickknacks I've picked up at flea markets, and random apothecary jars and bowls filled with found treasures from nature: feathers, a butterfly wing, a seashell from Myrtle Beach, antlers from my grandparents' farm. I slip out of my clothes and into an old comfy T-shirt. I crank open the foggy window by my bed to let a little breeze in and lie on top of the covers.

My thoughts cluster, knocking around in my head, swimming in their own tide. Plans for the house. Fear if I don't get the loan. Details for tomorrow's meeting with the Hawthornes. And an eeriness I'm unable to shake. Deep in my bones I know something isn't right tonight. Maybe it's the ghosts in my head coming to haunt. Or maybe it's the ominous unnerving feeling I've had ever since I smacked into Cain Landry. What if that grave bird he brought is right? What if dark times are about to befall our small town?

A storm is certainly brewing, and I can't help but feel like hell is coming to Hawthorne now the devil has come home to roost.

CHAPTER FOUR

I DREAM OF the dead sometimes. Often I am sitting at my grand-parents' old farm table. Bright morning sun beams through their kitchen windows. The fresh smell of biscuits is thick in the air. I can hear Granny humming some hymn as she cooks at the stove. My grandaddy sits across the table, sipping his coffee from the saucer since Granny made it too hot again. He smiles down at me, his broom mustache twitching when he does. I know we're about to spend a day outside doing chores, but it never felt like work with Grandaddy.

I miss him. My chest aches at the thought.

Then I remember he is dead.

Darkness slides over the sunny windows, and my joy is sucked down the drain of reality. His ghostly body fades until all that remains is his sad empty chair. The sobs rise up as the loss of him pours itself over me in ladles full of grief. My sleeping body fights to stay there in the dream state, trying to savor those last precious drops of time with him before I wake up.

Until I hear the pecking.

A peck-peck-peckety-peck type of urgent tapping on the window.

Quickly I stand, the veil of Granny's kitchen drops, and I find myself back home in my greenhouse studio. Night and the moon still linger outside, thick as thieves. My body is covered in sweat from the fitful sleep and the heat of the coming summer.

But the grief remains.

The lower windows, permanently tinged green from algae, fog my view, but I catch sight of a small silhouette, a fluttering bird on the other side, as if trying to get purchase on the thin lead line holding the glass. Gently, once more, the little bird taps its beak.

I swipe away the condensation on the window—moisture being an ever-occurring problem when you live in a greenhouse. It flies away before I can see if it's a real bird or a grave one. I peer out into the night toward the long rectangle of the reflecting pool that stretches across the rear lawn, searching the shrubbery and branches for my feathered friend. He's nowhere in sight.

A thought registers.

Slowly my eyes return to the reflecting pool. Its liquid surface, usually a flat black mirror, now ripples. A watery trail snails out from the side, onto the pavers, and over to the bare feet of a little girl.

I gasp, jumping back.

Watching her watching me.

Sopping wet, she stands there in her fine pink dress with its lacy white collar. Her long blond hair matted with sticks and leaves. Her skin a cold gray, something only the dead have. Fright sucks the words from my throat, and I can't find the will to scream.

She opens her mouth to speak, but instead of words, dirty water spills from her lips in a gushing rush. An overwhelming fears drowns me—

The loud roaring sound of a saw jars me awake. Men shout

with an urgent call. A shattering crash has me curling to the side protectively as shards of glass rain down on me.

Bright morning light spears through the open ceiling as a giant branch of an oak tree punches its way inside. It takes my brain a fogged moment to realize I'm awake, for real this time. And an actual tree branch has fallen onto my studio apartment.

"What the hell?" I peel back the covers, careful of the broken glass.

"What the hell!" Louisa shrieks. "What the hell!" she repeats over and over.

"It's okay, Louisa," I say then glance out the window, now full of daylight, and no little girl in sight. A dream, then? My subconscious fixated on the unnerving incident when I came home last night, has to be. My sober brain quickly dismisses the wet splotches on the pavement as Sampson's from his love escapade.

The jumping of panicked voices outside has me throwing on the closest pair of shorts I can find. I tiptoe around the stray shards on the floor and snag my sneakers.

At first I think they've started construction back up on the Greater Good subdivision, the last homes to be built on Grady Owens's property behind the house. But the chaos of noise erupts from the crew of men working in *this* yard. Hedge trimmers savagely shave the azalea bushes. A Weedwacker grinds away at clumps of grass encroaching on the paver walkway. I pinch the bridge of my nose to push back my screaming wine headache.

"Excuse me. *Excuse me!*" I'm forced to shout—to the detriment of my head—to get the attention of the workers who are staring in shock at the disaster they made of my glass roof. I hop on one foot to put on my sneaker, then the other. An errant thought passes that maybe I had in fact called the contractor to tell him to get started, assuming my loan would go through.

"Who's in charge?" I look around, trying to figure which one of these folks is going to receive my wrath. I pin my glare on a man with a hard hat who looks the part with the way everyone else is cowering. "Who are you? And what the hell are you doing?" It's one thing to be jarred awake, but they're cutting down my tree and destroying my home.

The big, burly man startles at my presence then cows for only a moment before he sizes me up like I'm some pesky neighbor complaining about the early morning noise. I cross my arms over my chest, realizing I don't have my bra on. "Again, what the hell are you doing?"

"I'm sorry, ma'am. We weren't aware anyone lived on the property. We were told the place was empty, and seeing how we're just here to landscape—"

"Who told you that?" I interrupt.

His bunched brow relaxes, and he turns toward the house, pointing. "The new owner."

Fear creeps up my neck, and I step to the side to peer past the man's broad frame. There, on the second-story balcony, is Cain Landry.

Suddenly, I feel as if I'm tumbling down Alice's rabbit hole, and maybe I *am* still dreaming—or rather nightmaring. My thoughts scrabble in the confusion. How can this be happening? Uncle Royce's will specifically gave me a one-year clause to buy. I know I'm nearly at the pinch point, but I still have time. No one else can buy the house yet.

No, this is not happening.

My feet start marching as my brain digests what the man said. *New owner.*

Who in the hell is this Cain Landry? He strolls into town, and not five minutes later he steals this house right from under me?

"Excuse me!" I yell up to the second-story balcony to get Cain's attention. He's deep in conversation with another man, wearing a hard hat. There's too much chaos in the yard for him to hear me. I wield a stern glare on the hedge trimmer guy, who fumbles and shuts it off rather sheepishly.

"Hey!" I try again, with every bit of bark I intend to bite him with.

Cain bristles, taken aback at the sight of me.

"I need a word with you." I point to the downstairs where I expect him to meet me. I don't bother waiting to see if he follows.

Inside there are already movers carrying in boxes and furniture. *What in the fresh hell is going on?*

"You can take that right on outside, back to the truck," I tell one guy, who hesitates until I stare him down long enough he decides to U-turn back through the front door. "You, too." I nod to another man with a load of boxes.

A fire lights in my chest as I see Cain descend the stairs. His crumpled brow lets me know he's not happy at this little disturbance I've caused. *Tough for you, buddy.*

He's more casually dressed than yesterday: sandy-colored slacks with a purplish-blue shirt remind me of the violas that used to grow in these gardens. It makes his devilishly gray eyes pop like they're plugged in.

I feel pretty tall at five-eight, but standing in front of all six-plus feet of him, it notches out a bit of my confidence. He sizes me up, seemingly confused about what a woman in her pajamas is doing in this house at the crack of dawn.

"Can I help you with something?" he asks, tilting his head slightly.

I catch no hint of an accent, Southern or otherwise. There is a slight spice to his voice, though, like he's well traveled. And a rich assuredness that typically comes with wealth. But ire underlines his pinched tone.

"What do you think you're doing here?" I bolt right out of the gate.

Cain casts a glance around, as if it's not obvious. "Moving in."

The reality of him confirming this feels like there's an anchor tied to my ankles and he's just tossed it overboard. I'm sinking, being dragged down into the depths of my worst fears.

"That's not possible." The words dry on my tongue.

He casually tucks his hands in his pockets. "I assure you it's very possible when you pay cash."

My eyes gobble up the flurry of activity around me: movers, landscapers, construction crew. No. Not happening.

"There's been a mistake." I find my anger again.

"Doubtful. The paperwork was all signed just yesterday. I myself was there. " Cain remains nonplussed by the situation. His stoic, emotionless composure digs under my skin.

"The house isn't for sale. Not for another seventeen days, anyway. And I'm going to buy it before then. Not you. *Me*." I jab a thumb into my chest.

"Well, I don't see how that could be since I've already bought it," he says rather flatly.

"Well, guess what, *buddy*?" I say. "Joke's on you because that's what was stated in the will. Time-stamped and everything. Besides, *I* already live on the property." I point to the greenhouse out back, the oak branch jammed in the glass roof.

He gawks with a disgusted shock. "You're a squatter?" The way he says it makes me sound like some vile creature.

"I . . . No. Of course not!" I balk. "I've lived here for three years. This," I say and wave my hands, "is my house. Not yours. *Mine*."

The electric gray of his eyes flickers, like a surge pulsing through a light bulb. The cold ache that's been locking up my right shoulder decides it's time to burn again. Absently, I reach across and begin to massage it out.

He watches as I do so, then stares at me a long, constrained moment. That nasty scowl finds home on his face again. "No. I'm sorry. You must be . . . mistaken." He waves an errant hand in the air toward me. "Please leave, or I'll be forced to call the authorities."

"Go ahead, call them. This is my home we're talking about here. Who do you think you are? You can't—"

"I'm the owner of this house," he cuts me off with his cool tone, but his patience has evaporated. "And you are trespassing on my property. Gather your things—whatever you might have scrounged in that tiny shed—"

"Greenhouse," I correct.

"And vacate the premises." He pauses a moment then adds, "I'll have you escorted away if I must." And that's all he has to say about that, because he turns on his heel and heads right back upstairs.

Oh, he's sadly mistaken if he thinks I'll bend easy. I know my rights. Uncle Royce gave me permission to live here as long as I needed to—or, rather, the full year he gave me to try and buy this place. I'm about to tell him just that, but then he hasn't listened to me yet, so why would he now?

"We'll see about that!" I holler at his back, then sharply turn to leave.

Cain thinks he knows what's what. Well, I'll go to the real estate office right this minute and get Landon Boucher to set him straight. I'll drag the estate lawyer into this as well if I have to. There's absolutely no way Cain Landry has legally bought it.

A mover wheels past with a dolly, almost knocking me on my ass. He's moving what appears to be a statue taller than me. I can't tell what it is through the Bubble Wrap. He strolls into the adjacent room, to an older woman who directs him where the piece should go. Her silky black dress is refined and looks like it was revived from the forties. Her strappy nude heels seem too formal for an early Saturday morning of moving furniture and boxes around.

As I walk across the back porch, I watch through the banquet of windows as she inspects a painting of an unusual white bird with a bare blue throat. From its squawking mouth comes a plume of smoke, the background a gorgeous jungle of green.

Then her shrewd eyes glide over to me.

Aware I was observing her the whole time.

I dash off the porch and out of her sight. A shiver ripples up my spine.

"WHAT IN THE hell do you mean it's sold?" I pull at the front of my moss-green dress, feeling like I'm about to burst into flames from all my anger. It doesn't help that Landon's office is stuffed to the brim with chunky furniture, heavy books and massive file cabinets. *Jesus, save a tree and go digital already.*

"Now, calm down, Hollis." Landon Boucher, the grand-son of the Boucher's Real Estate founder, pumps his hands at the air like he's trying to whoa a wild horse. I do feel like I'm about to buck. The thick cuff of his sleeves are pinched closed with chunky gold *B* cuff links. He reminds me of a lion with his sandy-blond mane and squared jaw. You'd know a Boucher if you saw one: they all have a thick build, strapping arms, and hair of gold. Not my type, but I can appreciate the appeal.

"I tell you what's going to get me to calm down is for you to march right back in there and tell your daddy and your gran-daddy they screwed up." I point to the office where the cowards have barricaded themselves. "It's in Uncle Royce's will as clear as daylight." I wave a hand to the copy on his desk, something he consulted before we made a more-than-fair offer to Royce's daughters.

Landon's gaze drops to the floor, and he lets out a long sigh, and I know I'm not going to like the sound of this. "Why don't you have a seat?" He fans a hand to the chair across from his desk.

"I'll stand," I grit through my teeth.

"Please?" If it wasn't for the tender way he said it, I probably would've kept standing.

So I sit. The last feather of hope I was holding on to flutters away.

He exhales and opens up a folder he brought from his father's office. "You are correct, his will states you have a year to submit an offer for fair market value, and they are required to accept it." He pulls out a letter and sets it in front of me, his college class ring a whopping gold nugget on his big hands. It's a letter from a law firm I've never heard of in Myrtle Beach.

"I know what the will says." I nod at the paper on the desk, too impatient to read the tangled-up legalese lawyers like to drown your brain in.

"As you know, in the last year we've received quite a few other offers, but none of them mattered because you had first right. But the will didn't say they couldn't have a backup offer on deck."

"A backup offer? My offer is good. They don't need a backup."

"They have a legal right to have one. And it seems Mr. Cain Landry offered them a considerable amount for the home, in cash, weeks ago. And your offer is contingent on a loan."

"I know, but all I need is a letter to clear my credit history and—"

"And before that," Landon interrupts me, "you had to put together itemized profit and loss statements from your business."

"Yeah, but Lizzy—"

"And before that, you said she wanted you to clean up your credit history so you would have a higher score and qualify for a better rate." Landon's tone is guiding me, but I can't see to where.

"Well, yeah, but Lizzy said—"

"Are you seeing a pattern here?" Landon cocks a brow.

The realization hits me like a mallet to a gong. "Damn her." If I could punch something I probably would.

For the last few weeks Lizzy Biggins has had me jumping through hoops, making me pull up reports and more paperwork, and every time I think I'm going to get the loan, she pulls the rug right out from underneath my feet.

I straighten in my chair. "You think she's been working with the sisters?" He doesn't even have to answer: I know they have. "Can we like, arrest them or charge them with tampering or something?" It feels desperate, but there's got to be some consequences here.

"Unfortunately, none of this is illegal."

"I have seventeen days left in my year," I say through gritted teeth.

"Look, Hollis . . . At this point the bank has no plans to approve your loan." His words hammer a spike in my chest. "The Gentry daughters could cripple the bank if they transferred their funds elsewhere, and I suspect they threatened to do as much. Lizzy simply delayed the process until Mr. Landry could arrive to sign the final paperwork. Gentry's daughters have gone ahead and moved forward with Cain's offer, knowing there's no way you can qualify for a loan elsewhere in the short time remaining."

"I'll sue them," I say, my anger tornadoing inside of me.

"You could try. But it'll cost you a pretty penny, and they have a lot more money to throw at it. And if you lose, the judge might force you to pay their legal fees. Courts tend to be more empathetic toward blood relatives than the deceased's godniece."

The anger and sadness rising in my chest is like a cold front that meets a summer storm. I don't mean to start crying, but the next thing I know there are huge tears forming blots on the lap of my dress.

Landon hands me his handkerchief—of course he carries one. I blow my nose on the embroidered *B* and wonder if it's customary to wash and return to the owner or if you keep it once you snot all over it.

I'm not even sure if he can understand half of my blabbering as I tell him all my dreams are ruined and that I don't know how I'm going to find a venue to host this gala because the last year of my life has been so wrapped up in buying this house, and I never even considered a plan B.

Landon sits there with his golden eyes and stubbled jaw and listens to every last word.

"And where am I gonna live?" I say, once I've managed to regain my composure. At Landon's confused face I add, "Cain told me I had to gather my belongings and be out of the greenhouse by the end of the day." Not my studio anymore, but Cain's. I'm terrified he will tear it down. What else is he planning for Uncle Royce's house?

God knows I'm not going to move back in with my parents or with Granny. Sure, I could crash at Nadine's or Calista's for a bit, but I need someplace to live for the long haul.

I've lost the house, my heart whispers to me. It's a harsh truth, dumping an ice-cold bucket of reality over my head.

Landon, with his scrunched up brow, nods, understanding the predicament I'm in. "Let me give him a call, see if we can't get him to give you at least until the end of the month to get your stuff out." He puts his desk phone on Speaker and dials a number from his file.

I feel eleven years old again, sitting in the back of Roy's Drugstore while Wilma Carver calls my grandaddy to let him know they've caught me stealing.

"Cain Landry." The voice on the other end answers. A fresh shot of anger bolts through me. Who answers the phone with their name?

Landon introduces himself and explains the circumstances around this whole mishap and that he would appreciate it—as a personal favor—if Cain would allow me to stay at my current residence until the end of the month.

A long silence lingers on the other end of the phone, until he finally speaks.

"It's a sad situation," Cain finally says. "But unfortunately, it's not my problem. I can't see how, after fairly purchasing a new home, I'm expected to allow some stranger to live on my property."

"I can assure you, sir," Landon rushes before Cain can hang up, "she's not a stranger at all. Hollis was born and raised here, and she's one of the town's preeminent event planners. She's a client of my wife's, Mary Beth Hawthorne, and I can guarantee you she's an honorable woman. She'll not give you a lick of trouble." Then Landon hikes up a single brow at me, warning me I better be on my best behavior. I simply stare back at him, unwilling to confirm one way or the other.

In the background a woman interrupts in another language, maybe Spanish.

There's a shuffling noise, then Cain responds in the same language. The conversation on his side gets a little heated.

I guess it's only fair he asks his—lady friend? His whatever—if she's comfortable with someone squatting in the backyard for a few weeks. It feels so wrong to have to ask for permission to stay at a place I've considered a second home for the last fifteen years.

"This woman . . ." Cain starts.

"Hollis Sutherland," Landon says, filling in my name for him.

"Right, Hollis Sutherland," Cain says. "She's close to your in-laws. Friends with your wife, a Hawthorne?"

"Yes, sir. Hollis comes from good people. I'm close friends with her younger brothers. Go duck hunting with them every winter. Like I said, you won't have any trouble out of her." This time Landon doesn't even bother sending me a warning glare.

"She can stay until the end of the month, not a day longer," Cain says rather quickly.

"Thank you, sir—" Landon tries to say, but Cain hangs up as he does. Landon shuts off the speakerphone. "There you go. You've got to the end of the month." There's a broad smile on Landon's face, like he's done me a huge favor. I suppose he has.

"Please don't tell Libby I lost the house," I say, my voice as grave as the night. I know he's not fond of his mother-in-law, so hopefully he will keep it quiet, at least until I can come up with a plan B.

"Ah," he says. "You were going to use the house for the gala."
Steepling his fingers, he sits back solemnly, now fully understanding this wasn't solely about me having a place to live. "You
know how this town is, Hollis. She'll find out soon enough."

"I know." I look at my watch. "I just need the next hour to
convince her to sign the gala contract with me. I can figure out
the venue afterward. Can you give me that?"

He throws his hands up innocently. "I know nothing."

"Thank you." I form prayer hands of gratitude.

Though I can't fathom finding another venue for the Hawthorne gala, Royce's place was so perfect. Something I'll have
to deal with soon, I suppose—once my heart gets over losing it.
I swallow the sadness and tell myself I can grieve later.

Right now I need to focus on winning this contract.

What in the hell else can go wrong?

A niggling feeling in my gut says *Everything*.

CHAPTER FIVE

HAWTHORNE MANOR IS one of those vastly ostentatious mansions straight out of a V. C. Andrews novel my mother loved to read. (Books I might have sneaked a peek at though I wasn't old enough.) The brown brick home sprawls upward and outward with steepled peaks of varying sizes from the many additions created since it was built in the early twentieth century.

I've only visited the Hawthornes' home once before. It was the summer after I died. The youth group of the Hawthorne Missionary Baptist Church was having a swim party at the house. I don't think the youth pastor or his wife expected a gay man to show up with a child who not only wasn't his but didn't belong to anyone who attended their church.

Uncle Royce didn't give a damn. He tithed more than the ten percent the good Lord asked for, and he had a youth, and I was going to their party, come hell or high water.

I was thrilled to go, but my bathing suit was a hand-me-down from my cousin. Whatever color it had started as had long faded to a sallow goose-turd green. A small problem Uncle Royce solved with a quick trip to the mall.

There I stood, in my new colorful polka-dotted swimsuit with a pale blue cover-up and a snazzy pair of white sunglasses perched on my head. I wasn't yet twelve, but I felt sixteen.

The youth pastor and his wife looked like a couple of over-eager cheerleaders. Those hundred-watt smiles of theirs beamed until they realized who we were. A blinking look of confusion curtained their faces. They stepped to block us as we tried to enter the home.

The wife crinkled her snub nose and leaned in slightly to whisper to Uncle Royce, "Maybe you've arrived at the wrong party?" She said it like she was giving him a proper out so he could leave without being embarrassed. As if there was another house in town that was having a swim party for the youth group and he accidently went to the wrong one.

Until that day, I had no idea anger had a taste. But it was fire and vinegar on my tongue.

Uncle Royce gently laid a hand on my shoulder, as if sensing the heat my small body was putting out.

At six foot three, Uncle Royce towered over most everyone, but especially this dinky Barbie and Ken. He cast down on them an exhausted look, as if he did not have the time or the inclination to deal with these peons.

"Don't be silly, Lauralee," he said, his voice smooth as velvet. "Why, there's all the pizza, cakes, and treats I told Noah and Libby I'd send over as a thanks to the church for hosting." His words went down like a smooth drink of ice tea whether they liked it or not. Then he strolled us right on past those two as if we were walking into his own house, and they were the hired help simply answering the door.

Shame crept over me, even when I told it not to. Uncle Royce had essentially bought me an entry ticket to *their* party, a country mouse from a poor country church didn't belong here with the elites.

"I'll have none of that," he said as we stepped outside into the joyous chaos of kids. He knelt in front of me and looked me square in the eye, cupped my face in his gentle hands and said, "You and your family are good people. Better than most. Don't you ever forget it. Now, go on out there and have a good time. Behave yourself. Careful of the trolls." His eyes swung over to a particularly self-important group of girls who seemed bored to be at one of the coolest parties in town.

I couldn't tell you much about the party, other than I had a blast. But I do remember leaving.

It's easy to get lost in a house that big. Eight bathrooms and still I couldn't find a one. Door after door, I eventually stumbled into a library. Or maybe it was an office? It was big and book-ish and stuffed full of stodgy furniture.

"Sorry, ma'am," I said to the woman frantically rifling through the desk drawers as I began to step out.

"It's here somewhere," she said, causing me to pause. "Come, child." She fanned me over. "Help me look."

I hesitated, unsure if she meant me. Plus, I didn't want to drip all over the beautiful green wool rug.

"Hurry, now, he said it's important." The authority in her voice had me hustling over there.

I wasn't sure whose mother she was, but in that moment I wanted her to be mine. Her dress, soft and flowing, was made for a summer breeze. Her rust-colored hair swept around her neck in long swooping waves. Her skin, kissed by the sun, caused the freckles to speckle across her nose and the bulbs of her cheeks to glow. Even with her eyes rimmed red and face splotchy from a recent cry, she was beautiful.

As I grabbed the drawer pull, a terrible feeling that I was snooping crept over me. "What are we looking for?" I asked, barely peeking inside.

"The key," she said, worry creasing between her brow. "It's here, somewhere. I'm sure of it," she said with convincing certainty.

"Hollis!" Miss Lauralee sharply called from the doorway.

I jumped back, knocking against the bookcase behind the desk. A wooden bookend toppled over and fell onto the plush oriental rug. Quickly, I bent to pick it up and gasped.

Leashed to the floor underneath the desk was a grave bird.

"You should not be in here!" Miss Lauralee wrenched me up by my elbow like I was an insolent child. She was scolding me something fierce as she dragged me toward the door. The sweet mourning dove waddled after me, but its tether quickly jerked it back. It wasn't until Miss Lauralee closed the door that I noticed there had been no one else in the room.

FIFTEEN YEARS LATER, I'm back in the Hawthorne mansion entryway, very happy that youth pastor and his wife aren't here to greet me. Silently, I wait as directed by the housekeeper, a withered thin woman with a stern back, while she goes to tell the family I've arrived.

Eight massive oil paintings hang on a grand wall before me. Generations of Hawthornes stare with their serious faces, scrutinizing and calculating. Posed in ornate gilded frames, the family members ranged from great-grandparents to the current grandchildren. One even features Noah Hawthorne's coon dog.

The oil painting of Jedidiah and Patsy Hawthorne is the mosaic replica that covers the exterior of the Hawthornes' massive church. It was commissioned as a loving gesture from the church members to the Hawthornes to honor Noah's parents. But the final result wasn't quite the masterpiece they expected. Instead it's more of a goofy, pixilated version of the couple. Too expensive to tear it down, too prideful to admit it's disturbingly ugly. Twenty-five years ago they were killed by a drunk driver on their way home from the Centennial Revival. Noah and

Libby Hawthorne had to end their eight-year-long mission trip to come home and run the church in the wake of his parents' deaths. I was only a year old when it all happened, but everyone who's raised in Hawthorne learns about the family's history, even if you don't care to.

"Creepy, isn't it?" a banjo-twangy thick voice says from the hallway. I turn to find Nikki Hawthorne, Noah and Libby's daughter-in-law, smacking on her gum like it's irresistibly tasty. Second wife to their son Jeremiah and ten years younger, she's closer to my age than his. He snagged her from a casino in Tunica, Mississippi. One minute she was serving cocktails to high rollers, the next she has a three carat rock on her finger and is celebrating Christmas in her new family's mansion. She looks—and sounds—like a black-haired Dolly Parton: petite, busty, and full of spunk.

"All those eyes staring at you as you walk into the house. It gives you the heebie-jeebies, doesn't it?" she asks.

"It's different, for certain," I say, trying to be polite.

"You don't want to see the portrait of Saint Constantine that hangs in the billiards room. Full-size painting of his old ass in nothing but a loincloth, holding a spear, out in the middle of the jungle, splotched with body paint. Something right out of *Lord of the Flies*. No matter where you are in the room, his eyes are always following you, I swear." She shivers at the thought.

"How eccentric," I say, then point to the young girl in Patsy and Jedidiah's family portrait. "I didn't realize Noah has an older sister." Noah graduated a few years before my mom; I don't ever remember her mentioning he had a sister.

"Girl, *yes*," she says from the side of her mouth. "Sarah, I think her name is." Nikki glances around to make sure no one is in earshot. "She's the black sheep of the family." She whispers like it's a sin to speak of her. "Lucy Carmichael, you know she runs the jewelry store uptown? She said Sarah Hawthorne and her deadbeat boyfriend stole a bunch of money from the church and got exiled from the family decades ago. Cut out of the will and everything." Nikki widens her eyes. "We don't talk about her. Like, at all. So . . . " She lays a finger on her lips with a *shhh*, then nods for me to follow her. "Where's your stuff?" she says, over her shoulder. "Don't you have presentation boards for us to look at?"

I pat my computer satchel and the gift bags I brought. "It's all right here."

"Huh," she says flatly, looking very unimpressed. And suddenly I'm nervous I've already lost.

When I first came to the home years ago, the wainscoted walls were a dark wood. Since then, they have been painted a bright white. The old wood floors have been replaced with gorgeous white Italian marble with a blue-pattern inlay. Even the artwork has changed, fresh and modern and very *en vogue*.

"Roy Wayne!" Nikki hollers, startling me half to death. "Get off that dadgum table. Jesus, you weren't raised in the wild." I wait while she goes in the other room and pulls her four-year-old son off the glass dining table.

A group of jovial voices travels down an adjacent hall. I turn to see who—and my heart sinks.

Walking out with Noah and Libby Hawthorne are the Richardsons, my competition. A pristine, fit older couple who look like they just came from brunch at the country club following a game of tennis. Him in his polo and starched shorts. Her in her pearls and yellow paisley capris. And they're all smiles and eager handshakes as they make their way out of the office, so you'd assume the deal was all but done.

But if this morning's taught me anything, when it comes to the rich, nothing is set in stone. Kind of like Royce's daughters who signed a deal with me then sold my house to the fattest check they could get.

I'm almost invisible as the group rounds the corner where the hallways join and walks right past me toward the front door.

Except, Mrs. Nanette Richardson notices: she cuts me a smug side-eye.

"Damn," I say under my breath.

Little Roy Wayne runs past toward the backyard, giggling like he's just robbed the cookie jar.

"Let's get you a mimosa," Nikki says, wagging her empty champagne flute. "Little liquid courage."

Memories of the past come floating back to life as we step into the backyard. Bunches of balloons sway around the long pool. Beautiful birthday presents huddle on a small table next to a mini buffet. A gorgeous custom floral cake, something fit for a small wedding, sits at the end with a HAPPY 35TH BIRTHDAY MARY BETH sign hanging above it.

"I didn't realize it was Mary Beth's birthday," I say, apologetically. "We can reschedule the presentation if we need to." Though, I don't want to give the Richardsons any more of an edge.

"Oh, it's fine." Nikki fans an indifferent hand. "It's more for the kids. Mary Beth hates birthdays." Then she turns to her husband, Jeremiah, who's acting as bartender. "A refill please," she hands him her empty glass.

Jeremiah, Noah and Libby's son, is a burly man with a beard and belly, and is as tall as his father. He's receding hairline makes him look older than late thirties. His Polynesian armband tattoo screams classic eighteen-year-old's mistake. All the waitstaff I've hired for events say he's pretty handsy with the female employees out at the country club. He's the one Hawthorne I want nothing to do with. But the family is a tight-knit group. You get on the bad side of one of them and you're screwed.

He points a finger to me. "Want a shot to loosen the nerves?" he asks. His eyes rove over the V-neck of my green dress.

"I'm good. Thanks." I doubt he offered the Richardsons a shot, doubt they had any nerves to battle. "Should I use the TV in the sunroom to link my computer up with?" I point to the bank of windows at the back of the house where a grand family room sits behind. Thankfully, the library I stumbled into all those years ago is at the other end of the house. Not sure I'll ever be ready to know what the little mourning dove had to show me.

"Do what you need to, doll." Jeremiah gives me a wink.

One of the grandkids cannonballs into the pool. A nanny tries to wrangle the other six grandchildren. A young high school kid, who looks like he was hired as a lifeguard, has become the unofficial babysitter/kids' toy. They both look exhausted.

Once I step inside, I find out exactly what I'm up against.

Propped on two giant easels are the presentation boards for the Richardsons' proposed event. DENIM AND DIAMONDS is plastered across the top. It looks luxurious and extravagant. Rhinestone and glass cowboy boots serve as vases for massive flower arrangements—though, I don't know how you have a conversation at your table around that. Champagne flutes are dripping with crystals. Everything has a very cohesive color palette of chambray blue denim and silver. It's not something I would plan—a little garish for my taste, but there's a level of sophistication despite its over-the-topness. Sparkle and glam does appeal to a lot of people. And guests are *suckers* for a good party theme to play into.

Not to mention, they have a guaranteed venue. The Serendipity Country Club might be run-down, but with all that glitz and glam the Richardsons have planned, people won't even notice.

Then my chest aches, as the reality of this morning hits me. I've lost the house that was supposed to be mine, not to mention a career-altering venue. Losing Uncle Royce's place, knowing someone else owns it—I can't go there. Not now. I have to land this job.

My hand trembles as I grab their master remote that controls the TV, surround sound, lights, shades, and probably the damn toaster, too. I'm pretty certain you need a PhD to operate it.

Just breathe, I tell myself.

There are only four Hawthornes who matter: Libby and Noah, and their two children Jeremiah and Mary Beth. But there's only one I have to convince: the kingmaker. Libby Hawthorne is the matriarch of the family. A Hawthorne by marriage, but she has the final say on everything the Hawthorne name touches: the church, the pastor, the missionary trips, and most especially the Greater Good housing development.

Everything lives or dies by Libby's hand.

If I can get her excited, I'll get the contract.

"Oh good, it's you," a light voice says. Mary Beth Hawthorne, married to my real estate agent Landon Boucher, glides into the room. Her arms spread open to give me a hug. She smells like lemon drops and sunshine and vodka. She's overly thin, like she favors a liquid diet more than food. Everything about her exudes kindness, but her threads are loose around the edges. Like she might come undone at any moment if the wind blows just right. I'm always running into her at the florist or Calista's salon or at Bren's bakery with her three children. Sweet as she is, there's a distracted whimsy about her.

"I was hoping Momma was considering your bid. Nadine's wedding was simply stunning, and I told her whatever you did would be perfection."

"Aw, thank you. I hope y'all are pleased with what I have planned. And happy birthday!" I say. "I had no idea it was today, or I would have brought you a little something."

Her smile softens, and she shrugs away the notion.

"The day doesn't feel like it really belongs to me, you know?" She stares off into space a moment, then shakes herself from a growing melancholy and heads to the bar cart. "Of course, life is a fickle thing if you think about it." The cubes of ice clink against the crystal as they fall into the glass. She pours herself a vodka with a conservative splash of club soda, then takes a long sip like it's medicine.

"I suppose it is," I say, unsure how to respond.

"Mm—" she stops middrink as she sees the master remote in my hand. "That thing is a beast. I don't know how Momma and Daddy ever get it to work. My six-year-old, Elijah, knows how to use it better than anyone, if you have trouble with it."

"Oh, I've just about got it figured out," I say, and on cue my computer desktop pops up on the flat-screen.

"Now we're cooking with gas," Mary Beth says, making her way to the couch. "And here comes the queen." She airs a hand toward her mother Libby, whose face sours at her daughter's introduction. Noah follows in behind her, holding a bouquet of birthday flowers.

"Farm fresh flowers," Mary Beth says and takes the bouquet, giving them a big sniff. "My favorite, Daddy."

Libby frowns at the bouquet. She is a long way off from the slim woman painted in the oil painting in the entryway. It's not just her weight: she's also gained a keen sharpness in her eyes, like she's always calculating her next move, and she's twelve steps ahead of you. Something I suppose anyone would master after years of running the Hawthorne empire. And Noah, he's a big, tall, and rotund man. A larger version of their son Jeremiah, minus the beard and less handsy with the ladies. His hair is a dark, monochromatic color that can only come from coloring his hair. He takes the whiskey Jeremiah offers as he and Nikki come in from the pool area. And who said Baptists don't drink?

"Hello, Hollis," Libby says as she makes her way over to me, her eyes quickly skimming me up and down. "Green suits you."

My sundress and nude heels got two thumbs-up earlier this week from Nadine when I tried on approximately nine hundred different outfits, prepping for this day.

"Thank you so much, Libby." I shake her outstretched hand. "It's my favorite color."

"You can call me Mrs. Hawthorne." She smiles pertly, holding my hand for a half second longer.

"Yes, ma'am. Mrs. Hawthorne. My apologies—"

"You know," she continues as if I didn't speak, grabbing the mimosa Nikki hands her. "Those Richardsons are a class act." She takes a sip and admires their presentation boards with a sense of pride. Then she turns to me. "So. Let's take a look at what you've got." As if she's simply following through on a formality and the gig is all but lost.

But a deal's not done until the deal is done. I learned that the hard way this morning.

"Only if you're interested in seeing the best," I give it right back to Libby, nailing her with the same square look and pert smile she gave me. And I'm pretty sure the corner of her mouth twitched with an impressed *touché*. With a click of the remote I cut out the lights and close the automated shades.

"What's the one takeaway you want your guests to have after the Twenty-fifth Hawthorne Missionary Gala?" I press Play on my presentation. A warm light of sunshine fans out across the giant flat-screen. Boka lights float and glow as ethereal music shimmers in the background.

"*Unforgettable,*" I say.

The dark screen explodes into a video of the cosmos. It's the closest visual I could re-create of my own experience in the afterlife. It's impossible to truly capture what I felt or saw, but this is a touch of what it was like.

"Welcome to the Empyrean Gala," my prerecorded voice says with a synthesized effect, as if spoken by angels. The words glimmer to life on the screen. "A place of pure happiness. A state of utter perfection."

And I let the video play out, showing each aspect of the gala, my voice narrating the details. A light speed–style tunnel entrance for the guests. Twinkling lights throughout the gardens like a starry night. Tables dressed in dark linens and fine stemware. Floral centerpieces in rich jewel tones. At the far end of the lawn in front of the privacy hedge a dressed-up stage with more flowers.

With each transition, Libby appears intrigued by the fresh, more modern vendor choices I've selected. Up-and-coming event professionals who make trends instead of chasing them—something I'm sure the Richardsons did not have.

Eventually the video fades to black, and I bring the lights up.

"The Empyrean Gala will be the event of the year, the decade even. And I would love an opportunity to do that for you," I conclude, leaving space for questions and discussion.

"Well," says Mary Beth, clearly wanting to show support for me, "that was certainly impressive."

"But the Denim and Diamonds theme seems so fun to dress up for," Nikki whines. "This feels like a typical suit and tie, generic, black cocktail dress type of event."

"Well, actually . . ." I bring up the slideshow portion of my presentation. "I envision ball gowns and tuxes. Full-on black tie. Mr. Hawthorne, might I suggest this midnight-blue tux with black meteorite cuff links. And Mrs. Hawthorne, one of these gowns would look stunning on you." All the long dresses I've suggested are in dark, rich colors with tasteful amounts of sparkle lining the seams.

"Very Gatsby," Libby purrs. "I love the celestial crown for that one."

"It's a vintage 1920s piece I found through an artist online."

"Splendid choices," Libby replies, and she sounds genuine.

"And your gift bag?" Nikki picks a fleck of something off her swimsuit cover-up. Her nasal tone suggests she's anticipating it to be something boring. I allow the briefest glance to the Richardsons' samples: crystal-and-denim jackets for the ladies and Western metal-studded denim shirts for the men.

I pass around the small gift bags from my satchel, confident now that this will wow them.

"Star constellation necklaces, personalized to the zodiac sign for each woman's birthday, made with delicate diamond chips and fourteen-karat gold. For the men, midnight-and-gold steel chronograph wristwatches from the Luminous collection by Matthew Gunn." Who just happens to be a friend of mine from college. He wants to be the next top designer of men's accessories, and what better way to showcase your product than at an event full of wealthy people. The Hawthornes are all murmuring as they evaluate the giveaways, and the general sound is (I allow myself to hope) positive.

"I still say the Denim and Diamonds theme is more fun," Nikki huffs, setting aside her necklace like it's an ordinary trinket. All other faces have returned stoic as they await my reply.

"Well," I start, "clearly the Richardsons put in a lot of work coming up with that theme," I gesture to the presentation boards. "And it's an *adorable* theme for sure. Something I've seen done *dozens* of times, and it's usually a crowd-pleaser, no matter how familiar it feels. I'm sure the Richardsons will manage quite easily at the *ole* Serendipity Country Club." I disconnect my laptop from the television. "But I was under the impression y'all wanted to hit the five million mark this year in fundraising, seeing as how this was the twenty-fifth anniversary and all. And throwing a spectacular, once-in-a-decade gala was part of that plan, as a real means to bring in enthusiastic donations in response. I apologize if I misunderstood." I slide my computer into my satchel, as though I'm ready to leave, but stop just short of picking it up. "I appreciate your time, though." I nod my thank-you.

"Five million?" Libby says surprised. She tilts her head unsure she heard me right.

Now I've got her attention.

They have never made more than two-point-eight million at an annual gala. When I dreamed up this event, I envisioned a top-tier guest list and designed around it.

I look Libby dead in the eye. "If you want to hook a few whales, you have to bring bigger bait. Something that will lure the likes of Charles Farandole or Virginia Boeing."

Two millionaire guests at Nadine's nuptials who personally complimented me on the *most gorgeous wedding of the century* and said that any event I planned they would happily attend. I'm hoping to get them to follow through on their pronouncement.

A long, quiet moment stretches where everyone watches Libby. Her eyes narrow on me, considering.

Laughter and splashes from the kids in the pool out back eats up the growing silence. The ice in Noah's glass rattles as he finishes off the last of his drink. I feel as tight as an overwound clock about to spring loose.

The Richardsons are a guaranteed nice time; it would be a lovely gala for sure. The foundation could achieve similar fundraising numbers of years past if they choose them.

I'm a risk. Young, new to the game, promising big results, but I don't have a proven track record to substantiate what I'm projecting. Nadine's wedding was a game changer for me and my career, but can I replicate that kind of success again? *I* know I can. I know myself and what I'm capable of.

I just need them to believe it, too.

"And you can guarantee Royce Gentry's place can hold that many people?" Libby asks.

A knot yanks in my stomach. I didn't declare a venue in my presentation, thankfully. But everyone in town knows I'm trying to buy Uncle Royce's place and what I plan to do with it. Heck, Mary Beth is married to the real estate agent I was working with.

"If you sign with me, I guarantee there will be plenty of space for each guest."

"All right, then, send over the contract. We'll take a look. I like your vision. We'll see if you can follow through."

It takes all my willpower to not pump a fist in victory.

"Thank you, Mrs. Hawthorne. I won't disappoint you." I'm trying to contain my smile, but I'm fit to burst. Even this morning's events can't sour the moment.

The house erupts in chaos as the kids flood the room. One

child declares they're hungry. Another wants to know when they can have cake. One has stubbed a toe and runs over to *Naymee*, that is, Libby. The men decide it's time to light the grill.

"Oh, don't forget about the awards," Mary Beth stops me as I'm headed toward the front entryway. "Every year we honor an exemplary missionary family who serves for the church. Named after me."

"Momma. Uppie." Her little girl tugs at her sundress.

"A *Mary Beth award*?" I ask her. Of all the family members, it's not her I would've pegged as the vain type.

"Give Momma a minute, Ruthie." Mary Beth nuzzles noses with her toddler. "Go see, Naymee. She's got cookies." She nudges her back to the others. "More precisely it's a *Mary of Bethany Award*," she says to me. "After Mary of Bethany. She demonstrated a great love for Jesus, according to scripture. Isn't that something?" A thoughtful smile tugs at the corners of her mouth. "To love your children so much you'd give them biblical names. What special children, you know?"

"Very special indeed. I'm guessing you were named after Mary of Bethany."

"Was I?" Before I can even figure out how to respond, she says, "Your presentation was truly beautiful. You have a real *vision*, don't you? You can see things more . . . more clearly?" Mary Beth quirks her head. Her question throws me for a loop.

I don't talk to people about being brought back from the dead. Not that I mind; most conversations just tend not to go there. Sure, plenty of people know what happened to me. Heck, my own momma paraded me around our country church as the so-called miracle child for months afterward. I became a status symbol for her, like it made her holier by association. Not hardly. But this was fifteen years ago, and no one has talked about it in years.

For some reason, Mary Beth's question makes me uneasy.

She steps in closer, the smell the vodka strong on her breath. Mary Beth drops her voice so only I can hear. "Is it peaceful over there, after you're . . . gone? You were like, ten years old or so at the time, right? Is it a place a little girl could be happy?" Fear prickles up my spine. At my wary expression she adds, "I mean, you see awful stuff on the news all the time. And I hope there's peace after—"

Something crashes into the back window and causes one of the children to scream. Mary Beth and I jerk our attention to the rear of the house.

A darkness blocks out the sun as a shadow falls upon the home. Like a storm of hail, birds crash into the windows. Smashing into the glass like fists of anger. Tiny splatters of blood spray from their impact. Spiderweb fractures weaken the glass. Brutal, relentless thuds pound one after the other as it seems an entire flock has set upon the house.

The children erupt into fits of tears and screams. The adults do their best to shield their innocence, covering their eyes. But none of us can look away. The crack of glass, the screams, the darkness that's enveloped the room, and then—

It finally stops.

We stand there, drowning in the cries of the children, frozen from shock.

Slowly, I edge to the windows. I'm the only one who dares move, and I peer out.

Hundreds of red cardinals litter the back patio, sopping wet, yet there's not been a drop of rain all day. Their small bodies lie loose and limp in an unnatural way that only comes with death. A few twitch with spasms, their last fight for life.

"Cardinals don't flock," I hear one of the men say.

The nanny is frantically ushering the children into another room, with Libby and Nikki following. Jeremiah and Noah are slowly making their way toward the back door, unsure if it's safe but knowing they have to do something. It's time for me to go, too. The experience of it edging my nerves.

Only Mary Beth remains in the room as I leave, satchel over my shoulder, my legs antsy with the need to get going. She makes no move, no sound as I brush past her.

Something tugs at me as I get to the entry hall.

I turn to go back, to ask if she needs anything, if there's anything I can do, when I notice the family portrait from when she was younger. Something is different about this one. I move closer; it's almost like a pull as I'm now inches away from the oil-painted surface. I scan Jeremiah's face, Libby's, Noah's, and then I get to Mary Beth: she must only be about nine she looks so young. But as I'm searching her face it starts to move, like it's melting, like it's going to slide right off the canvas.

I hear a door slam shut, and it knocks me out of my trance. I glance back down the hall as Mary Beth presses her hand to one of the smears of blood on the window with a soft smile on her face.

 # CHAPTER
SIX

I'VE COME TO learn that death has a heavy hand, and it will take what it wants, when it wants. God might have something to do with it, I suppose. At least Grandaddy would preach it was the good Lord's decision when it was time for us to go. But it's hard to see anything of God in the death of hundreds of innocent cardinals. Drowned in the sky on a clear, sunny day.

A few years ago on the news, they showed a video from Mexico where a flock of blackbirds dropped down out of the sky so fast hundreds crashed to their death as they hit the ground. Scientists later said it was probably a predator who caused the synchronized flock to swoop so erratically and the earth was too close for them to dodge. Is there a predator in Hawthorne?

Let the skies darken and their wings of death rain upon them. Is this what that grave bird on Cain's shoulder meant? Surely not.

Mary Beth's face as she approached the broken windows still haunts my thoughts this morning. Though, my dreams, thankfully, were free of drowning girls . . .

Early this morning I snuck out of the greenhouse, hoping to avoid my new landlord, and headed to the bakery. There's nothing a sugarboo—or three—can't fix. The pink sugar-sprinkled rainbow muffin-cupcakes are something made from unicorn magic. Bren Dawson is the best baker I've ever worked with. Sweet Salvations used to be Berlant & Co. Fine Furnishings back in the forties. The historical, two-story corner building is painted a ridiculous shade of bubblegum pink. An arc of billowing flowers frames the stone-columned doorway and changes with the seasons. Inside is the downstairs bakery mixed seating of pastel pink and pale aqua. Giant rose-patterned wallpaper covers the walls. The tearoom upstairs, bistro-style more for light dining, is *the* spot for rubbing elbows with the who's who ladies of Hawthorne—or a great place to have brunch and mimosas. The whole place smells like cookies and hugs and dreams come true.

From my favorite spot at the marble window counter, I can see the whole of Main Street. Most of the stores are closed on Sunday; typically only those who serve food stay open. The Methodist church always dismisses its congregation early—Jesus must like them the most, because the Baptists are always running late.

"Between you, me, and the fence post," I overhear one of the ladies sitting at the bistro table behind me say, "that Landry fellow has a house in California *and* New York—or that's what Joanna said she heard."

"He doesn't look more than thirty. Surely he didn't make all that money on his own," the second woman says, sipping her tea. I keep my eyes on my computer screen but my ear stretched their direction.

"I bet he's a trust-fund baby," the first one says.

"Well, you know how June Monroe is—any single male under the age of forty, she's gonna push her daughter on them."

"Oh, bless her. She can't help it she's got her mother's bushy brows and mustache. I don't know why that child doesn't get it waxed. They're not broke."

"Speaking of broke," the second lady says, and then her voice quiets so low I can't hear the rest.

That Landry fellow also ruined my gala plans. I've spent all morning trying to find an alternate venue. Prospects are slim pickings around here. Every place within a fifty-mile radius is either too small, not nice enough, or already booked for the date. I've even resolved to search again for other properties for sale on Boucher's Real Estate website that are too big or out of my price range to buy. It takes a special house to be converted into a premiere venue; I have yet to find a suitable equivalent. I don't want to have to think about the alternative, having to make nice with the Richardsons and use the Serendipity Country Club.

All of this to say nothing of needing a place to live now, too.

"Can't you stay with Granny?" my younger brother, Denny, asks over the phone. Twenty-two with a set of twins and another baby on the way, I have no desire to trade shoes with him. I can hear my cute but terror-prone nephews wreaking havoc in the background.

"You know I can't stand to sleep in her spare room, with all those creepy dolls," I say, then mouth *thank you* to the server who drops off my muffin and refills my coffee. Not only that, too long at Granny's and the guilt would start to eat away at me. Everywhere you look in her house there are pictures of Grandaddy, who I took from her.

"Sorry, Holls, but Katie got rid of the futon to make room for the crib. You know Mom is here, watching the boys. I could ask her—"

"No! *Do not* tell her I don't have a place to live." For the love of God, the fastest way for Libby Hawthorne to get the news I've lost the venue would be a direct line from my mother. "Just tell her—" There's a fumble on the other end of the phone.

"You've got yourself in a fix again, Hollis, dear?" My mother's nasally voice pushes through.

"Hi, Debra Jean. No, I'm good." I fork a consoling bite of pink sprinkles and pray something will save me from this conversation.

"I can ask Barnaby if you'd like to stay with us? But I'm not sure how keen your stepfather will be on the idea. Honestly, dear, you don't anticipate your twenty-six-year-old child needing to move back home. You raise your kids, you expect them to stay gone."

I don't bother to correct her that Granny and Grandaddy mostly raised me. And Uncle Royce, too, after Grandaddy passed. Trying to find her next husband, my mother was too busy to raise her children.

"Your brothers are doing so well," she continues on. I can feel my body go cold with anger and frustration. "I don't know why you can't get a good job like them and stop with this play tea-party mess you've gotten yourself into."

I love my brothers, and they're hard workers, for sure, but I put myself through college to get a business degree to someday run my own event planning company. And still it's not enough for her.

My shoulder tenses up with an ache as she lectures me about needing to get my life in order. Which is rich, coming from a woman on her fourth marriage with debt up to her ears and three months jail time for credit card fraud—for opening an account in *my* name and the whole reason why I couldn't get my bank loan.

"Can't have you living with us for free. So, we'd have to charge you rent," my mother continues on as if I've already asked her. Her generosity is a desert.

My composure is hanging on by a thread, and I'm barely listening at this point as she drones on about my stepfather and what he'll have to say. I lean forward and press my forehead against the cool windowpane. My mother mentions something else about my brothers, and I chuff. A foggy spot of white forms on the glass.

Tiny cracks zipper out in little fuzzy lines from the center.

No, not cracks.

Frost.

Crystalline ice grows and melts and regrows on the window. I press a finger to the spot; it's now frigid. Reminding me of the afternoon Uncle Royce pulled me from the frozen river.

The tiny cracks alight at my touch. A panicked frenzy of what looks like electricity has formed, as if trying to get to me. It gathers in the center. And then it reforms and spreads, covering the tip of my finger. I yank my hand away from the glass. The cracks have grown and rip down the glass like icy veins onto the pristine white marble countertop toward me. They root across the marble, colliding into my pink teacup. The furry white frost grows over the lip of my saucer and up the side of my cup to the hot tea—

"You're so ungrateful for what's offered to you," my mother finishes in her snide tone.

The cup fractures with a *pop*. I jump back to avoid the splash of hot tea. The porcelain splits, and the shards fall away. A curved shape of frozen tea slides off the counter and onto the floor, shattering with a crash.

"What the hell?"

"Hollis, are you listening to me?" I hear my mother's voice push through the phone I'd nearly forgotten I was holding.

"Look, don't worry about it. I'll figure something out. Gotta go. Tell Denny I'll call him later," I say to my mother and hang up.

Scattered bits of teacup litter the parquet floor. I'm down on my knees, picking up the pieces, apologizing to the waitress for breaking it when Libby Hawthorne passes by the window. She does a double take when she sees me. I whisper a curse under my breath and quickly stand as she enters. A preemptive knot locks up my stomach.

"Mrs. Hawthorne, it's nice to see you today," I use my most casual, cheery voice like I wasn't just crawling all over the floor. I brush the dust off my pants.

"Is it true?" Her sharp tone takes me by surprise. My body tightens. *Damn, she knows.*

"Is what true?" I say, trying my hardest to sound earnest. I knew it would be a miracle if I made it past the Sunday morning service without her finding out.

"Don't play games with me," she says, an edge to her voice now. The hostess snaps her head our direction only briefly, then makes herself busy with cleaning menus. "We signed a contract with you, based on certain assumptions. If you can't deliver, I'll end your little soiree company before it has a chance to take off. Someone else bought the Gentry Mansion, and I want to know what you're going to do about it."

I take a measured breath before I respond. "As our contract states," I say in a firm, clear voice, "the venue is to be determined and finalized within two weeks of a signed contract. As the contract was only signed yesterday, we still have plenty of time to hammer out the details." The ladies at the bistro table gossiping earlier quickly glance at each other.

"You're supposed to have it at the Gentry Mansion, and from what I recall a significant portion of your presentation relied on that space being the final venue. Or is there some other spot in Hawthorne I'm somehow unaware of?"

"The Gentry home would certainly make for an excellent venue, and Mr. Landry and I are in talks to discuss its potential use."

"So you're working with this Landry fellow, then?"

I say a quick prayer to the good Lord above He doesn't strike me down for the lies I'm telling. "I prefer to think of him as a partner." And I wonder if maybe there is actually an angle there

I can work through with him. "We're negotiating the terms and its final design in more detail," I lie, leaving it as vague as I can without it sounding fishy. "I hope to have something to present to you by the end of the week." And before she can pry any further I say, "Now, if you'll excuse me, I'm on my way to a client meeting. I was simply stopping to pick up some refreshments. I'll be in touch." I close up my laptop and put it in my bag and walk over to the bakery display case.

"Hey, CeCe," I say to the young girl behind the counter. I feel Libby Hawthorne's eyes burning a hole in my back. "I'm going to need a dozen sugarboos to go. And put them in the fanciest box you got," I tell her, hoping this fake display of a robust client list buys me enough leeway. The entrance bells ching, and I hope it means Libby has left but I don't tempt a look.

Now I have to find a way to convince Cain to let me borrow his home for one night in September. This is going to take a miracle.

CHAPTER
SEVEN

IT WAS IN Uncle Royce's attic where I found the pair of finches.
I had never come across a pair of grave birds before, but there
they were, attached to a rocking chair that looked as if it belonged to a child from the sheer smallness of it. Dark cherry-
wood with roses carved into the top rail on the back. The seat,
embroidered by someone older than the house, is where they
sat. Chatterboxes, those finches were, the second I discovered
them up there. It was the chair's tendency to rock when no one
was in it that forever banished it to the attic.

I could hear the rocking through the ceiling whenever I slept
in the guest room. The slow back and forth sound of wood on
wood, it reminded me of my granny's rolling pin when she
worked piecrust dough. Uncle Royce's ex-wife had bought the
chair somewhere in New England at an estate sale for the nursery.

I couldn't figure out how two people could have died in such
a small chair until the grave birds showed me. Side by side, two
lives were shared. One in darkness. The other to a fullness as best

as she could. But a loneliness trailed beside the woman as she showed me her life. Snippets of time, all the brightest and darkest moments. It wasn't until she gave birth to her first children, a set of twins, that it occurred to the woman—and to me—what she was missing her whole life. Her own twin. Vanishing-twin syndrome, I'd venture to guess. When one embryo absorbs another. When she died in the chair, so did her absorbed twin. I can't be certain, but it's the only thing that makes any kind of sense with those two finches.

The rocking chair is long gone from the house. Sold at an estate sale by Uncle Royce's daughters.

As for those finches, they're long gone, too. All the dead woman wanted was to be heard, for someone to know her story. Then they disappeared.

That fresh box of sugarboos sits innocently on my greenhouse dining table, unaware of who they are going to be sacrificed to as soon as I can work up the nerve to ask Cain if he will let me rent the Gentry Mansion for one night in September.

"I was thinking of wearing one of my nice jumpsuits." I pull one from a large French armoire. The vintage piece I stripped down to raw wood and left unfinished is the only place I have to put clothes in this tiny studio. My brothers even installed a light inside. With its double doors, it's almost like a walk-in closet . . . almost, but not really.

"I hope not the orange one," Calista says over the speaker-phone. "You look like you have jaundice when you wear it." I put the outfit back and opt for a simple sundress.

When I was younger, picking out a dress for one of Uncle Royce's dinner parties felt like preparing to dine with royalty. Uncle Royce spoke three different languages: Finnish, German, and enough French to get himself into trouble, he used to say. Working as a consultant for foreign companies, he always had someone important in attendance, if not several important someones. Senators, oil tycoons, foreign dignitaries, and once we were honored by the prince of Asfedonia. (A small country I had never heard of, and to my tween self's dismay, he was not nearly as young nor as handsome as I'd been led to believe a prince would be.)

Tonight feels paramount compared to those evenings of the past. If I handle this right and win Cain over, maybe I can convince him to let me have the gala in *his* home. My stomach roils at the thought.

"It says here," Nadine, the internet sleuth, chimes in on the group call, "a company from Panama hired Cain as a consultant for imports."

"Of what?" I slip into the sundress. It flatters, narrowing at my waist, the color brightening my eyes. The dainty ruffled sleeve shows off my shoulders nicely.

"Grain. But then another website says sugar from Guyana. And then another website about an Orange County foundation says he's a board member of the Good Water Institute, which is worldwide. Oh, and he has a house in Belize, too—or so the *OC Weekly* mentions it's his *new home* in their recent 'Bachelors of Orange County' article."

"Hello, Mr. Hot and Single," Calista sings out.

"Hello!" Louisa shrieks. "Knock-knock. Hello." She dances back and forth on her perch, repeating it a few times.

"Makes sense. He doesn't sound Southern in the slightest," I say, thinking about the coldness in his voice. Southerners have a way of sounding warm, like maple syrup on a stack of pancakes. And I thoroughly ignore Calista's *single* comment, since it's only applicable to me *and* not something I'd even remotely consider.

I slip my foot into a nude sandal to see if it works with the dress. When I glance to check myself in the mirror, I catch sight of the second-story bedroom window. Only a sliver of a view but I can see his window through my greenhouse's glass roof when I stand near the front door.

His greenhouse now.

Cain's silhouette moves past a time or two. I doubt he has any idea what this house means to me and all the rich memories I have inside there. I bet for him, it was just a beautiful home he could add to his collection of other beautiful homes. A part-time place to live when he has a hankering to be somewhere else.

His silhouette pauses again.

And then a thought sneaks up on me. *I wonder what he smells like.*

In two strides Cain is back at his window, peering out to the gardens. I tense.

His eyes swing across the yard and find me. The cocktail glasses on my bar cart rattle lightly. A low buzz emanates from the floor, tickling the bottom of my feet, like the purring hum of a race car engine. The greenhouse feels like a furnace turned on High.

"Are you seriously going to ask him to borrow his house?" Calista's voice pulls me back.

I break eye contact with him and shake off the gnawing unease that's creeping up my arms.

"Not borrow. Rent." I grab my other shoe, then check my makeup once more. "People do it all the time with vacation homes. Sometimes movie companies rent a place out for filming. All I need is a week: a few days to set things up and a day or two to take it all down." And I'm not above guilting him about the situation either. "Shit. It's after seven. I better go before it's too late." Or before I chicken out. "Wish me luck, ladies!" They echo their wishes as I hang up. I grab the box of sugarboos.

Outside a light breeze swirls around my ankles, flirting with the bottom of my dress. The neighbor's wind chime tinkles *Good evening.* I try not to be too judgmental about the landscaping of the rear gardens as I head to the house's back door. It's only been twenty-four hours, and it seems the crew does have some semblance of an approach to return it to its former glory. Even the old oak tree looks a heck of a lot better trimmed up, though there is a matter of the unsightly blue tarp, covering the hole in the roof of my greenhouse—

His greenhouse—damn, it's going to take a lot of practice to get used to those words. I wonder if he'll keep it as a studio. I'd always planned to turn it into a guest rental. And I hope he appreciates these rear gardens once they're restored: they're perfection this time of day. The Carolina sun looks so beautiful when it hangs low in the sky, golden and nostalgic. The glow it casts right before sunset makes everything crisp and vivid, perfect lighting for a photo shoot.

A wedding out here would be a dream.

But I swallow that dream and lightly knock on the back door of a house that's not going to be mine.

The ballroom has always been my favorite part of this place. A vast open room that spans the width of the back of the house. With the twenty-foot floor-to-ceiling windows that make the gardens always feel like a part of the room. At one end, Uncle Royce had a backlit marble-and-onyx bar with custom honeycomb shelves to display the liquor. In the center sat a grand dining table for twenty that was the centerpiece for all those dinner parties. On the opposite side, a lounge area for cognac and cigars.

While I wait, I take a peek through a window to see what's been done to the place.

I can see a dark green velvet sofa. And a gorgeous carved wood coffee table, something vintage.

From my right, I hear a clatter of a door from the side of the house. I turn to see Cain walking barefoot toward the outside trash cans with a small bag he quickly tosses inside. My footing on the porch causes the wood to creak, and he sharply turns his head toward the sound.

Cain balks at the sight of me. He jogs up the side steps and heads across the porch toward me with purpose. As he does, out of the trees a small bird swoops down and gently lands on his left shoulder.

Not any bird. A robin.

His grave bird.

Cain doesn't seem to notice the bird, but he pauses to look over his left shoulder and scans the yard, like maybe there's something else out here with us.

In a few strides he reaches me. "Can I help you?" His voice is a clash of steel and silk, and I am not ready for it to run through me like it does.

Then, there's his grave bird, watching me watching it.

I force myself to focus on Cain and not the bird. "Hi, Mr. Landry. I'm Hollis, Hollis Sutherland. I believe Landon Boucher gave you a little bit of a spiel on me and the fact that I live in the greenhouse out back?" I pause, waiting for any kind of recognition that he knows who I am or what I'm even talking about. When he doesn't say anything, I press on.

"Yesterday we got off to a bad start, and I'm hoping we can try this again. Sugarboo?" At the questioning look on his face I open the bakery box. "They're like a muffin mixed with a cupcake, with a colorful happy interior, topped with sugar sprinkles and a *tiny* icing rose. Sin, in other words, in the form of a baked good." I flap the lid shut and push it toward him.

"I don't like sweets." His flat tone hits like a hammer to an anvil.

"Oh." I have never understood—or trusted—people who say they don't like sweets.

"Well, maybe your lady friend does?" I sugar up my accent and add a little extra nice on top, then push the box at him again, into that uncomfortable space where he has to take it: a real Southern gentleman would have been taught by his momma to simply accept the gift and say thank you.

He eventually does.

I leave my hand outstretched, now that it's free, and it's hard for him to ignore, even though you can tell he wants to.

"Cain Landry." He balances the Sweet Salvations box in one

hand and offers me his other, his little grave bird tottering with the movement. "Thanks," he says, gesturing to the box and opens the back door to head back inside.

"I was also stopping by to ask a favor." I wedge my foot against the door in case he started to close it. He turns around reluctantly. "A proposition, really. There's no short way around this, and I'm a get-to-the-point kind of woman, but I was wondering if you'd consider—"

"No," he cuts me off before I can even ask. "I said end of the month. It's the best I can offer. Good night—"

"Who's here?" someone interrupts. The woman in the black dress comes up from behind him. "Oh. It's you, the spitfire who caused a big ruckus yesterday," she says, with an impressed glint in her eye. "Come back for more?" Her voice is full of flavor and spice. "But I suppose we've not yet been properly introduced. I'm Paloma Cabrera," she says and smiles, reserved but polite. She steps underneath his arm to greet me, which causes his arm to flail upward and his little grave bird to fly.

I flinch as it swoops past.

My eyes dart to him, back to her: neither seemed to notice. Then I shake her outstretched hand. "Hollis Sutherland."

"I believe my godson might have gotten off on the wrong foot with you yesterday." Godson? I'm surprisingly pleased to know they aren't in an intimate relationship, but I don't want to read into what that means.

"It's an unfortunate thing, this business with the house," she says. "We were not aware that you were in process to purchase it."

"It wouldn't have stopped me from buying it," Cain adds, but Paloma spears him a look, something my granny used to do as a reminder to be on my best behavior or else.

No, I doubt it would have stopped him. He comes off as an assured, take-what-I-want kind of man.

"We don't want there to be any . . . awkwardness," she tacks on. There's a reserved quality about her: she's polite enough to be respectable without overdoing it. But I'm here on a mission, and I plan to kill them with kindness to accomplish it.

"No worries at all. As my granny would say," I offer my politest smile, "that was last week's supper, no sense trying to chew on a meal that's already been eaten. I should probably apologize for how hotheaded I was yesterday morning. Hopefully y'all can understand, seeing as I was taken by surprise by the tree almost murdering me in my sleep and all." I give an obviously fake little chuckle and cut a look to Cain when I say it. "Which brings me to why I've come today," I say. "I was hoping to share a little about the history I have with this house. Maybe talk to you about—"

"Have you found a new place to live?" Cain interrupts. "The end of the month will be here before you know it."

Paloma clears her throat. "What my godson means to say is we hope your search for a place is going smoothly."

"It's going" is all I say.

Tension builds in the air between us. It's so thick I could slice it with a knife. Cain's armored up behind a wall, and no one, not even with my sugary-sweet facade, is going to get past it. Whatever I'm trying to sell, he's not buying.

It was stupid to even think I could speak from my heart and tell him my life plan and he'd rent me the place, let alone hand over the key to his house.

So I step back and smile. "I appreciate the extra time y'all are allowing me to gather my things. I'll be packed and out by the end of the month. Y'all have yourself a good evening. A pleasure to meet you, ma'am," I say directly to Paloma and walk away.

From behind I hear her snip at Cain in another language. My Spanish is rusty, and I don't recognize any of the words. Portuguese? Or maybe something else. He responds, and it sounds like he doesn't agree with what she's saying.

Then silence.

I'm almost to the safety of the greenhouse when I hear the hurried steps coming up from behind.

"Hollis, please wait," Cain calls.

The nice-girl act is quickly losing steam. I slow my steps but don't turn around. He'll have to work harder than that if he wants my attention.

"Please," he says again as he catches up to me. "Look, I'm sorry about the way you found out about all this. I'm sure it must be tough to move when you'd so nearly snatched this house up from—"

"*Snatched?* As though it wasn't mine?"

"Well, it wasn't, was it? That's why I didn't buy it from you, I bought it from—"

"I know damn well who you bought it from," I spit, and he flinches, taken aback by my brashness. He opens his mouth again but nothing comes out, and I pounce on the cat-got-your-tongue moment. "You bought it from two ungrateful leeches who never gave a damn about this house or the man who lived here. I grew up here. I was supposed to buy this place, had been banking on that for months. I had plans for this house. Did you know that? I wanted to make this *the* venue for Hawthornians to celebrate life—for weddings and anniversary parties and retirement celebrations and fundraiser galas and whatever else. Then you come in here with your big fat wallet and your I-take-what-I-want attitude. And like that—" I snap my fingers "—it's gone. Everything I've dreamed of. Worked for. This house means something to me. My uncle raised me here. I loved his home and . . . and I had plans, plans to turn this place into something grand." Goddamn if my emotions don't teeter at the surface. "And for you to have an attitude about it, like I did something to personally offend you. What could I have possibly done to you? Because I apologized already for the way I behaved."

"You suggested it," he says.

"What? Suggested?"

"You said 'I *should probably* apologize.' That's not an apology, that's a proposition to an apology. A suggestion, but you didn't actually follow through."

I stare at him a long quiet moment, flabbergasted that *this* is the point he's focused on. And in that instant I hate him—his presence in my town, his money, his godmother, his goddamn grave bird, and the fact that he is right.

Then I burst with an incredulous laugh. "You know what? *Fuck off.*" As I turn to walk away, his hand catches my elbow, and the anger I was feeling drains out of me. I turn back to face him, and an icy chill spreads up my arm.

"You've seen her, haven't you?" His words shudder through me.

It's not what he says, but it's the calculating way those stormy gray eyes of his watch for my reaction that makes me feel . . . seen. Exposed. Like he knows everything he needs to know about me in this single moment.

His grip remains firm on my arm, even as I pull back. Everything around us has gone dark, and I can't look away from his eyes. I swallow hard. "Seen who?" But the effort in my voice is weak, and it gives away the lie I'm trying to spin.

He gently lets go of my elbow, and the rest of the world rushes back in, and all is as it was before. "I know she's here," he simply says. Slowly he turns, leaving me to stand in the gardens with nothing but my racing thoughts. They stumble on top of each other, trying to get to the front of the line.

How could he know about the ghost of a drowned little girl? That I dreamed of her? Is she visiting him, too? Has she been here before? Or did she follow him here?

A gust of irritated wind whips through the gardens. The sunset-stained sky has transitioned from orange to deep purple. I try to shrug off the shock of what he said—what I think he meant—and head back into the greenhouse.

"Good night!" Louisa says, when I enter. "Good night," she cries again until I slip her a cracker.

"No, Louisa, it was not a good night."

I walk past her cage and slip on a wet spot on the floor, landing hard on my ass, almost breaking my neck. "What the hell?" I stagger to my feet and flick on the light and find a puddle of water in the middle of the room.

The blue tarp covering the glass roof flaps from the wind, but the puddle's on the opposite side of the room. There are no ceiling cracks for this water to have leaked from. It didn't even rain today. I grab a towel from the bathroom, wondering if the water was there before and I just hadn't noticed it.

I kneel down to mop it up, and as I bend over the water the drowned little girl stares up at me from the reflection. I feel my soul slip loose.

"Fuck!" I scramble backward and crack my head against the glass coffee table, knocking over the vase. My heart jackhammers in my chest and jumps into my throat.

Suddenly, the room grows ice-cold. The windows fog over with a layer of frost. My breath puffs white.

I am no longer alone.

I can't see anyone, but I can feel them. *Her.* She's here.

The wind picks up outside. It whistles through the cracks of the windows, scratching to come in. The tarp on the roof ripples in waves until it peels back and rips right off as the floor lamp crashes to the ground and swipes a glass jar off my dresser on its way.

"Goddamn it, Hollis!" Louisa shrieks. I curl myself around her cage. The wind rages against the windows of the tiny studio, threatening to break them wide open, until the chaos simply stops and the room goes still, as if the wind was never there.

"You okay, girl?" I say, patting Louisa's cage then pulling down her cover so the darkness can soothe her. I turn around and take in the tornadoed mess of my apartment.

A tiny bird chirps above me. Slowly, I look up to the opening in the ceiling.

The fat little robin attached to Cain perches on the window frame of the roof. He tilts his little head back and forth with a curious nature. Looking at me.

"Oh, no you don't," I say, floundering to get away from it. I stumble backward over the fallen lamp and onto the couch, but my eyes never leave the bird. I try desperately to back away, but I'm too late. He hops down and lands upon my hand with a soft tweet.

The world tilts, and the fall through time is like a drop off a cliff in slow motion. My flailing arms are useless.

She smells of bubble gum and sweat. Her blond hair tickles my face. I squeeze tight around her neck as she struggles to carry me on her back over the burbling creek. The darkness grows thick around us. The jungle alive with the night. The pulse of her heart thrums under my arm. Fear. I've never seen her so scared. I only wanted to visit the cows, I didn't know they would make me sick. I don't want her to tattle on me to Mother. I tell her I'm sorry, over and over. My words murmur as the fever eats up my strength.

I know what this means. They will go on their trip without me, and I will have to stay home.

I dream of her. Later. Days later. Years later. I dream of her.

I miss her.

The room comes back into focus as I lie in the center of the greenhouse, staring up through the glass roof at a partial moon that's frowning at me. Regret anchors me to the floor, not mine but his. *I miss her* whirls in my head, a hushed repeat. Emotions scatter to the corners of my thoughts. Wispy threads. I try to capture them before they slip away. *Love. Adoration. She was my favorite, and I was hers.* It's just something I know. Truest of anything.

Then it's gone.

All of it. Wiped away like windshield wipers on a misty day, all that's left is a blurry smear.

Cautiously, I sit up. The night is deep in its thoughts as I am in mine. My fingertips touch the thin puddle of water still on my floor. *I miss her* echoes in my brain. I glance around the room and find the robin is gone.

I can't say for certain if the little robin is Cain's. I think maybe, but what I do know is that the owner of that grave bird personally knows the drowned little girl I've seen twice now. It won't be set free until I figure out what it wants. It's going to have to give me a better clue if it expects my help.

On the floor, the feathers I collect that used to reside in the now-broken jar are strewn about from the whirlwind that whipped through. A cardinal feather, the size of my pinky, the one I found outside after her first visit, lies near my foot. I pick it up and stare at it, hoping it will give me the answers to who she might be. How I can find her. What it is she's trying to tell me.

I have never had the dead come to me. They have always kept to their resting places with their grave birds. But a ghost seeking me out like this—it's never happened before. And it's hard not to notice that this coincides with the arrival of Cain Landry.

I go about picking up the pieces of my room. Parts of my heart feel scattered in the mess. It's hard to separate out if the lingering emotion is mine or the tattered remnants of the grave bird's.

After a moment I stop and look up to the second-floor window to Cain's room. I don't know why I do it, but when I do, I find him there, staring back at me.

CHAPTER EIGHT

MURDER FEELS LIKE a viable option today. Or at least assault, because I want to throttle Libby Hawthorne. She has needled me to death about amending the contract to include the Richardsons and have the venue at the Serendipity Country Club.

With only three days before my two weeks is up, I have no other choice.

"Granny, it wouldn't be for more than a week . . . maybe two," I say to her over the phone as I turn down the long and winding Country Club Lane. If I'm resigned to using the country club, I at least need to tour it, to know what I have to work with. I dread telling Granny I've signed a contract with the Hawthornes to plan their gala. I doubt she can imagine why I would do such a thing, and for *those* people. But she has a spare bedroom—filled to the brim with eerie dolls, sure—and it's rent free and the least likely option to give me a headache (as long as I don't mention the Hawthornes).

Of course, there's the small issue with my grave bird who likes to hang out with Granny. It used to be attached to the riverbank

where I died. I was happy for it to stay there. But then somewhere around eighteen years old, Uncle Royce convinced me I
needed to set right my own wrongs. That ended in a big disaster
when all it showed me was the day Grandaddy died, reminding me of what I regret most in life, like I didn't already know.
Now that little bastard always shows up whenever I visit her. It
makes it hard to stick around her long. But I'm in a pinch, and
that sparrow and I are just going to have to figure out how to
dwell in the same space.

"Well, sweet thing, you know I'd love me some company.
Bring your boxes over tonight, and I'll whip you up some real
supper. None of that microwave crap you usually eat."

My stomach gurgles in appreciation.

"Yes, ma'am. I have an appointment this afternoon, then
I'll come over afterward." The boxes in the back of my Honda
Civic sway as I turn into the valet's circle drive. "I have until the end of the month, so I'll bring over a few every day this
week. I gotta go, Granny. Love you." I roll down my window
to speak with the valet. "I'm here to drop off some boxes for
Libby Hawthorne. Can't I park in the staff—"

"Twenty dollars." The young punk rips off a ticket and hands
it to me.

"It says ten dollars right here." I point to the price on the ticket.

The boy is barely old enough to have a license, but he glowers
at me with an old man's exhaustion.

"We only get paid in tips," he says with a grunt as he opens
the door.

"Dear Lord," I say, grabbing my computer satchel as I get out
of the car. "You're Delaney Newberry's boy, right?" He stares,
waiting for me to go on. "How about you take those boxes inside and drop them off at the manager's office, and I won't tell
your momma you're scamming people at ten bucks a pop? That
sound good?"

He slips me an annoyed side-eye then groans.

Oh, I'm going to make him earn every cent of his tip.

The air outside is thick and dry, reminds me of the heat from the Arizona desert the time we went to see the Grand Canyon. It holds a static quality, too, like it's edging on a big storm. The stillness makes the hairs on my arms stand. The meteorologist didn't mention any rain, but they've been wrong before.

"Just a few more days in the greenhouse, Lord," I say to the gray sky. "Can you hold off on anymore catastrophes in my life for a few more days?"

The Serendipity Country Club is one of the historic land-marks in Hawthorne that once epitomized the wealth in this town. It used to be called the Royal Oaks, named after the huge oak trees that flank the front. A grand manor of an estate, once white, it's anchored by four pavilions. (Though the fourth pa-vilion is an unfortunate addition that departs from the original building's style.) Stately pillars hold up generous porticos that open up to dramatic views of the golf course and a pinch of the Carolina swamps. Then sometime during the eighties it got a name change and a not-so-grand facelift. The crisp white was changed to a dull Nantucket yellow, the beautiful rose brick now a mud brown. The grass on the golf course looks dead no matter the time of year. The swamps are so overgrown you're likely to find a gator in the water hazards every other week.

If I could get my hands on this place, I'd turn back time and go back to its glory days of the forties. At least the original chan-deliers are still here, one last vestige they didn't ruin.

"I'm here to meet Libby Hawthorne," I say to the hostess, who looks to be about fifteen.

I follow her along a hallway toward the back. You can tell exactly when they added this dining room pavilion. The navy-and-gold paisley carpet, worn and exhausted, looks like it came from an economy motel and easily dates the addition back to the late eighties. We're going to need a lot more midnight fabric to hide the ugly wallpaper in here.

This place is in serious need of a facelift.

The hostess gestures to the table when we arrive, leaving me with a faux smile plastered across my face. "Good afternoon, Mrs. Hawthorne."

"Did you bring the place settings for me to review?" she asks as a waiter brings her dessert. I check my watch to make sure I haven't arrived at the wrong time. But classic Libby with no regard to other people's schedule has ordered dinner . . . for just herself.

"Yes, I had the valet take it to the manager's office. And I have a meeting set up with the Richardsons later, so I'll get you an amended contract once I get clarity from them."

"Wonderful," she says blandly. "As you can see I'm finishing my dessert," Libby says in a rather snooty fashion, as if my presence is a nuisance.

I re-up my fake smile and quite literally bite my tongue as I say, "No problem. I wanted to check some things while I'm here. I'll meet you in the manager's office."

Once I'm done, I head up to said office where Libby is reviewing the flatware options. She's slightly hunched over the table, seemingly deep in thought about the weight of the utensils. "Did you pick out which place setting you wanted to use?" I ask.

She whips around suddenly with a blazing look on her face, and I'm taken aback.

"Is there something wrong with the samples?" It should all be perfect. I checked everything myself this morning.

She flips open one of the boxes and fetches an envelope from inside. "Who in the hell do you think you are?" Her face is almost wild, her glare full of anger.

"Excuse me?" I can feel my pulse start to race, and I take a small step back.

"Don't think me a fool. I know who your grandmother is. What she blames me—my family—for. So you think you can—what, bully me with this?" She flaps a handful of photos at me. I barely catch sight of the images, but it looks like family photos, maybe on vacation somewhere. "Whatever it is you think you know, you don't. Whatever game you're playing here, you're gonna lose. I will not be blackmailed." She bites out the last part.

"*What?*" I yawp, still trying to get a better look at what she's holding. "I've no idea what you're talking about. Mrs. Hawthorne—"

"You expect me to believe you had nothing to do with this? These were in the sample boxes, your sample boxes, clearly meant for me."

"Mrs. Hawthorne, I have no idea what's going on. If you'd just . . ." I reach out so I can take a closer look at the pictures, but she quickly yanks her hand back, clutching those photos to her chest.

She studies me a second, trying to decide if I'm telling the truth or not.

"This must be some kind of mix-up. Maybe the staff switched up the boxes? Or those photos fell in by mistake? I'm sure it's nothing. If you let me see, I can probably clear this up."

Libby glances to the boxes then back to me, still wondering if she's pegged this wrong.

"Yes," she draws the word out. "The staff. Yes. I . . . I suppose," but her unsure tone isn't convincing. Then she hurriedly stuffs the pictures back into the white envelope, but her hand shakes as she does so.

A single photo falls to the floor. I bend to get it; our heads almost butt. She snatches it from me.

But not before I saw.

It was a quick glimpse but there's no denying the beautiful, rusty-haired woman in the photo.

Someone I've seen once before.

The ghost woman at Hawthorne Manor.

We stand there, scrutinizing each other, neither of us sure what to say.

Quickly, I school my face to appear nonplussed by the unusual exchange.

"Well, let me know what place setting you decide on." I nod toward the boxes and try to pretend that's all I'm concerned with. "Once you do, I'll reserve them for the event."

"Let's hope there won't be any more hiccups from here on out," she says with a bit of haughtiness returned to her tone.

My eyes dart to the envelope she's clinging to, even though I tell them not to.

"If that's all you need," she says rather dismissively.

"That's all." I force a polite smile and leave.

But the image of the woman gnaws at my thoughts like a dog with a bone. I can still see her grave bird leashed to the floor under the desk, a mourning dove. A woman died in the room or else a little bird wouldn't be there.

Blackmail. That's what Libby said. If someone died at Hawthorne Manor, wouldn't it have been front page news? Those kind of rumors are hard to tamp down. Maybe old news, and I've just never heard about it?

Or maybe it happened, and the Hawthornes had it erased.

I didn't know Noah Hawthorne had a sister until a few days ago when I saw Sarah Hawthorne in their family's oil painting. Deep pockets can erase all kinds of secrets.

When I step outside to get my car from the valet, a hot wind shoves itself into my face. The gray clouds, now roiling with vigor, look like they're about to unleash themselves on the town. No sooner does the thought cross my mind, the sky splits open and spits out a fierce bolt of heat lightning. The vein rips a jagged line straight to the earth. It cracks with a thundering boom as it hits the ground.

A collective gasp comes from the handful of us who were caught standing outside. The valet's umbrella crashes over. I grab the keys from the valet's hand and whip my Honda Civic out of the circular driveway as fast as I can, the ghost woman in the photo heavy in my thoughts.

What was it she asked me to help her find in the desk all those years ago? *A key.* A key to what? A drawer? A door? A lockbox? She said it was important. I wonder if she ever found that key.

But what would cause Libby to be so upset? What is in those pictures that Libby's so scared of?

As I drive away from the country club, leaves skitter across the road like they're running for their lives. Trees on the side of the road shake like angry fists raised to the sky. The air is so dry my mouth feels like I'm sucking on cotton.

I adjust the rearview mirror. Behind the darkening clouds is a red glow, as if the sun is bleeding.

I was headed home to finish packing, but the woman in the photo has a hold on my mind. And the grave bird.

That's how I find myself turning toward the historical district.

Down Hawthorne Lane.

To Libby Hawthorne's house.

CHAPTER NINE

THE DAY IS fighting to stay alive with the almost black clouds blocking the sun. A fiery red strains to break through. I park in the street, eager to get inside the Hawthorne mansion and find that mourning dove grave bird and see what it has to say.

The wind whips my hair across my face, and I fish strands of it out of my mouth. I stand at the grand doorway with my prop, a box with nothing in it, and a bag of courage that feels damn near empty.

The door swings open to the lovely older woman who let me in last Saturday.

"Linda," I say.

"Lydia," she corrects, shying away from the harsh wind. She sneaks a peek of the sky, not liking what she sees.

"Yes, that's right. Lydia. So sorry. I'm here for a meeting with Libby." I move as if to enter the house, but Lydia steps to block me.

"Mrs. Hawthorne isn't here."

"Oh." I frown and check my watch. "I'm a little early. I'm sure she'll be along soon." I can feel my pulse jump into my throat. Silently I'm willing her to let me in.

When she doesn't budge, I glance warily over my shoulder at the growing storm. "Maybe I could just wait in her office until she gets here?"

Out back a man hollers for Lydia's help because the patio furniture is blowing into the pool. She sighs. "I suppose." Reluctantly she allows me inside.

"I know the way," I assure her. She hurries out back to help the man chase the tumbling pieces.

All those oil paintings in the entryway seem to watch me as I walk past them; I suppress a shiver. I disappear down the right hallway in the vague direction of the office where I found the ghost woman that day. East wing, back of the house, is as much as I can remember.

With the chaos of the outside shut out, the silence in the home is unnerving.

The walls and floors are different, but the energy is the same, hollow and sad. The stark quiet feeds my fear. Or maybe it's nervous anticipation. Time seems to slow. My senses tighten, narrowly focused on where I'm going. All I can hear are the slow ins and outs of my steadying breaths.

Down the hall I pass a bathroom and a billiards room, and then I see the door at the end of the hall.

This is it. I can feel it.

I grip the doorknob and turn.

The office has changed drastically in the last fifteen years. The shutters are drawn, but I can still tell: the mahogany wall of bookshelves are now painted a fresh white and filled with feminine decor, not the stodgy books that used to live here. The substantial desk that once floated in the middle of the room is gone, and now there sits an antique writing desk with wooden claw feet that grip glass balls.

And underneath . . .

Gently, I exhale a measured breath, then kneel.

Sure enough, just where I expected her to be, the mourning dove soundly sleeping under the desk. Waiting, for at least fifteen years—or maybe longer. Her transparent gray body almost invisible in the darkness of the room. But her outline is there. Her eyes pop open as she senses me. Black beady orbs scan me, confused.

"I'm sorry you had to wait so long," I whisper to her. She coos a soothing sound. "I'm ready now." I open my palm to her.

She works to push herself up onto her feet, like she's too old and her legs too stiff. She waddles over into my hand.

And I fall back in time.

We land just after midnight. A storm, wicked and ornery, brews in the sky. Rain so thick the driver can barely see a car's length in front of us.

"She wants to meet," my husband whispers.

A knot catches in my stomach. "I don't like this. Not with the children." I glance over the back seat to the SUV's third row, the children sleeping soundly from the long trip.

"I agree," he says. "Driver?" he calls to the man the housekeeper sent to pick us up.

The man's dark eyes glance upward to the rearview mirror, cutting and emotionless.

"Do you know of a Johnson's Autobody near Camden?"

The man simply nods.

"Good, then. Drop me off there. Then take my wife and children to the house." My husband turns to me. "When you get to the house, go to the office . . ."

My fear gobbles up every bit of his instructions. Separating seems like a bad idea, but he wants to make sure we're safe.

At the house, darkness eats up the room. Only the shallow glow of the green lamp hovers close to the desk. My heart gallops. My hands are clammy. All I can think is We shouldn't be here. *My husband has never been wrong about these things, though. His worry was so serious when we dropped him off.*

I say a small prayer to our dear Lord, asking him to put a protective hand down upon our family.

"Mother?" my son calls from the hallway. His voice croaking from exhaustion and adolescence.

"In here," I answer. A moment later his silhouette blocks the hall light that barely bleeds into the room, as if scared to enter the space. "Come, child." I fan him over. "Help me look."

"Are we staying here?"

It's hard to explain to a child who has never experienced anything but love why someone would have so much hate in their heart.

"No. Your father doesn't trust her," I simply say. It's not fair the children have been thrust into this situation. They've been away now longer than they were ever here. But God doesn't give us more than we can handle, I remind myself. We will fare through this together.

"Is this it?" He holds up the small plastic trout key chain with the number 14 etched in black. A single silver key dangles from the mouth.

"Yes, love." I sigh with a huge relief. "Now, go fetch your sister. The driver will take you both there. As soon as your father returns, we will come straightaway." Down the hall he gathers his sister; I go about putting the desk back as we found it. The corner of an envelope catches my eye. A stack of letters accumulated over the years. Years of fond memories. I miss our life. My boy. The simplicity. Soon, I tell myself. Soon we will all be back home, together.

Heavy footsteps fall outside the door. I only half glance behind me. "You're back already? I still need to pack our things, then we can go." I return the letters to the drawer and douse the lamplight.

"No problem." His rusty voice cleaves the dark. That's not my husband.

The man's shadow inches into the room. For a breath, he looks to have horns. The light from the hallway slowly retreats. Then a soft click snaps the silence as the door latches shut. Trapping me in with him.

Quickly I whir on the man. "What do you—"

I don't even feel the crack against my head. Just hear the loud, suctioned knock as wood meets skull. Then I spin. Face hitting the floor. Fibers from the wool carpet stab my eye through the hurried blinks—the only eye I can see from now.

Words are rendered useless as my brain stutters in disjointed code. It rifles through the files of my life, shoving forward scrambled chunks and erratic bits. I feel my tongue pushing at the back of my throat as I choke on a scream.

Jolted awake. An electric shock of stark fear bolts me upright as if thrust from a nightmare. Panic holds my brain hostage. *The children. The children. The children.* It's all I can cycle through. *Were the children far enough away?*

My breath comes in quick sharp huffs as I reorient my senses to the here and now and let go of the past. The two briefly overlap until they drift further and further apart and all that's left is the present. This tangle of emotions is not mine, but it clings to me as if I gave it life.

This moment, *this* is the moment in her life she regrets the most. I can taste it on my tongue, acrid and bitter like the shell of a pecan.

I close my eyes and try to squeeze out a few more drops of the memory before it vanishes.

The letters, wrapped in soft ribbon and well-worn from being read repeatedly. The man, he had a slim build from the silhouette I glimpsed. The sour smell of his sweat mixed with the sweet scent of whiskey and motor oil. His voice was steel wool and smoke.

And those devil horns.

I saw them, too. Their spiky shadows were there, then they weren't. Gone in a blink. But I saw them. What it means, I don't know.

What did her husband know? Whatever it was, it worried him. Worried her. Enough to make their family run. From what?

There was a murder in this house. Whether the Hawthornes know it or not, it happened. That grave bird has been there fifteen years at least, maybe years longer. Could have been there decades, even. It's hard to say for sure when she lived.

Blackmail was the word Libby used. Does she know something about this house and what happened a long time ago? Did she have something to do with it?

There's something familiar about the trout key chain. Like a ghost of the image already exists in the back of my mind, waiting for me to rediscover it. I can't put my finger on why it would be there, hanging out in my thoughts. Unless I had seen it once before.

The mourning dove flutters on top of the desk, now free. Then it flies over to the closed window and turns back toward me. It simply looks at me and gives a soft coo, as if to say *I've given you what you need.* Then it disappears through the glass and out into the world.

I hope that little bird is right. I push myself up back onto my feet.

At the commotion down the hall I stop to listen. Off in the distance I hear the crooning wail of a siren. A tornado warning. Followed by the frantic voices of others.

I rush to get outside.

The front door already flung wide open. A violent, hot wind whips down the hall and licks my face with the heat of a too-close bonfire.

Up in the sky a blazing, bloodred sun. Gray smoke swirls in funnels as three fire tornadoes rage through town.

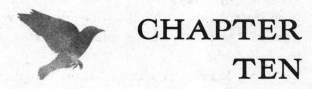

CHAPTER TEN

LIKE A HELLCAT I tear through the streets, trying to get home. Ash falls like a dingy snow. Sirens cry for help all over town.

I get stuck behind a cluster of abandoned vehicles at the four-way stop as a few lookie-loos are out of their cars filming the whirling flames dance through town. Skinny ribbons of fire whip out with erratic movement then suck back up into the clouds, only to dart down again.

Never, in all my days, have I seen such a sight.

My sinner's heart skips through passages in Revelation.

The Second Coming. The Four Horsemen. The end of times.

Fear prickles over my skin like a cold douse of water. I grab my phone and call my Granny. Then my brothers. Nadine.

Finally Calista answers. "Holy fuck! Are you seeing this?"

"Yeah. Are you safe?" I cough as the air thickens with smoke. A police officer directs the others to get back in their cars and head back the way we came. I wind through the side streets to see if I can get home the long way.

"Yes. We were at the bakery when it hit. They're evacuating

people from Main Street to the football stadium. It came so fast. And it skipped!" Her voice pitches with shock. "It literally skipped down the freaking center of town, picking off stores with the flick of its fingers. It got the hardware store across from us. I think maybe the bank. Someone said multiple have touched down."

"Yeah, I saw three when I left the Hawthornes'. Have you heard from Nadine?" Every street I turn down I get redirected farther and farther away from home.

"I got a text. She was on her way home from Mauldin when Jackson called her and said stay away until we figure out what's going on."

"What *is* going on?" My words sound lost and broken.

A stitch of silence tightens between us.

I can hear the gathering of people in the background on her end. Worry layered in their voices as they attempt to comfort each other.

"I don't know, love," she eventually answers. Her heart sounds as heavy as mine feels. Another long pause, as we both swallow terrifying thoughts. "But we're going to be okay."

"Yeah?" But will the town?

"Beau's calling me," Calista says. "I'll call you back."

I try my family again, but all I get is a generic *We're sorry. All circuits are busy now. Please try your call again later.*

At another roadblock, I loop the back through a quiet cul-de-sac when a call finally comes through. Both my brothers and Denny's family are okay; they're headed out to Granny's since she's far enough away from the chaos, thankfully. I promise to be there as soon as I grab Louisa and Sampson. A ripple of fear for the worst tries to hijack my thoughts. What if it's too late?

"They're going to be fine," I say aloud to reassure myself. "You don't know if the fire is even near the house. Just stop it."

Then I wonder how Cain and Paloma are faring. It's one thing to know this town and the many roads you can take to safety. It's another to have no idea where to go during an emergency.

On the bypass I get hung up with everyone else who had the same brilliant idea to navigate around the town. We're all driving at a snail's pace, watching as a billow of black smoke chugs into the sky. From this direction, it's hard to say what's burning. Something near town, for sure. And something east, out by the levee where two smaller whitish-gray plumes seem to be dying down.

A narrow sliver of space where Uncle Royce's and Nadine's houses sit is wedged somewhere in between. I can't be certain it's safe.

Suddenly the traffic ahead diverts. "Are you kidding me?" I steer slightly to the side to see the fire marshals redirecting everyone to exit the bypass.

Far off on the right, out in the middle of acres and acres of land, fat and happy and well away from any danger, sits Hawthorne Missionary Baptist. It's a massive brick building that looks like any other Southern church but magnified by ten. Inside three seating levels break up the congregation. Church bells in the massive white steeple can be heard for miles. The parking lot wraps around it like a fanned concrete collar. The memorial mural on the side of the church looks morbid the way the big smiling faces of Jedidiah and Patsy Hawthorne gaze toward town, as if they're enjoying the fire show, eager to see it all burn to the ground.

They file us into the church parking lot like cattle. Clusters of people gather outside their cars and huddle close, whispering prayers of comfort. Only a thin, fiery tail of one tornado dangles from the sky, slowly losing its enthusiasm. Eventually it dissipates. Only dark, brooding clouds remain. The red glow hiding behind, that seems to be the culprit in all this, has calmed to a simmering orange.

I wind my way to the rear of the parking lot, not in the mood to be commiserating with the masses. Bren Dawson, my neighbor and baker friend, texts to let me know they aren't letting people in the neighborhood yet—and no word on Sampson or Louisa. I overhear one of the others waiting say they're only letting essential personnel back in town tonight, so I call my little brother to come pick me up.

Twenty minutes later, Dylan arrives on the Gator, an all-terrain utility vehicle. A country boy will always find a way. It's three farms between the church and Granny's house, but back roads are easy to travel if you have the right transportation.

You could call Granny's property a family compound, really. Granny and the farm sit in the middle. Denny and his wife and kids live in the small white house down on the corner. Dylan lives the other way in a two-bedroom trailer. There's an empty plot of land saved for me, like a splinter in your thumb you can't get out. That empty plot of land has been festering away at me for years. But it's going to stay empty.

Both my brothers help Granny manage the farm on the weekends. Not the land—she rents it to the Callahans who rotate crops between cotton and soybeans. But there's a smattering of animals she maintains: a cow named Myrtle, two miniature donkeys, an ornery goose she rescued from a petting zoo, and a handful of hens.

By the time we get to Granny's, everyone is gathered up for dinner.

"Ho-Ho!" my little nephew Jack screams as we walk in. He hops off his momma's lap and tackles me with a hug. His brother, Finn, follows right behind him, waddling in his diaper. I hold them tight as I can, so grateful they're safe. I hope others in town are as lucky as I am. Katie stays home with the boys since they don't start preschool until next year. I'm glad they live way out here, far enough from the danger that all you can see from here are the trails of smoke in the distance.

"It's fire," Finn says. His eyes bulge big as he points toward the television.

"Big fire." Jack arcs his arms over his head; it pushes his little potbelly out. I can't resist a poke.

"Scary stuff, right? You keep Momma safe?" They nod eager yeses. "Good boys."

Jack and Finn look like their daddy and Uncle Dylan did when they were little. Wild brown tufts of hair, perfect pudgy noses, and eyes that smile with mischief. Katie and Denny were high school sweethearts, and then *Whoops, it's twins!* Now they're married with a third on the way.

Granny's place is classic grandmother. Everything is decades old, but looks like she bought it yesterday, it's been so well-preserved. A moss-green sofa butts up to a floral wingback chair. Handmade doilies, like cobwebs, cling to every table as if they're coasters for the decor. An eclectic mix of figurines and photographs suffocate every available surface.

We all gather around the television in the living room, fear and worry huddling us together as we watch the news, trying to make sense of what's happening. Denny wonders aloud if the water treatment plant blew up, but Dylan confirms it was fine as he passed it leaving the factory. The evacuation orders make it difficult for reporters to sort out the chaos going on in town. We even discuss the possibility of arson, but the authorities can't determine exactly where the fires started, much less the cause. While the twisters seem to have subsided, there are still lots of small fires that have crews racing around to stamp them out. Locals have even taken to using their own water hoses to assist.

"Are there wildfires in the area?" Denny asks, taking Finn from Katie's arms. "Because these fire funnels don't make sense. There's no ground source or any strong winds, for that matter."

That's something I'd wondered, too.

"This all feels so . . ." Katie starts, rubbing her cross pendant between her fingers, "so ominous . . . like Revelation-type stuff." She finally lands, and I couldn't agree more.

The bizarreness of it all has an eeriness creeping up my spine. I'm not sure what to make of it myself, but my gut tells me something more is at play.

"What do y'all think it means?" Katie asks. None of us have an answer.

"Come on, now," Granny says as she steps from the kitchen, drying her hands on a dish towel. "Let's take a break from all that . . ." she fans a wayward hand, not sure how to label it either ". . . and have something to eat, settle our nerves."

A breather from all the dark news is a welcome break.

"Let Ho-Ho get a plate." Katie pulls Jack from my lap. I follow Granny into the kitchen, where she takes the cornbread from the oven.

"Did you call your father?" she asks, setting the iron skillet on the stove to cool. "He'll see it on the news and worry."

"Dylan said he told Sherrie." My father and stepmother moved to Gulf Shores years ago to take care of her parents. If we didn't make the effort to see him, he sure wouldn't. So I doubt he'll fret one bit.

"And your momma?" she asks. I shrug. She grunts a disapproving sound.

If there's one thing I can be certain of, we'll never starve as long as Granny's alive. You can guarantee there will be a full course meal even if you're only stopping by. I pinch a piece of coconut icing off the cake she clearly baked this morning.

"I'll probably stay tonight, if it's all right?"

"Of course, sweet thing." Granny rests a hand on my cheek, getting a good look at me through those pearl-rimmed glasses of hers. The kind of sight only a grandmother can have, where she can look into your eyes and know exactly what's ailing your heart. "Where are your things? Could you get back to your place? How's that nasty kitty and that foulmouthed little bird holding up?"

I sigh. "I don't know, Granny. Haven't heard anything other than they're not letting people back in the neighborhood. I hope they're okay. I hope the house is still there."

She lowers her voice slightly. "I'm sorry you weren't able to buy Royce's place." Her words are so tender it causes those few threads that are barely holding me together to loosen. "I know what it means to you."

I don't know if I fall into her arms or if she pulls me in for a hug, but I needed this, a soft place to land.

From the corner of my eye, I catch a small flutter. It swoops into the room and lands on Granny's recipe stand. I tense and quickly shrug away from her.

A small house sparrow.

My sparrow. My grave bird.

Always around to ruin a good moment.

"Thanks, Granny," I say. It's a bitter sound to my own ears.

I ignore that damn little sparrow as best I can, pretend like it doesn't exist. But for some reason it enjoys reminding me of that fateful day. Like I need a reminder.

I remember that day clearly. It's seared in my brain like a brand to cattle. I was nervous as hell, browsing through Roy's Drugstore, like I was deciding on what I wanted to buy when what I was really waiting on was Mr. Pattinson to tend to Libby Hawthorne and stop paying attention to me.

I had eyed it the week before knowing it was the perfect Christmas gift for Granny. She had recently knitted a sweater of blue teal and rich green. I imagined her walking into our simple country church, looking like a queen wearing her fine jewels.

But the tables turned, as two weeks after Grandaddy died, we celebrated Christmas—as best one can under the circumstances.

Wrapped up with a pretty bow under the Christmas tree, a present for me.

From Grandaddy.

My heart ached knowing he bought me something even though he was no longer here. It's like God was giving me one last gift to keep.

A gift it was indeed.

My stomach clenched when I unwrapped the little teal velvet pouch and emptied the contents into my hand.

The peacock haircomb.

"We found it in the truck," Granny said with every bit of love in her heart. "He bought it for you for Christmas," she said. "It's going to look so good with the sweater I knitted you."

Sick I was. Heartsick and nauseous. I wanted to crawl under a rock and die. I didn't do so well acting like I was happy about the gift. The sorrowed look in Granny's eyes near broke me.

Grandaddy must have bought the haircomb from Roy's Drugstore as an apology for having a horrible granddaughter. And Granny obviously thought he bought it for me as a Christmas gift.

And God wanted to make sure I never forgot it.

I swallow down the memory and try not to get choked on my feelings as we carry the food to the supper table. Denny says the blessing with a thoughtful prayer for those who might have been affected today. He reminds me of Grandaddy, the way he used to pour his heart out to God over every meal, even if it was just bologna and crackers. Then we dig into the evening dinner of black-eyed peas, mashed potatoes, country-fried steak, and a skillet full of cornbread. And try to set aside our worry and pretend everything is normal, if only for a few minutes

After everyone is gone, it's just Granny and me and the *Wheel of Fortune* as we wait for the news to come on. She's sewing away at one of her sassy cross-stitch patterns. Last time it was IF YOU'RE HAPPY AND YOU KNOW IT, IT'S YOUR MEDS. Tonight's piece: HOME IS WHERE YOU TAKE YOUR BRA OFF. She sells them at the church bake sell to help fund her Soul-Glam Sisters choir trips. Like the time they went to the casinos in Tunica. Granny *swears* they only played bingo.

I'm sitting on the couch drawing in a notepad I took from the kitchen junk drawer. There's too many thoughts in my head right now, too much swirling around, and I can't make sense of any it. Fire tornadoes? In Hawthorne? Sounds like something straight out of scripture. My mind jumps to the earthquake a couple days before, when I was at the bank. Not something we typically see here either. Neither were the hundreds of cardinals that nearly bashed through the window at the Hawthorne place. And then there's the cicadas—right on time, according to their seventeen-year cycle. But still: a plague of bugs, an earthquake, a mass death of wildlife, fire raining from the sky.

Vengeance will be mine.

That's what the grave bird on Cain's shoulder shared with me the day he arrived. It spoke of the rattling earth, raining wings of death, fire from the sky. All of it has come true.

"Whatcha drawing there?" Granny looks up from her stitching to ask me.

"Something I happened upon earlier today." Before all the chaos. "I know I've seen this before. I can't recall where, though." I hold up the notepad. It's the trout key chain the grave bird showed me.

"That's the Kappy's Campground trout." An inkling of what she's saying starts to form. "You know, the old billboard used to be out on Highway 19, right after you pass Good Eats."

"Oh yeah!" That's how I know it. When we were kids, Granny and Grandaddy would take us out to the Good Eats restaurant for the all-you-can-eat buffet of home cooking; it's long closed up now. There was an old billboard with a faded Kappy the Trout, who pointed his fin down the road to THE BEST FISHING HOLE IN THE COUNTY! "Is Kappy's Campgrounds still a thing?"

Granny shakes her head as she knots her last stitch and snips off the excess thread. "Not for a long time. It's been shut down for more than thirty years now, back when the water treatment plant diverted the river. Now it's a bunch of abandoned camp houses where pockets of water collect when it rains good enough." Granny narrows her focus on the needle she's threading. "You know what a little bird told me?"

From her tone alone, I have a pretty good idea what she's heard. I close my eyes and prepare myself for a tongue-lashing.

"That you've landed yourself *the* event of the year." She glares at me over the top of her glasses, daring me to lie to her face.

"Granny, this is just—"

"Hush, now," she chides. "You think you know what I'm going to say, but you're wrong. Now, I can handle you prospering your business—even if it means you're working with those awful folks, but what I will not tolerate is my granddaughter thinking she can't tell me herself. I had to go and hear it from Big Mouth Barbara Jean . . . Of all the people in this town, I'd rather not hear it from a woman who spreads gossip in the form of a prayer request."

"I'm sorry, Granny. I was going to tell you when I got here."

"Days later? That's no excuse, Hollis."

"I know, it's just . . . I knew you weren't going to love the idea."

"And what should I love about it, exactly? You working with those terrible, greedy, no-good people."

"But, Granny, this is such a big opportunity for me. And the gala is for a good cause."

"Patsy and Jedidiah would roll over in their graves if they knew about that monstrosity of a church their children built in their name. Look at how much money they rake in from the gala alone. It's vulgar. What kind of so-called church needs that much money?" Granny smarts her head.

"Well, they do good with it, don't they? Send people on mission trips, fund charities—that sort of thing."

Granny leans forward, resting her elbows on the arms of her brown recliner. Her eyes narrow on "Name one."

"Name one what?"

She smirks, knowing she's about to take me somewhere. "Name a single missionary they've sent. Or a place they send them."

"Well . . . I don't know. I don't go to their church. The funds raised from the gala aren't really related to the work I'm doing for the Hawthornes."

"You know Gloria Marie? Pete and Marsha's kid?" she asks. I sort of know her, still in college I think, but the name is definitely familiar. "Where did she go on her mission trip last year?"

"To Habitat for Humanity down in Mexico."

"Exactly. And you don't go to her church either. But you knew about the mission—it was all over town, posters and flyers and kids stopping in businesses, trying to raise awareness." Granny has a small point, just not sure it's strong enough to support what she's insinuating here. "People love to brag about the lives they're touching, the good they think they're doing. You'd think someone from their church would be proud of the missionaries they support. At least invite them to guest-speak and share their testimony with the congregation. Yet, you never hear nothing about them. Just a generic *We're doing good work here, now give us your money.* I'll tell you what. Your grandaddy knew exactly what they were up to. No good! That's why they got him. Shut him up permanently, they did. Who does construction on a Sunday? That truck had no business being out on the road the day you and your grandaddy got hit. No business whatsoever."

I mull over the point she's trying to make. Maybe it is a little odd; I can't think of a single mission coming out of Hawthorne Missionary Baptist . . . maybe ever? Maybe they keep quiet for a reason, trying not to brag or boast? But surely I would know something about their efforts. I mean, damn, the whole town is named after the family. You'd think they want to fund half the charities here, and yet all they focus on is the missionaries they send out. I'm still racking my brain for any known charitable work the Hawthornes do, when the late news comes on.

"Meteorologist Consuela Alverez is an expert in weather phenomena," the newscaster says, bringing my attention to the television. "She's here to explain the natural disaster that occurred today over in Hawthorne."

The weather expert explains fire tornadoes are rare and usually occur with severe winds that can accompany wildfires. But it's not fire season, and there have been no reports of fires lately. She's going on about how the most likely explanation is that an electrical storm ignited a natural gas source. Pockets of methane gas have been known to hiccup, as she calls it, from the ground when tectonic plates shift, as in theory they would have done after the earthquake a few days ago. Most occurrences go unknown with little to no harm. But when it coincides with an electrical storm, it's prime conditions for something like this. But still . . .

"Has she not watched the video?" I ask Granny. They replay someone's shaky cell phone footage, and it's exactly what I saw, too. "See, the funnels are coming down, not up. They came from the sky."

"*He maketh fire come down from heaven on the earth in the sight of men,*" Granny quotes the Bible. I'm a little rusty with my scripture, but I'm pretty sure it's from Revelation.

"He who, Granny?"

"The false prophet," she says. "Jesus warned us the devil would return someday. Performing great signs to trick you, like fire from the sky."

Immediately my thoughts race to Cain Landry. He was there when the cicadas started waking up. He was there when I felt the earthquake. And I'm assuming he's still here in town, as fire rains down on us.

And yet for some reason, I'm not scared. If anything, I'm

curious. *You've seen her.* His words whisper in my head. I know he was talking about the little girl's ghost. There's a connection there. Between him and me. Between him and her, I suspect. Maybe he died before, like me, and the dead are drawn to him. Or maybe he's something else entirely. Either way I need to know.

None of this feels like coincidence. Not Cain's sudden arrival. Not the drowned cardinals. Not the fire tornadoes.

Something big is happening here in Hawthorne.

CHAPTER ELEVEN

I FOUND MYSELF wandering the fiery streets of Hawthorne in my dream last night. The star-filled night placid and tranquil. The evening air laced with smoke and sin.

Flames licked at my sides, guiding me down the dark throat of Main Street to the center of town. To the bronze statue of Saint Constantine's fountain. The statue's head turned my direction, and it's Cain Landry. A lazy smile touched his lips. He stepped down from the fountain, unfazed by the ombré waves of red and orange that ravaged the buildings surrounding us.

In a stitch he stood before me. Steel eyes grazed over my skin with a careful scrap of a blade's edge. It made me burn like a sip of smooth whiskey. He stepped closer to me. He smelled of ash and amber and wickedness.

He lowered his mouth close to my ear and hummed a faint tune, something familiar, but I couldn't place it. The music drummed from his chest against mine. A rhythmic *thump-thump. Thump-thump.*

His lips grazed over my cheek. The warmth of his breath tickled my ear as he said, *Come find me.*

"Knock-knock, sweetheart," Granny's voice pierces my dream. "Breakfast is ready."

I wake to the smell of warm biscuits and the sizzle of bacon . . . and to the lazy-eyed vintage doll who sits crooked in her red high chair next to my bed, staring at me.

"Mind your business." I push her face away. It's one cross-eye joggles with a fluttering blink, then rolls, finding its way back to me.

I turn over to a wall audience of eager-eyed doll faces. A collection of kitschy, crocheted pot holders with a plastic face sewn in the center. Ranging from generic babies to Pocahontas to Mr. and Mrs. Claus. The bookshelf is no worse with a vintage collection of Barbie toilet paper covers, their skirts crocheted antebellum gowns.

How am I going to live here? Even temporarily. I grumble and drag myself out of the bed.

I make my way to the kitchen and take a seat at the table, still foggy from the remnants of my dream. Granny's loading eggs onto my plate when my phone buzzes. She gives me a sidelong glare and a brief tsk as I take out my phone at the table. Nadine texted. They're allowing residents back into most of the neighborhoods. I finish shoveling down my breakfast and offer Granny a big hug and thanks, then rush off to get dressed.

"Did you make it home yet?" I say to Nadine after she answers the phone. I wave goodbye to Dylan as I pull out of the church parking lot onto the bypass, grateful that he was already up and able to take me back to my car.

"Jackson and I are headed there after we check out of our hotel. I just still can't believe it, never seen anything like it around here. But seriously, how are you holding up?"

"I mean, I guess the same as we all are." I would wager that everyone is still shocked by the town's catastrophe.

"Oh." There's a marked note in her tone that doesn't sit well with me. "You haven't heard yet."

A cold fear floods my body. "Did they find Sampson? Is the house okay?" My heart jumps in my throat.

"Oh God, no! Sorry. I think the house is fine, though I haven't laid eyes on it yet. No word on Sampson. It's the country club."

"What's wrong with the country club?" I pull over onto the shoulder of the road.

"It burned down."

My hope drops in my stomach with a hard thud.

Hurriedly I pull up the local news on my phone. Storefronts along the main street were singed by the twister. Poe's Hardware receiving the worst of it but saved, thanks to the sprinkler system—though, the water damage will be something to deal with as well. Cars were torched, trees and bushes incinerated. But the Serendipity Country Club suffered the most damage. There's a picture: the fourth pavilion, with the dining room I sat in not hours before it all happened, seems to be sliced in half. Like a sword of fire cut through the middle. What if I had stayed? Oh God, what if the Hawthornes were still there? The punk valet kid? Anyone, really.

No fatalities have been reported, but twelve people were taken to the hospital with injuries ranging from mild to moderate. The Serendipity owners are unsure of the full extent of the damages but anticipate they will be closed through the whole of the summer and most likely into the fall.

I feel numb to my core.

"Hollis, honey?" Nadine says through the phone, drawing me back to reality. "Are you there?"

"Yeah. I'm here." I pull back onto the road. "It says some people were injured. Do we know who?"

She tells me a few people we know but are not close to. "And Jeremiah Hawthorne, Libby's son. Bad burn on his right arm. Somebody said the tornado chased him across the golf course, and he had to jump in one of the water traps to escape the flames."

"Oh my word. Is he okay?"

"I think so. No surgery or anything. But they are going to keep him a few days, do the protective wet wrap thing they do. I can't remember what it's called."

"Good, he won't be there long." I make a mental note to call Libby later and check on him. Of course, I have no idea what to tell her about the venue. "What about the gala? What am I supposed to do now, Nadine?" It's one thing to remodel a place, but to rebuild it? There's no way the country club will be ready for the gala by September.

"Come over tonight. The three of us girls will put our heads together. Besides, I need to put my hands on y'all to assure myself you're safe. This whole ordeal has me shook."

As I DRIVE through town to get home, there are signs of the twister's path everywhere. Roasted trees, black and bare, curl like skeletal fingers toward the sky. Plastic signage bubbled into blobs. The occasional forlorn shed that didn't stand a chance.

I'm relieved to find Uncle Royce's house still standing, perfectly intact and untouched by the disaster. I can't tell for sure, but I don't think Cain and Paloma are in there.

"Sampson," I sing out to him as I walk to the gardens. "Here kitty, kitty, kitty." No sight or sound of him.

Inside the greenhouse I find Louisa's birdcage lying on the floor, its door flung wide open and Louisa nowhere in sight.

Panic forks inside me. "Louisa!" I scream and head back outside to the gardens. "Louisa!" I call out. "Where are you, pretty girl?" I whistle a few tweets, our playful little tunes. My eyes comb the trees for her gray body and yellow crest. "Pretty girl?"

Then I hear something.

"Pretty girl?" I say again, frozen to the spot. Listening. Hoping.

"Goddamn it, Hollis," comes a far-off squawk.

Oh, thank God! I sag with relief and call out, "Pretty girl?" as I head down the hill behind the house where I heard her.

The iron gate to the rear of the gardens yelps when I yank it open. The sloped embankment leads to a small patch of woods, no more than a hundred feet deep. A buffer between the historical community and the cookie-cutter new homes of the Hawthornes' planned housing development. It's the third expansion from Grady Owens's original land.

"Louisa?" I sing out to her again as I search through the narrow strip of trees. Ordinary birds flit here and there in normal patterns, causing me to turn at every fractional movement.

Six months ago, construction crews were chewing up the streets here, building these new houses like breathing depended on it. Then one day they stopped showing up. It's like they put down their tools and walked off the job. Now it's a dead zone with half-built homes in varying stages from plots that haven't even had ground broken yet to two-by-four framing to finished houses with naked insides. Building supplies lay to waste in piles, rotting out in the weather. Weeds swallow up abandoned heavy equipment.

The fluttering of a small gray bird flies toward the edge of the woods. I stiffen.

Not any bird. A wren. Faded gray brown and transparent.

Grady Owens's grave bird.

I follow as it darts back and forth through the trees. The moment I stop, it looks back at me with a tweet. So I go deeper.

As I approach a thatch of bushes, I hear the bark of a woman's voice. Farther down the empty street, standing next to their cars, are two women. I'm about to ask if they've seen a cockatiel fly through here when I realize one of the ladies is Libby Hawthorne. She throws out her hands in an agitated flare. Their heated talk causes me to hesitate.

I don't recognize the older woman she's talking to, but it wouldn't be hard: her pale pink hair looks like an oversized dollop of cotton candy stuck on her head. Marker-thick liner rims her eyes, and garish pink lipstick coats her lips. Her zebra-striped off-the-shoulder T-shirt partially covers a sparkly purple tank top. Those long, manicured nails look like glittery knives.

Curious, I sneak closer and duck behind a thick batch of bushes and watch them through the branches. I'm too far off to hear what they're arguing about, only catching every fifth word, but it's clear Libby is upset. She gets so worked up and pushes herself into the woman's face, threateningly close.

The woman doesn't back down, her voice deepens into a growl. A fraction of a hesitation passes where I fear they're going to tussle.

Until eventually Libby throws a fed-up hand in the air and gets back in her car. A moment later she reappears with a Sweet Salvations pink paper sack and shoves it at the woman—who is more than happy to take it.

For some reason, I don't think it's a box of sugarboos in there.

Without saying another word, Libby gets back in her custom blush-pink Cadillac SUV and whips out of there, faster than lightning. The woman climbs into her PT Cruiser and heads out the opposite direction. Her car sports as much personality as her clothes with its hot-pink rims, leopard-print seat covers, and Toot If You're a Tit bluebird bumper sticker.

What is Libby Hawthorne doing out here in a deserted housing development meeting up with this woman?

"What are you doing?" comes a voice from behind.

I let out a goosed scream and turn to find Cain Landry, towering over me. I've been caught like some kind of Peeping Tom, cowering in the bushes.

"I think I found your bird," he says. Louisa sits on his shoulder like a traitor.

"Goddamn it, Hollis," she says.

CHAPTER
TWELVE

"Is SWEARING SOMETHING the bird naturally picked up from you?" Cain asks. I can't tell if he's offended or impressed. "Or is it something you've taught it?" A slight twinkle glimmers in his eye as he says it.

"It's not on purpose, I swear." I laugh. "She's like a toddler. The second she learns it's a naughty word, it's all she wants to say. Then she's a broken record." I get up from the bushes and brush myself off, hoping there's nothing tangled up in my hair. I reach out for Louisa to come to me, but she refuses and climbs around the backside of Cain's neck to his other shoulder. From how agile she appears, it doesn't seem like she injured herself escaping her cage.

"Where did you find her?" I reach around the other way as she tries to evade me again, his warm amber scent stirring up images from my dream last night. His eyes scan my face, but what he's searching for I don't know.

I take a step back in surrender and give up on capturing Louisa myself.

"I saw you had returned home," he says. "So I came to check on you. I found the cage knocked over but no sign of you. When I came out into the gardens, this bird flew out of the trees and landed on my shoulder. I assumed it was yours."

Louisa sits there, snuggled up close to his neck, quite smitten with her rescuer.

"You were checking on me? To see if I was okay, or in hopes that your pesky renter issues had been taken care of by an act of God?" I wait for his reply, the crook of my mouth edging to a grin.

His lips twitch, as if a smile is itching to come out and play. "Fair enough. I haven't been the most approachable," he says. He manages to cup Louisa in his hands and then hands her to me.

I huff a laugh.

"Pretty bird." Louisa whistles a catcall, disrupting the quiet between us. I glower at her, as Cain turns to head back up the hill toward *his* house.

"Pretty bird," Louisa squawks again, the only sound in what has otherwise developed into a comfortable silence as we near the back of the house.

"Your family is okay after yesterday?" he asks, opening the rear gate for me.

"They are. Thank you for asking," I say, though I'm a little surprised at his kindness. I offer a smile, an actual genuine one. "We gathered out at my grandmother's as she lives away from town. You and Paloma kept out of harm's way all right?"

As pass we the reflecting pool, a whisper image of the little girl eclipses my thoughts. I side-glance to Cain, who watches the water with concern as well.

"Yes," he says, seeming to pull himself from his thoughts. "I was at the Chamber of Commerce when I got the call from Paloma. She was at the teahouse in town when it hit."

"Bren's place? Sweet Salvations?" He nods. "I heard their front door and awning caught on fire. Paloma's okay, though?"

"Yes, she's fine. The owner took them out through the alleyway, and they were directed to the high school for shelter."

"I'm glad. Good to hear." I walk into the greenhouse, expecting him to follow. When he doesn't, I turn and find him standing there, his feet seeming to be stuck at the doorway.

"I could use your help with the cage." I hold up my occupied hands with Louisa, then tip my chin toward the cage sprawled out on its back with its doors flung wide open.

"Are you giving me permission to come in?"

I spike a single eyebrow. "You own the place. You don't need my permission."

He waits a breath longer, seeming to contemplate my answer, then steps over the threshold.

He rights Louisa's cage and sets it in the corner where I direct. Still cupped in my hands, I gently place her back inside.

"Good night, Hollis." Louisa snakes her head in a circle.

"Yes, girl. I know. It was a long night outside, wasn't it?" After I refill her water and seed, I cover her cage so she can rest.

I glance up to find Cain surveying my private space. I take in the totality of my studio. It's not just the whirlwind that came through here yesterday: I've been a living a by-the-seat-of-my-pants existence for a while now.

"Sorry for the mess. I didn't expect company." I immediately attempt to straighten the place. My bed is a disheveled nest. The comforter a wrinkled white cloud. A small mountain of coffee cups pile in the sink, threatening to avalanche. And of course I have a pink bra air-drying on the doorknob of my bathroom. I yank it off the nob and toss it into the shower and close the door behind me. It then hits me that I'm wearing the same dress I had on yesterday, and I haven't showered. Lovely.

"What's this?" He nods to the vision board for the gala taped on one of the windows. Not the specific cake or table-scape or flowers, but the feeling—the embodiment—of what I'm hoping to capture that night. The colorful clouds of a nebulous galaxy, personifying an infinite space. An image of warm bathing light that seems to emanate from everywhere.

A reflection of the afterlife I experienced for thirty-two minutes.

"It's a project I'm working on—*was* working on," I correct. I don't expect the weight of my voice to come through so strong, but there I go, darning my emotions to my sleeve again. I clear my throat. "I'm an event planner. Just started my business, actually. I had landed a big contract for a fundraising gala—the Hawthornes raise money for the missionaries they support. I'm not sure it's going to happen now, considering the venue was badly burned." And the fact he bought the house and not me. I have *got* to come up with a plan C since the country club isn't an option. Or am I on plan D now? I can't keep track at this point. "You said you were at the Chamber of Commerce yesterday?" I switch subjects before he can ask any more questions. I grab a broom and clean up the seed spilled on the floor from Louisa's cage.

"Ah, yes." He tucks his hands in his khaki pants pockets. "I was speaking with Lyle Wyderman about possibly partnering up with a few of the soybean farmers." He peruses my bookshelf that runs along the bottom half of the room.

"Really? My grandmother's farm is rented out to soybean farmers. Partnering how?"

"We're looking to get exclusive sales to us, a five-year commitment with a guaranteed price, even if the market drops."

"Do you run a nonprofit, then?" From what Nadine found out about him on the internet, this would align.

"No. My company works as consultant contractor. I'm the intermediary, the person who pairs the resource with the need."

It sounds like smart positioning, to know who has the product and who has the need and negotiate the two so both are happy. It's impressive.

"You collect these yourself?" He points to my apothecary jars full of feathers.

"Yeah." I lightly pause. "I have a fascination with birds." His demeanor doesn't change. No hint that he understands why.

"They are beautiful," he says, a bit of marvel in his voice. "I meant to ask you, if you have the time, there's something at the house I wanted to talk to you about—"

Outside a warbled cry that sounds like a broken ambulance. Trotting through the garden is an overwrought Sampson. You wouldn't know it from the ungodly yowl he's setting free, but not a hair on his pretty butterscotch head has been harmed.

He strolls right inside the greenhouse's open door and straight up to me with a petulant flick of his tail. Then he proceeds to maw and chuff and chirr, disgruntled about being left alone during yesterday's traumatic event.

At Cain's light chuckle, Sampson startles and turns with a sharp stare. He pauses, then trills a pretty purr and slinks right over to Cain. The zigzag he winds around Cain's legs, you'd think the man was catnip.

Maybe he is.

"*That* melodramatic furball is Sampson."

"Hello, Sampson." Cain kneels and begins to scratch Sampson behind the ears. You can tell when someone was raised with pets by the casual ease at which they regard them, something Cain seems comfortable with. He hits the sweet spot as Sampson purrs like he's fallen in love. He rolls onto his back and lets him rub his belly. "This explains it." Cain seems relieved.

"Explains what?" I ask.

"I found a dead bird inside the house—inside my bed. I believe your friend here gave me a gift."

"Oh God! I'm so sorry. That's disgusting but definitely possible. I get a half-eaten lizard or mouse on occasion."

"No worries." He smiles up at me. "I'm relieved to know it was him."

I quirk my head and spear him with a curious look. "You sure have changed your tune in the last twenty-four hours. One minute I'm getting evicted and the next you're seducing my pets."

"Are you complaining?" A smirk slides across his face.

I suck in my cheeks to keep from smiling. "No, but I don't want you spoiling my cat."

He gives Sampson one last good rub then stands. "Look, I should probably apologize."

"Is this a *suggestion* of an apology? Or an actual apology?"

This time his smile comes out to play. "This is bona fide *I'm sorry*. I can be an ass sometimes—"

""Only sometimes?"

"Touché—hold on," he says and turns around. "Let's try this again." He steps outside the greenhouse door and then lightly knocks. "Hi, I'm Cain Landry, your new landlord. Just wanted to come over and introduce myself, now that I'm settling in."

The morning sun lights across his face, seeming to purify him, absolving him of his sins.

"*New landlord*?" I ask. "Because previously I was told I had to the end of the month to get out."

"The guy who said that? He's fired. You won't be seeing him again," he says with every ounce of seriousness, until the corner of his mouth curls slightly. "I'm truly sorry how I behaved." His eyes speak a sincerity I'm forced to believe. "Paloma and I were thinking, in light of what this town got hit with yesterday, the least we can do is assure you a safe place to stay for a little while longer. We can sort out some kind of official arrangement if you want."

"I appreciate that. I'm not sure how much rent I can afford. My next job," I say and nod to the vision board taped on the window, "is up in the air now. But I appreciate your change of heart." I straighten a pillow on my couch for no other reason than to not have to look him in the eyes.

"Let's just say Paloma has a way of setting things straight, so you never know. Speaking of, she found something in the garage, and I was wondering if you could help us sort it out."

Sampson makes a protesting meow as Cain and I leave and head toward the carriage house.

It's a small two-car garage next to the main house that still has a functioning horse stall. Technically, you could legally keep a horse here since the livestock rights were grandfathered in with the property. The mason stone building has two large green wooden doors with Gothic peaks. They split down the middle and open wide enough to park a car. As soon as he opens the left side, I know what he's referring to.

There are five huge shipping containers sent from California stacked in the corner. They hold the light fixtures I had planned to install in the ballroom.

"My Uncle Royce bought them from an auction. He thought they'd be incredible in the ballroom." They were his last Christmas gift to me before he passed away. I don't tell Cain this. "He owned this place, until he died last year. And boy did he love it. We both did. He loved hosting dinner parties. He truly made use of the place." I've no idea why I'm telling him all this, though. "Hawthornians love a good party—the whole town is like that. When I thought I would end up buying the house, I had planned for it to be *the* premiere venue in town. But plans don't always work out, do they?" I try to smile.

"Is that the favor you came over to ask me?" Cain asks. "If you could use the home for your gala?"

I lightly laugh, nudging my toe at the nothing on the floor. "Yeah. Bit of a foolish idea. I didn't really think it through. Would take a lot more than just renting out your home for a week. I had all these grand plans to remodel the place and bring it to a standard that would make Charleston green with envy."

There's a silence that follows when my mind drifts to what might have been.

"Maybe we can do something like that," he says, calling me back from my daydream. But he actually sounds serious.

"What? No, I couldn't impose like that. Really, I didn't think it through. To host a gala here—it would be a huge undertaking, not to mention disruptive. And this is your home now."

"Well, it sounds like it was once your home as well. Maybe that's the proper way you should get to say goodbye to it."

My jaw actually drops open a little in response. Could this maybe work?

"You'd have to be one hundred percent sure, because there's a lot I'd need to do to get this place in shape for something like a gala."

"I wouldn't mind changing a few things about the place. I'd love to see what you had planned."

"You're sure?"

He shrugs. "I need to convince the local soybean farmers to sell and export their crops to the world hunger organization I'm working with. What better way to win over locals than to host their biggest party of the year?"

I should be thrilled he's offering his home for the gala. Ecstatic, even.

But then his grave bird lands on his shoulder, and I'm left feeling like I just signed a deal with the devil.

CHAPTER THIRTEEN

SPENCER LEVY AND I shared a kiss once. It was the last day of sixth grade. It seemed I was the last person on the planet who hadn't gone to first base, not with tongue anyway. Spencer was cute, I guess. But we lived on the same street, so mostly he was convenient.

We stood behind a fat tree at the end of the street; at least six other kids hung out across the street in his yard, waiting for us to do the deed.

His tongue felt like a slug in my mouth, and all I could think of was how much I wanted it to be over.

As soon as we stepped out from behind the tree, the other boys congratulated him. Like he was a man now. I shrank with embarrassment. All I wanted to do was run away.

So I did. I took off behind our houses and into the woods. I thought if I ran hard enough the feeling would leave me. Instead, every dreadful thought I'd ever felt tangled itself inside my head until eventually I was good and lost.

I paused in the woods with only my ragged breaths to keep me company. A wisp of a thought spoke to me. It made me think of my grandaddy. It said *follow the rain*.

I leaned into the shushing sound of water that I could hear, faint but there, deeper in the woods until I came upon an ancient oak tree. Dangling from the limbs were hundreds of ribbons with objects tied to the ends. They shimmered in the breeze with a tinkling pitter-patter.

The Mourning Tree.

I'd heard about it but never seen it. People tied trinkets of a lost loved one to the tree, as a send-off, as a way to say goodbye, to help with their grief.

There were also at least fifteen grave birds on the branches of the tree. Never had I seen them gathered like this. Old and transparent, thin—more than usual, that is—piled on top of each other at the base of the tree, too, like they were there on purpose. I wasn't sure what it meant. something about the cluster of them made me feel safe despite being lost.

It was a beautiful yet haunting sight.

That's when I heard the singing.

Quietly I peeked around the wide tree trunk. A young woman, old enough for college, sat cross-legged on the ground with a fancy cupcake in front of her and a single flickering candle stuck in the middle. She sang Happy Birthday to absolutely no one.

"Make a wish," she said as she finished.

On command a soft breeze gently blew out the candle.

I don't know who Mary Beth Hawthorne was mourning over out there, but the sight of her drenched my heart with sadness. To this day I can still feel the ache.

"Could I get your signature, ma'am?" Spencer's voice snaps me back to the present. He taps the pen on the delivery order from the tree nursery where I'm to sign. He's a lot more toothy than back then. I doubt he remembers it.

"I'll take that." Cain reaches from behind me and grabs the clipboard. He quickly scribbles across the bottom. "There." He shoves it back at Spencer and watches him walk away with a hard glare. "Who was that?" Cain asks, a hammer in his voice, looking for a nail.

An unsettling ire radiates off his body, like he can sense the something more I'm not speaking about. That's how it's been these last three weeks working together on the house. Like every time my mind wanders, he can somehow read it. There's a deeper connection building underneath the surface but neither of us are allowing it to emerge.

Doesn't stop it from existing.

"No one important," I say and walk back to the greenhouse.

It took some time to coordinate enough construction workers to help patch the burned scars from the town's fire tornadoes. Cain, not wanting to take away from the locals' restoration efforts, hired a company from Alabama to work on his house. Thankfully we haven't suffered any more bizarre disasters. It's like Mother Nature—or hell—is satisfied now that Cain and I are working together. Something about what that means should probably bother me.

The first week I laid out my plans for what I had always wanted to do in order to make the house a perfect venue, except it will no longer be just a venue but a home, *his* home. Even though he's offered to host the gala, I have to keep in mind what changes could be made to maintain its original purpose. Lucky for me, a good portion of my plans fit.

By the second week the landscapers were in full swing, bringing back the gardens to their formal glory.

Now that we're in the third week, we begin to redesign the inside.

Cain and I stand in Uncle Royce's grand kitchen, picking out decorating touches. An avant-garde twist on a classic, historical Southern mansion. The kitchen is already an incredible start. From its stately floor-to-ceiling cabinetry to its spacious white marble countertops to the French double-oven range that could cook a feast. A good kitchen was the secret to a grand party, Uncle Royce had always believed.

"I think this wallpaper captures the Art Deco look of the chandeliers." I point to what's always been my favorite design, scalloped spoonflowers of black and teal and blush.

"It feels very Gatsby," Cain says, stretching the word, trying on our Southern accent for size—and mimicking it nicely. "I like it." He reaches around to give me the last pour of wine.

"It's my favorite. I think it works the best with the honeycomb black shelves behind the bar." I take a sip and melt, the cabernet heaven in my mouth.

He chuckles under his breath. "That good?"

A heat creeps up my neck as I realize I've moaned my pleasure out loud.

"Let's just say I'm going to be a wine snob by the time we're finished here."

"Then I'll grab another bottle." He fans off my protests that it's too late in the evening to open more wine. He pads barefoot to the library where Uncle Royce had a windowed wine closet installed. Books and wine, a perfect pairing.

At the sounds of footsteps I look up to find Paloma, wandering into the kitchen in a fine silk robe, poking around the cupboards for a bedtime cup of tea.

I straighten up and switch my smile from casual to business-professional.

"Good evening, Ms. Cabrera."

She lightly tsks. "I've told you before. Call me Paloma." Her eyes trail over the samples laid out on the kitchen island, not missing the two wineglasses side by side. "Working late again?" She fills the teakettle then sets it on the stove. I can't tell if her cool tone is disapproving or impressed.

"Yes, ma'am. Picking wallpaper. Which do you prefer?" I spread the five samples out for her review.

Paloma is probably my mother's age, but her skin is flawless and she looks much younger. Her rich brown hair is long and cut in playful layers to her chest.

She contemplates all the samples before settling on my favorite. My pride beams—I'm like a child, relishing in any favor she casts my way.

Paloma pulls a teacup from the cabinet. I can't help but notice her manicure is perfection, as always. I also notice her fine rings, especially the sapphire solitaire paired with a gold wedding band, but no spouse has ever been mentioned.

"And by September, we will be far enough along to impress the great people of Hawthorne?" she asks.

I mentally run through everything we need to do in the two months to get us there. And even I think it might actually be doable. "Yes, ma'am. I believe so. I think it's wonderful for y'all to let me use your home in this way."

Cain insisted on calling the Hawthornes and personally asking if he could host their gala as a way to build the community's optimism after suffering from the devastating fire tornadoes. Smart, honestly. I get the sense he's going to close the deal with the farmers any day now.

"Where I'm from," Paloma starts, "community was always the most important. And we want to be part of the community here. It's the least we can do."

"Where is home?" I ask her, putting the wallpaper samples back in a folder.

"Southern California the last twenty years. Originally, a small village in South America."

"Do you get home often?"

"There's no home for me to go to anymore. Cattle farming claimed the forest and surrounding lands. Most of the people were forced out, my family included." She looks up at Cain who's returned with another bottle of wine. "Of course, now *mi ahijado* is my home. Wherever he goes, he insists I go with him."

"Because she's a great negotiator," Cain says, then leans in conspiratorially. "My secret weapon when I need to close a deal." He grabs the corkscrew to open the bottle.

"Soybean farms are all over the South," I say. "What makes Hawthorne so special?"

"It's the rich—"

"Soil," Cain interrupts her. "We want to take advantage of the rich soil. Its nutritional value impacts the food security for so many third world countries. The organization we're work-ing with wants the top product to be shipped out. We think it's right here. If it goes well, I'll stay a few years to oversee the production. Make sure everything runs smooth." Cain finally pops the cork. "Speaking of, *Madrina* has a great proposition for you." He goes to poor more wine. I've learned over these last few weeks *Madrina* is the Spanish endearment for *godmother*.

"Seriously," I say and lay a hand over the top of my glass. "No more. But thank you. What's your proposition?"

She smiles at Cain. "We want to hire you to plan a party for us. So we can invite the farmers and other influential people in town, like the Hawthornes."

"Here?" There's so much remodeling going on it would be a nightmare.

"No, no. Not here," she says. "Someplace that reflects how much we care about the land. The people."

"Something intimate," Cain adds. "An opportunity for ev-eryone to get to know me, see that I have their best interests at heart. Is that something you'd be able to do?"

"Sure, I'd love to. I have a few places in mind. When were you thinking?"

"A week from Saturday," Paloma says as if she's suggested something quite reasonable.

"Oh wow. That quick. Okay. Um, let me see what I can put together."

"Wonderful," Paloma says. "Just no balloons. This one is scared of balloons."

"Why would you out me like that?" Cain jests in reply.

"This I have to hear." I sit up taller, eager to listen. Cain groans, covering his face.

The teakettle whistles. Paloma removes it from the burner and pours the hot water into her cup. The comforting smell of lavender drifts through the air. She proceeds to tell a story of Cain's third birthday where they took him to a petting zoo and decided to tie red balloons to his belt loop so they wouldn't lose him. But an angry emu chased him down.

"Determined to pop each balloon!" Cain throws his hands in the air. "Twenty-five years later, and I have managed to have nothing but balloon-free birthdays. No balloons for me. Ever."

"And no emus either?" I say, laughing.

"Ha ha." He shakes his head at Paloma.

"It was just before you went to the hospital." She pats his hand affectionately.

"Hospital? Another emu attack?" I smirk. Cain scowls.

"No, it was more serious than that," Paloma says. "He was a sick, sick boy. He was in the hospital for three weeks. They wouldn't let anyone in to see him, no family at all, scared we'd catch the *tifoidea*."

"Typhoid fever," Cain clarifies.

"And so I told his mother I would wait at the hospital, even if it was just in the waiting room, and they could go, do whatever they needed to do. But after a while, with still nothing from the doctor, I needed coffee. The machine there was terrible. So I went to the market to get a cup. Then I had something to eat. I took a little longer than I should have but was sorely in need of the fresh air. Maybe I was gone an hour? I knew something was horribly wrong as soon as I got back. I could hear people wailing before I could see them, crying and screaming. Then I saw the smoke. Then the flames. So I ran. They were saying all of the quarantine patients, none of them made it, they had all died, almost all at once. The nurses were weeping. They'd never seen anything like it. The doctors had no explanation. And they couldn't keep the bodies so they had to burn them. What did they call it?" She waves her hand for Cain to find the words for her.

"Incineration," Cain fills in for her. "To keep the sickness from spreading."

"Yes. So I fell to my knees and cried. These uncontrollable sobs."

Cain has a light, loving smile on his face as he listens to her retell the story.

"And all I can think is *How am I going to tell his mother and father?* They will blame me. I never should have left. I should have stayed with Cain the whole time. Then I heard something tiny. So tiny I almost thought it was in my mind." She points to her head. "But then I heard it again. *'Madrina.'* I stop crying and listen. *Escuchar.*" She holds a hand around her ear as if straining to here. "And then again, *'Mi madrina.'* And I turn to see my godson, naked. Unharmed. The sickness gone. His arms spread wide, like the Christ."

Cain closes his eyes and spreads his arms dramatically to imitate.

"You can laugh all you want." She swats a playful hand at Cain. "But God saved you. *Milagro michĩmi,*" Paloma says affectionately

"Is that Spanish?" I ask.

"Guarani. It means *little miracle.*" She turns to Cain, cupping her hand on his cheek.

"All this happened on vacation? What a nightmare," I say.

She exchanges a quick look with Cain. "It was a long trip, you could say. A long trip with my late *esposo* and Cain's *familia.*

But now I've stayed up too late. We have a cocktail party to plan and a gala to host, all with the help of a beautiful young woman." She winks at me.

"Aw. Thank you. I'm so happy we're having the gala here, and I know the Hawthornes are thrilled," I say.

"Are they good people?" Paloma asks. It feels like I've been thrown a curveball. "The Hawthornes, are they friends of yours?" She dunks her tea bag a few times. The kitchen is suddenly devoid of noise. Both of them watch me, waiting for my response.

"More like clients than friends, but I . . . I like to believe they're good people. They raise millions of dollars every year to send missionaries out into the world and support local charities. That counts for something." Despite my personal criticism of how they don't quite live up to the Christian standard, their philanthropic work kind of makes up for it. Right?

"Millions?" Paloma bobs an impressed eyebrow to Cain. "So quite a lot of money. I guess we'll find out next Saturday what kind of people they are." She adds a sugar cube to her tea and stirs. "A dear friend of mine once said you can tell a person's soul by the type of eyes they have. So I will know."

The hairs on my neck stand.

Cain watches his godmother cautiously.

"Just like I know what type of eyes you have," she says.

"And what type do I have?" I ask, nervous about the answer.

She pauses before taking a sip of her tea, then locks her eyes with mine. It feels like she can see every lie I've told. Every secret I've held. Every ounce of guilt that seeps from my soul.

"Spirit," she says. "You have spirit eyes, just like Cain." The bob in her brow speaks of something more. And without another word she quietly heads back to her room.

"Did I pass?" I ask Cain after she's long out of earshot. "I feel like I took a test I didn't know I had to take."

"*Madrina* likes to keep us on our toes," Cain says with an amused twist in his smile.

"Now I can see why she's your secret weapon." I load my samples and design plans back into the box I lug them around in.

"My business partners never see her coming," he says. I laugh.

"Where do your parents live? Are y'all still close?"

A heaviness softens Cain's posture. "It would have been nice to have a traditional relationship with my parents, but they weren't really there for me."

My parents weren't the most involved either, especially my self-absorbed mother, but at least I had my grandparents and Uncle Royce. I can't imagine my life without them. "I'm sorry you didn't have that."

He shrugs. "Life doesn't always give you what you want. But I can't complain. Paloma has been an incredible surrogate." Cain picks up my box to carry it out for me.

Those seventeen-year cicadas are in full force tonight, their incessant chatter like a static noise, ringing in your ears until it settles into the background. Somewhere far off two dogs are saying good-night to one another. My skin feels dewy from the humid summer night. The energy of the outdoors is open and ripe and full of possibility.

"How about your parents. Are they local?" he asks.

"My mom and stepfather are. My father lives in Gulf Shores with my stepmom, taking care of her parents. My parents were checked out a lot, my grandparents mostly raised me. I have my twin brothers here in town, and their families. I absolutely love my nephews. And my granny is amazing. She lives here, too."

"What was it like growing up with siblings?" he asks. My thoughts flit to all our explorations in nature, catching lightning bugs, climbing trees, digging in the cool creek water for arrowheads.

But then I say, honestly, "Denny and Dylan, my younger brothers, were pains in my ass." Cain stares at me, unsure if I'm joking, until I crack a smile. "But they were really fun, too. Lots of adventure with those boys. No brothers or sisters for you?"

"Never had the opportunity," he says. "Mostly raised as an only child. But *Madrina* has lots of nieces and nephews that I connected with over the years. Nothing close like siblings, though."

I'm hung up on the way he phrased his answer: *never had the opportunity.* To have siblings? I'm still turning it over in my head as we approach the studio and Louisa's squawk greets me.

"Pretty bird," Louisa whistles as soon as Cain and I walk inside.

I scowl at Cain. "Have you been teaching her that when I'm not around?"

"Absolutely not." He sets my box down on my two-person dining table. "She must have picked it up from you." He sends a sly smirk my way. Then he leans toward her cage and calls her over with little kissy noises. Of course she rushes to him. He sneaks her a sunflower seed from his pocket.

"You are incorrigible, you know that?" I slip off my sandals and flick on the floor lamp.

He holds up his hands in innocence. "It's not my fault she has good taste."

"Or maybe she just loves sunflower seeds."

"What do *you* think?" Cain asks. "Does Louisa have good taste?" He quirks his head, waiting for an actual response.

A soft smile touches my lips. I take the opportunity to fluff the pillows on my velvet love seat. "I don't think I really know you well enough to say."

He chuckles. "Okay. Fair enough. What do you want to know?" he says, casual as a breeze. He fans his hand as if to say he's an open book.

I turn and eye him momentarily. There's plenty I want to know, but there's something more pressing I need to know. Something that might help me piece together what's been happening.

"Did you die?" I ask him, and he looks genuinely confused.

"In the hospital, in the fire? What Paloma said about how the sickness had killed everyone. Did you die that day?"

He lightly chuckles. "I'm here. So nope, not dead," he says, his smile broad.

"Right, it's just . . . The only reason I ask is because—" How do you tell someone you died before, and now you can see grave birds? "I died. When I was eleven." I tell him about the drive home that winter day, and the construction truck that hit Grandaddy and me, pushing us into the river. I leave off the part about the stealing of the haircomb. Then I explain how Uncle Royce happened by and dove into the freezing river and saved me. "But in those thirty-two minutes, I crossed over to this . . . this place. Somewhere filled with light. It's hard to describe."

His eyes slide over to the gala vision board I have taped on the window, and he considers it thoughtfully for a moment. "I had this dream once," he says, "when I was little." And then he proceeds to tell me about the vision I saw the first time his grave bird landed on my shoulder. "These birds . . . they seemed to be roped to the ground, but somehow they lifted me up and told me to go home. When I woke up, I found myself walking down the main road through town. There was *Madrina*, on her knees, sobbing in the street. The dream reminds me of that," he says and points to the vision board.

Now his vision makes complete sense. The giant silk worm cocoons wrapped in muslin were probably the the bodies bound in white sheets, piled for a mass burn that Paloma spoke of. All those grave birds literally lifted him back to life.

When I was brought back to life by Uncle Royce, I woke up with the gift of the grave birds. What kind of gift do you get when the grave birds bring you back to life?

Or what if the grave birds brought back something more than just a boy?

"I'll let you get to bed," Cain says turning toward the door.

"Thank you," I say, yet I don't want him to leave. He stops at the door, looking back at me. "For trusting me with your dream."

He stands there a moment. "Maybe *Madrina* is right, maybe I am a miracle boy." He steps back toward me. "Good night." He leans forward and presses a soft kiss to my mouth. I swim in the heat and scent of him. Then he slips out the door, his good-night lingering on my lips.

"Good night, pretty bird," Louisa squawks.

"You hush up." I wash my face and brush my teeth. Eventually I flip off the light and crawl into bed, my head full of Cain and his stories. As I pull the covers up over my legs I feel something scrape against my foot.

"What the hell?" I unearth a torn piece of paper. I flip my bedside lamp back on and freeze. It's the sketch of Kappy's Campgrounds number 14 key.

The piece of paper I doodled on and left behind at Granny's house has now found its way into my bed.

CHAPTER
FOURTEEN

I'VE ONLY WITNESSED one person die. It was before I had died myself, so I didn't get the opportunity to see their grave bird. Granny and Grandaddy had taken my brothers and me out to Good Eats for their after-church buffet. A man passed by our table with his plate of food from the buffet table while we were saying a quick grace over our meal. He wobbled in his step, and I thought he had tripped on something on the floor. Then he simply fell over, taking out a table with him. A loud clattering of dishes and the distinct snap of splintered wood, followed by the desperate cry of his wife.

Fear came out of her, so raw it was like she knew he was gone before she actually knew what was happening.

My grandaddy and a few others rushed over to help, of course. Though, it was quickly obvious there was no help to be given.

The whole restaurant went quiet. All you could hear was the frantic murmurings of the hostess at the cash register speaking to 9–1–1. Then we all waited for the authorities to show up and officially declare what we already knew.

I didn't know the man; he wasn't local. He was an older person, around my grandaddy's age. Later that night on the news we found out his name, Chester Willisham, and learned he'd had a massive heart attack. Granny never took us back there again. It closed up a few years later, then reopened for a short life as a catfish place. But like all things on the edge of the highway, they don't live long. I've always wondered if I went into that abandoned building now whether I'd find the man's grave bird on the floor.

As I'm driving along the highway, I pass the old Good Eats on the right. Boards are nailed over its windows. Tufts of weeds are eating away at the crumbling asphalt parking lot. My heart is a little heavy, longing for the good memories we shared there once with my grandaddy.

"You're cutting out, Mrs. Hawthorne," I say through the phone as I keep looking for the exit sign I need. "You want to invite another couple to Cain's party tonight?" I'm all the way out in the boonies and only catch every other word. I check the signal bars and barely have one. "That should be fine," I yell into the phone as if me being louder improves the signal coverage. "I'll try you back when I have reception again." But I've already lost the call.

Shit. I don't think I've ordered enough food. I tap out a text to Nadine, asking if she'd mind making her famous crunchy wings and bring them out to the conservation center for the party. I hold my breath, praying the text goes through. But I can't worry too much about that now. I need to find the exit for the campgrounds.

As I get closer I focus my attention on the left side of the highway, searching for the old Kappy's billboard.

Eventually I spot it—or a sliver of it. The long furry arms of a pine tree shield the bulk of what's left. Kudzu vines gobble up the stilt legs and beard the base of the sign. But I catch sight of the faded cartoon trout with a wide, friendly smile and a glint in his eye.

His fin points to an exit a mile down the road. The off-ramp is clumped with weeds, long forgotten. A gas station sits on the corner all by itself. It isn't more than a cracker box building with two pumps and looks like it belongs in a museum. Parked out front, a beater of a car and Cain's pristine new Range Rover. *What's he doing getting gas all the way out here?* If he's going to the conservation center, he's headed the wrong way.

I half consider turning around to see if he needs help, but my curiosity for what's waiting at the campground is too strong to change course now.

Trees narrow on the road as it snakes through the country-side where houses are as rare as a passing car. Eventually I come upon a wooden sign that reads CRYER'S LAKE, overtaken by the weeds and lost to the past. The former Kappy's Campgrounds sprawl out behind it. A hundred feet in I reach an X-bar gate that shackles the road closed.

This place was never open in my lifetime. But there's an old picture in a box at Granny's with a thinner, more fun version of my mother in a high-cut bathing suit lounging on the lake's shore next to my dad who's sporting a goatee. The lake started with an earthquake, over a hundred years ago, opening up a vein to an underground water source. Then someone got the bright idea to flood the forest and make it into a lake, something to attract tourists. At some point the water treatment plant filled in the man-made gap, and this place dried up.

I park my car and continue forward on foot. Honestly I have no idea what I'm looking for other than the number four-teen. A thin path of asphalt splits off into two trails. Scattered empty campsites pop up as I go deeper into the woods toward the lake. Eventually a clearing opens up to a sloping valley of cypress trees.

Cryer's Lake has been reduced to nothing but shallow pockets of water that collect in the dips. Skeleton docks stand naked without any water, marking off the now-gone shoreline.

At the sound of a large splash not too far off, I recognize the chance of something bigger than a catfish living here.

Nestled in the woods are small cabins. Hunter-green boxes that blend in so well it's only by their squareness that they stand out. A blue jay cries a distress call somewhere off in the distance. Sticks crack under my weight as I make my way to the closest building.

To my delight, it's numbered: cabin 3. Mostly empty, besides a forlorn plastic white lawn chair lying on its side, one leg broken. I head up the two short steps and try the door. It opens and I peek inside. The place is one large giant room with a small kitchen wall where the appliances have been removed. Cabin 4 is pretty much the same layout, except it has a floral sofa with all the cushions missing. A plastic bucket of toys rots on the lemon-yellow stove in cabin 5.

Systematically I go to each one, looking for number 14, though they're not neatly lined up. A barely there road ribbons around. It zigzags deeper into the woods to the odd numbered cabins, then back toward the shore for the even numbers. Each one in various states of neglect, all abandoned decades ago. Eventually I come upon cabin 12, half-submerged in stagnant water as the shoreline has shifted. Farther into the woods I suspect a splintering pile of limbs is cabin 13 collapsed upon itself.

My heart picks up in pace as I near what must be cabin 14. I don't even care I'm ruining a perfectly good pair of sneakers, trudging through the soggy earth to get to it. I still don't know what I expect. Maybe for all the answers to come spilling out of its front door.

My expectations are sorely disappointed as I am met with the stench of stagnate scum water, skimming with fuzzy green algae. Walls empty of photos. A dirty bucket and floating detergent bottle are the only items remaining.

No clue as to who might have stayed here. This cabin is as equally uninformative as the previous ones.

I don't even know if these cabins were owned or rented out short-term.

The wind blows, and the small noises of the woods close in around me. As I stand there, I can't help but feel like I've failed the little mourning dove in the Hawthornes' office. The ghost woman showed me this trout key, but nothing is here for me to help her. Was she ever even here?

Back outside, a clear plastic sheet flutters in the breeze on dock 14. The dock, like an outstretched arm over a small basin of water, looks sturdier than most. I don't trust my weight on it, but I get close enough that I see a rotted bouquet of flowers. Probably a few weeks old and totally out of place. Who would have brought this out here? Why?

Something breaks the surface of the water not far out, and it reminds me the occasional gator is not unheard of in these parts, and I might want to head on back.

I return via the short side of the lake, seeing as I easily covered half of it in my search already. But something inside me tells me to slow up.

A sixth sense.

The woods hush to utter stillness.

Then I hear a caw.

Loud and direct, but not of this world. It cries out, reverberating inside my head, and I turn toward the direction from which it came.

Off the main pathway, a tall stone fireplace stands. In the middle of the forest, like it had once belonged to a house but the house had long since packed its bags and moved away. With its huge size and central location, I suspect this was a communal lodge for the campgrounds.

Barely a few remnants of the once-surrounding structure remain. Kudzu vines have grown thick over the grounds, covering the area like green hair.

It takes until I'm right upon it before I see the grave bird.

It's perched on a fallen branch. A thin, inky-black crow. Proud and stern, a sentinel to his post. It quirks its head at the sight of me, unsure if I am the messenger he was meant to wait for.

Carefully I step through the debris of the building. He caws again, his fierce cry commanding me to ready myself.

I kneel and hold my hand out. It shakes its feathers. A cloud of soot puffs around him. Then he hops from the branch and into my palm. I am sucked into the past with such a force I actually feel the hard punch as my body hits the ground.

The concrete floor is cold against the side of my face. Hog-tied with rope, the weight of the boy's arm pinned across my neck makes it difficult to breathe. His breath smells of soured bologna. Flecks of spit hit my cheek with every angry word. I don't understand what I have done to deserve his hate. It's vile and vicious and whips me with every lash of his tongue. He blames me and my family for every misfortune that he has suffered.

Today is the first we have ever met.

Stupid, that's what he calls me. Because I don't own an Xbox or watch something called South Park, *two things I've never heard of. But Mother has me reading at the high school level, I have mastered geometry, and I am a whiz at science, even though I've just turned fourteen.*

This only feeds his anger when I tell him, and another swift kick lands in my side, fracturing a rib. There's a glint of joy at the pain he inflicts, like he was born to do this. The driver barks for the boy to get out of the abandoned building. Shuffling feet scurry around the large room of the lodge as something splashes against the floor, followed by the sharp fumes of gasoline.

A crack of thunder breaks the night in half. A flash of lightning finishes it off. It seems as if the heavens have disappeared with a roar. A harsh storm hides the sin occurring here tonight. I doze in and out of consciousness, as the thickening smoke burns my eyes. My heart hammers at the reality of what's happening. But my body is too weighted from the soda pop the man let us drink to react—one more thing I should have never done. I close my eyes and say a prayer to

Jesus that they don't notice the blanket my sister was sleeping under is now a bundled-up plastic tarp with only her shoes sticking out from the end. Run, *I told her.* No matter what she hears, no matter what she sees . . . Run!

And then I feel the flames, burning at my back.

I gasp awake with a bellowing cry that echoes out through the trees. A flash of hot pain shoots to my nerve endings, as vibrant as testing the water from the faucet and discovering it's scalding. I shudder as my body lets go of the past and the pain. Then I puke. A gut-wrenching purge I cannot stop. I keep at it until there's nothing more for my body to give up, and I dryheave. I curl in the fetal position and wrap an arm around my abdomen where the phantom kicks still linger. I sob. The grief of what I believe I witnessed is too much to bear. Huge gasping breaths accompany the tears. The anguish is suffocating.

It's my fault, the young boy's thoughts whisper. *All my fault. I beg my mother to forgive me.* I plead to God for his forgiveness as well. *I was a stupid,* stupid *boy.*

His feelings are hard to untangle. So raw they feel as if they are my own. I lie there, numb from what I have experienced. Surely, I'm wrong. Surely, a boy was not murdered here.

I reach a shaky hand out to a vine snaked around a board. The black char, like fertilizer to the plants growing here, confirms my fears.

I don't know who this little boy is. I have no way of knowing if he's connected to the woman or if it's sheer coincidence this happened out here.

If there was a fire here—if a boy died here—the authorities would know about it.

There will be a record of this place. Of his death.

And I have to find it.

CHAPTER FIFTEEN

THE SECOND I reach a hint of civilization my phone explodes with texts notifications from Libby, informing me she's invited a couple of big donors and interested farmers to join us tonight.

A little soiree before the soiree, her final text reads.

I definitely did not order enough food for additional guests. Corky's Barbecue has the best pork sliders, bite-size macaroni and cheese bombs, and mini cups of mayonnaise coleslaw. But they won't be able to double my order on a busy Saturday. And much to my Granny's disappointment, I don't cook. It's the one Southern gene I didn't inherit. So I do the next best thing and call Nadine.

"I know the real reason Libby invited the Carmichaels and the Prescotts," I say to her over the phone. "Because they are her nosy, busybody friends. Plain and simple. They want to get a closer look for themselves and meet this *mysterious Cain Landry*."

"Is that a note of jealousy I hear?" Nadine asks after agreeing to bake her crunchy chicken wings for me, then she's gracious enough to listen to me vent. "Because you can't keep Cain to yourself forever. Every mother with a single daughter under the age of thirty is trying to play matchmaker."

I don't care to label any of the pesky feelings I've developed for Cain. They nibble at me, though. But dang, every woman I know has poked and prodded me for some juicy morsel about Cain Landry.

Did he inherit his money or is he a self-made man?

He isn't in a long-distance relationship, is he?

Is he looking for a plus-one for the gala?

It's bad enough with me still living in the greenhouse these last several weeks, I'm the only one who seems to have gotten to know him at all, outside of some soybean farmers. Pretty sure people already assume we're sleeping together.

We aren't.

"Yet." Nadine adds, and I can hear her smirk through the phone.

After picking up the food from Corky's, I rush home, shower and change into something pretty, and barely make it to the wildlife habitat an hour before the guests are set to arrive. Cain suggested we host his cocktail party for the farmers at a place that was focused on conservation efforts. The Cypress Grove Wildlife Center was perfect. It's a sleepy building nestled in the swamp groves with two-mile boardwalk trails throughout. There's a raptor rescue for injured birds, and a pond with a viewing tower that overlooks the whole grove. The visitors' center building has a decent-size room, which was recently renovated and will hold sixty people easily. The back deck overlooks the knobby-kneed cypress trees, their roots look wrung-out like a dishrag. And I've set up enough citronella candles that mosquitoes don't have a chance. With a small donation to their conservation efforts guaranteed, they allowed us to have our cocktail party out here.

I'm running around like a chicken with its head cut off, trying to get the bar and tables set up for tonight. But all I can think about is the poor little boy. Why was the older child so angry at him? Angry enough to beat him and leave him for dead. Where did his sister go? Did she get away?

"Where do you want these?" Nadine asks, jarring me from my thoughts. She carries in a huge tray full of her famous wings. "Ms. Cabrera has the other tray."

"Please, ladies," she chides Nadine. "Call me Paloma. *Missus* makes me feel old," she says with a smile.

"Paloma, you're in for a treat with Nadine's wings. They're like little bites of heaven."

"Then, I look forward to trying them," she says. "I take this to the buffet table, *sí*?" I nod and thank her.

"This is going to work out, right?" I ask Nadine once it's just us.

"You're going to knock their socks off," Nadine says with conviction.

"Hello, ladies." Cain steps into the visitors' center from the observation deck wearing a blush-pink button-up oxford shirt and white linen pants. He looks like a Carolina dream.

"How can I help?" Cain asks after he makes it over to us. Sandalwood and citrus waft off him in the night's breeze.

"Ice. Two bags," I say and point toward the nature center's kitchenette. "For the big cooler over at the bar." I thank him as he goes to fetch it.

Paloma returns, taking the second tray of wings Nadine is still holding.

"Oh, Paloma, I don't mind," she protests but Paloma insists.

"Hello! Hello!" Libby Hawthorne's voice echoes as she enters the center. "Noah's parking the Hummer."

Libby may be a buxom woman, but she carries her weight well. She's in a beautiful eggplant-colored dress tonight, with a caramel belt wrapped right under her large chest. Her nose is a bit broader than most, and her eyebrows are penciled but skillfully done. Her voice has a light husk to it, like maybe she smoked when she was younger and never quite got rid of the gravel. Her dyed-blond hair is a bit on the brassy side, something Calista could tone out for her if she wanted.

"*Hola*," Paloma greets Libby with a warm smile. "Welcome."

"A wine spritzer, if you don't mind," Libby says to Paloma.

"Oh, she's not—"

"Nadine, it's lovely to see you here. How's your father? I sure hope he plans to attend the gala. We're counting on his donation." Libby holds out her small clutch purse for Paloma to take.

Oh dear Lord. I swoop in and take the clutch. "Paloma is one of our hosts tonight, Mrs. Hawthorne," I say with a forced chuckle, then tuck the purse under my arm and pull the tray of chicken wings from Paloma's hands.

"Oh." Libby's face sours. "My mistake. Wait a minute—" She takes a second, longer look at Paloma like she's trying to pull her from a memory. "Do I know you?"

"I don't know . . . *Do you?*" Paloma's flat tone almost feels like a challenge.

Libby's brow perks, picking up on the same note. "I must be mistaken," she says and saunters off into the room, setting the tone for what's sure to be an unforgettable evening.

AND SO THE night goes. The Carmichaels invited the Duvalls, and the Prescotts invited the Vaughns, and the next thing I know we're entertaining forty couples instead of twenty.

Hawthornians do love their parties.

"I'm sorry there's so many people," I whisper to Cain as I dump some empty plates into the bus tub behind the bar and give the bartender a quick break. Cain props an elbow on the corner, observing the group like a wily coyote searching for a way in. His thumb fidgets with the gold college ring on his finger, an alumnus of USC in Los Angeles.

"Not a bother at all," he says, taking another sip of his neat, eighteen-year blended scotch. The bottle costs more than a cut-

and-color with Calista. "Just more people who can help convince the farming commission I'm what Hawthorne needs. What's her story?" Cain tips his chin toward Mary Beth.

Currently, she's the fifth wheel to a four-person conversation and only pretending to pay attention when someone notices she's not. She absent-mindedly stirs her third martini with the toothpicked olive.

A cloud of melancholy always seems to hover over her. She has a flighty, distracted quality about her, like her thoughts are always elsewhere. She's got an incredible husband, three wonderful children, a beautiful home, and a mountain of money, but some people can't seem to find joy no matter how much they have.

"There's not much to tell about her. She's married to Landon—you know his father from the real estate agency." I nod to him talking with a group of men. "She's a stay-at-home mom. Three sweet kids. I've always found her pleasant. A bit odd but nice. Not too involved in the family's church affairs."

"Interesting," Cain says more to himself than me. Then he straightens as Noah Hawthorne and his son, Jeremiah, approach for a refill. "Enjoying yourselves, gentlemen?" he says to them.

Cain's pretty tall at six feet, but they both have a couple of inches on him and probably double the pounds—soft pounds, though.

"Yes sirree." Noah shoves his empty bourbon glass at me. "Maker's. Skip the ice."

"Sure thing," I say through a biting smile.

Noah Hawthorne is one of those men who likes to shake your hand with a death grip to prove he's more man than most. He might have been handsome when he was younger, but it's hard to see past the sneakiness that hovers at the corners of his eyes now. He likes to act like he's the big man on campus, but Libby runs the show, and everybody knows it.

"Did you get the investor portfolio I sent you?" Noah asks Cain.

"Yes," he says rather dryly. "The courier copy *and* the email.

I'll give it a read when I have the chance." Cain points to the bandage Jeremiah has wrapped around his hand and forearm. "Looks like there's a story attached to that."

Jeremiah glances down at his arm, the color leaving his face. "Firestorm a few weeks back." Fresh fear fills his eyes. "I thought it was going to burn me alive." Nadine told me something about the tornado chasing him across the golf course, like it was on a mission.

"Wouldn't that be awful," Cain says, "to be eaten alive by flames." The eeriness in his voice causes me to look up from fixing Noah's drink, the boy out at Kappy's fresh in my thoughts. The pain he suffered there at the end.

Just what was Cain doing at the gas station out there?

After a pause, I hand Noah his drink and offer to fix Jeremiah one.

"Tell me, now, Jeremy." Cain leans lazily on the bar, giving off the most earnest yet mocking air of curiosity. "What is it exactly that you do for the family?"

Jeremiah, with his thinning hair and bulging belly—and that ridiculous surf band tattoo on his bicep—puffs up his chest like he's about to inform us how important he is. "I do the stuff for the missionaries."

Cain nods as if it sounds most impressive. I bite the inside of my cheeks to hold back a smile.

Noah steps up and pats his son on the shoulders like a *Good try, buddy.* "Jer here helps me run the back end of the mission trips for the church. We coordinate the supply shipments. Set up assets on the ground for the families. Pretty much the engine that keeps it running."

"Now, how does exporting work through a church?" Cain asks. "Do you have LLCs set up for each country? Or do you have a nonprofit umbrella corporation for the church so it doesn't get hit with high tariffs?"

Larry Prescott comes over to join the conversation. Cain gives him a quick nod hello.

"Um . . ." Noah swallows hard, looking to Larry for the answers. Cain waits patiently. "Well, there's a couple of ways to avoid fees when you're a nonprofit."

"Like offshore S corps?" Cain says, crossing his arms over his chest, intently interested.

Noah's eyes narrow. "That could work, as long as you keep things legal-like."

Cain's face lights up. "Well, the law is flexible—as far as you can bend it. Am I right, boys?" He beams a smile over to the other men who chuckle in agreement.

Like ants to candy, one by one the group meanders over to the bar, and before you know it Cain is holding court for his new, adoring loyal subjects.

He's captivating the men with his wild tales of his trips abroad. Building a water system in Honduras and getting trapped in the underground tunnels for a week with nothing but water and the granola bar he had in his pocket. Or stumbling upon a Thai prince's pet tiger in the palace and feeding it honeyed apricots all night to keep it from eating him. Then he throws in one for the women, a story about a foreign dignitary's soon-to-be-wed daughter in Bali, who snuck into his bedroom the night before her wedding, looking for a way out of her arranged marriage.

"Tell me there's a dignitary's grandson out there with light gray eyes," John Vaughn says, and the crowd bursts into laughter.

"There is not. I was a complete gentleman." Cain holds up a hand with an oath on his honor. "Though, gentlemen never kiss and tell." He winks, and all the ladies giggle in return.

"Bullshit!" one of the men calls, and more laughter erupts.

While they prattle on about Cain's tall tales, he slips a sultry look over to me. Those gray eyes turn to a sinful black. A trick of the light, maybe.

"Tell Cain about the time you gave preaching a go." Larry Prescott nudges Noah with a jesting elbow, laughing.

I pull myself out from under whatever spell Cain has cast over me.

"Can you believe this bastard tried to be a pastor?" another man says to Cain. They all join in. Whatever magic Noah may have possessed during his eight years as a missionary did not translate to *pastor*.

"Better Noah than his wildcat sister!" Larry Prescott and a few other burst out in laughter, but the smile on Noah's face quickly fades, and his eyes grow dark, like the sheer mention of his sister scares him. Odd, seeing as how she's the one who wronged the family.

So some people seem to know about Noah's sister, Sarah Hawthorne. Makes what Nikki said about her getting in trouble with the church money more likely.

"What are you gentlemen getting all rowdy about over here?" Libby says as she walks up, almost to rescue Noah. She slides her empty wineglass toward me and flicks her wrist, inferring she needs a refill. I can see Cain watching the exchange out of the corner of my eye.

The men continue on, sharing embarrassing, scandalous stories about one another. I slip out from behind the bar and make my way over to a small group of women that's formed and is now deep in conversation.

"Well, Teenie Simmons's son said they walked from the job because they hadn't got paid in three months."

"What job?" I ask. Lindsey looks around to see who's in earshot.

"The Greater Good subdivision." Lindsey says. "They were supposed to be houses. Then apartments. Now they're sitting there, wasting away."

"It's probably a lot of red tape and hoops to jump through for the permits," Joanna says. "They always slow up Mitch's investments. You know how these things take forever to get approved."

Lindsey raises a skeptical brow. Both women straighten at the sight of Libby coming over.

"What's the word, ladies?" Libby asks. The other two women shrug, awkwardly quiet.

"We're discussing how lovely the new homes behind Cain's house will be," I say to cover for them. "Didn't I see you over there the other day, checking on the property?"

Libby watches me a careful moment, then turns her scrutiny on the other women as if she suspects the previous conversation was indeed about her. They find sudden interest in their wine. Libby wields her skepticism back onto me. "Well now, I don't think so. We put a hold on the construction a while back. We felt the company we had hired was underperforming and overcharging. I haven't been over to the lot in ages."

"I see," I say, not breaking eye contact with her. "Must have been someone else's Cadillac I saw out there." Swiftly, I shift my attention to the ladies and their empty wineglasses. "Let me get y'all a refill." I turn toward the bar to get a bottle, but I don't get more than two steps when Libby comes following, tight on my heels.

"I need a word," Libby says, causing me to stop. "This Paloma woman, Cain's friend, was telling me a moment ago about her idea—"

"You mean Cain's godmother?" I sense my voice edging on caution, feeling protective of Paloma.

Libby sighs with restrained patience. "Yes, his godmother. She suggested having families bring their children to the gala. Please tell me that's *not* going to happen."

Paloma suddenly appears, either having overheard or guessed at what Libby brought up. "You do not like this idea?" she says straight to Libby.

"It's an adult evening," Libby says with a smile. "Guests don't want to be bothered with children when they're trying to have a night of adult fun."

"But to share the joy of giving is a beautiful thing for a child to see," Paloma says. "I've cared for lots of children. It could be wonderful to have them join."

"Did you nanny for someone around here? Because I'm sure I've seen you before."

"Have you?" Paloma says, and there's a glint in her eye.

"Remind me again. Who did you say you used to know from Hawthorne?" Libby asks her.

"I didn't." Paloma looks off past Libby's shoulder. "If you will excuse me." She makes her way over to William Parsons, the farming commissioner.

Libby watches her with scrutiny, then turns to me again. "We can table it for now, but this conversation isn't over." She takes off to find someone else to chat up.

I pause for just a moment, stuck on the interaction that just played out. Paloma mentioned she'd traveled to this area of the country decades ago. Could she have meant Hawthorne? And she and Libby could have met? I guess the bigger question would be why she's not saying so.

THE NIGHT WINDS down later than I expected. Across the room I can tell Cain is on his last polite smile as he finishes saying his goodbyes.

"Well, this was a lovely evening," Libby says. "For a smaller-scale event. I look forward to seeing you try to manage something more substantial."

I try not to let the whiplash from the backhanded compliment deter me. "Thank you, Mrs. Hawthorne. I'll certainly strive to meet the mark." As she turns to go, an idea strikes me. "I also wanted to ask . . . I was thinking, as a part of the gala's evening, we should have one of the church's missionaries speak. They could talk about the work of the missions. Maybe have their family there. Bring photos and share stories. It could be a really good opportunity, something to further inspire donations."

She pauses for the smallest moment. "I think we will be fine without it," she says dismissively and proceeds to walk out.

I follow her and Noah onto the conservatory's porch. "But think of the impact it could have. You know there's nothing more powerful than a one-on-one connection with someone who's doing such wonderful work. We could—"

"The cost to bring an entire family back from overseas is not cheap. It's not feasible."

"Surely the few hundred dollars it would take to fly someone here would more than be made up for in donations."

Libby exhales, exasperated. "Do you have any idea the challenges Christian missionaries face dealing with government regulations in countries like China?"

"Wait." I give her a quizzical look. "Aren't missionaries forbidden in China?"

Noah and Libby exchange a brief look. Then Libby shrugs her shoulders. "My point is I find it a tad vulgar you're suggesting we *rip* a missionary and their family from the important work they're doing for God simply to come back here and entertain us for an evening with tales from their little adventure out of the country."

"I see." I keep the light smile on my face. "Mary Beth said she wanted to have a Mary of Bethany Award to honor a missionary family. Surely it's not too much bother for them to send a few videos? Maybe some photos? Write down a few thoughts from the experience to share before we hand out the award?" I dash a look between Noah and Libby. "I'm just trying to bring in as much money as I can. For the church."

Libby stares at me a stiff moment, her eyes narrowing. Then suddenly everything about her softens. "You know, that's actually a wonderful idea. I'll have Jeremiah get in touch with

Thomas Watterman. Lovely family. They've been in the Philippines for . . . two years?" she confirms with Noah.

"It might be going on four," Noah says, his eyebrows stretching high with recollection.

"Yes, you might be right," she says to him, then turns to me. "It's hard to keep them all straight with so many missions spread all over the world. But we will get you something for sure." She pats my hand. It almost feels like a swat.

"Wonderful," I say, inflecting it with the fullest of my Carolina manners.

I watch them as they climb into their too-high Hummer. Those custom white rims could probably pay my rent for the next six months. I turn back toward the building to find Paloma watching me from the doorway. I'm not sure how long she's been there, but there's a keenness in her eyes.

Inside, Joanna Prescott leans precariously close to Cain, an evening's worth of wine having loosened her up. "Thank you, hon, for such a lovely night," she tells him.

"Mrs. Prescott, it was my pleasure to have you," Cain says.

"Please," she lays a hand on his arm, "call me Joanna." Her eyes are all sparkle and shine. I feel myself rile.

"Joanna," he says her name like he's savoring a bite of chocolate cake. "What a lovely name. I had a great-grandmother named Joanna."

You can see the sparkle shrivel up like a dried apple left to rot on the ground.

IT'S LATE BY the time we all get home. My feet ache from being in heels the last four hours, but I insist on helping Cain carry in the bottles of wine and booze we didn't drink.

"Did you really have a great-grandmother named Joanna?" I ask him. The kitchen's stone floor is cool beneath my bare feet. It's just the two of us now, Paloma having gone to bed almost immediately once we arrived.

A grin slivers onto Cain's mouth. "No, but I wanted to let her down easy."

The smile I give him is a little smug, I have to admit.

"You put on an incredible evening." He sets his box of booze on the counter next to the wine I've carried in. "I think we've convinced the farming commissioner and the guys who run the co-op to sell their crops to us over the next four years. It'll mean less in taxes and more money in their pockets. And a better deal for us and the organization."

"Oh, that's a big deal, then. The co-op men are tough to win over. What did you think of the Hawthornes? Are you still comfortable with hosting their gala here?" I ask, hoping they didn't rub him the wrong way tonight. "Of course, we'll rope off the private quarters upstairs. The bulk of it will be in the ballroom and out in the gardens. I just want to make sure you're all right with everything. That this still works for you. And Paloma."

"Everything is going according to plan. Better than I could have imagined, really." The assuredness in his words causes me to pause.

"*According to plan?*" I ask, lightly laughing. "What plan? To charm the pants off everyone?"

"Not everyone," he says low and quiet, leaving no room for question.

"It's late," Paloma says, startling us. She stands at the kitchen door with a watchful eye. I take a professional step back from Cain and thank them both for trusting me with their party.

Back in the greenhouse, my thoughts are swimming as I brush my teeth. So many little crumbs gathered from the evening, and no clue what they are falling from. I grab my phone and start jotting them down in Notes.

- Kappy's Campground burned down.
- Construction stopped on the new housing development.
- Pink-haired woman with Libby, tense discussion.
- Cain Landry had a plan.

CHAPTER SIXTEEN

"You need me at the auction meeting?" I ask Ada Grace, balancing the phone between my shoulder and ear as I drop three hundred and twenty-five gala invitations into the post office box. I thought Libby would never finalize the guest list. Eight weeks should be plenty of time for guests to make travel plans, considering two-thirds of the guests are coming from out of town.

I have a list of a gazillion things to do today and appeasing Ada Grace Huntly is not on it. I check my watch. I had hoped I'd have some time to research the fire out at Kappy's, but instead I'm being summoned to oversee the silent auction entries. Besides, Ada Grace is proving to be a proverbial thorn in my side. She's hired me to plan her daughter's eighth birthday party next month. It's not something I'd typically take on, but I didn't have the gala booked when she asked, and I needed the money. It was supposed to be a catered barbecue with a fun cake and twenty-five people total but has morphed to include a petting zoo, two bouncy houses, three live princesses, and at least thirty children plus their parents.

"Yes, I can swing by Sweet Salvations. I'm just down the street at the post office. I'll be there in a few."

Wednesdays at the bakery are usually pretty quiet; it's where I typically get my work done when I need a break from the cramped space of the greenhouse. But this morning the ruckus upstairs from the auction committee ladies sounds like they're knee-deep in mimosas with their bursts of laughter and louder-than-deemed-proper chatter. I find the group of women on the second-story balcony that overlooks Main Street.

I try not to feel self-conscious about the athleisure I'm wearing, but these ladies are dressed as if they're having brunch at a café in Beverly Hills: summer dresses, espadrilles, and two of the eight women are wearing wide-brim floppy hats. They take fundraising to a whole new level. It's a healthy competition of who can raise more money for their favorite organization with bragging rights as the prize. It's a full-time job for most them, which makes sense seeing as how none of them work, and their husbands have more money than they know what to do with.

"Hollis, darling," Ada Grace says halfway through a laugh. "You would not believe the ridiculousness of these women. Do sit. So good of you to finally make it to the meeting," she says as if I was supposed to attend all along.

"Happy to swing by on such short notice," I say and sit next to Geraldine Thurmond, the least pretentious in the bunch. "What can I help you ladies with?"

For the most part they want to know what the auction tables setup is going to look like. I promise to send over the venue layout as soon as it's complete. They go on to offer a few suggestions for the event's emcee: one is known for being too in his cups by the end of the evening, and the other is very yuckety-yuck with all his jokes. I'm hoping Parker Mason can do it: he's a great personality on the morning radio and the best fit for the tone I'm trying to set.

"So the ladies and I had an incredible idea," Ada Grace starts. "And we wanted to ask you a *big* favor."

I hold in a groan. My event business isn't even established enough to make a profit yet, but they're going to ask me to donate my services—and I doubt we're talking a simple birthday party either.

"Susanna here had a fantastic idea for an add-on to the gala—another way to bring in some *real* money for the church." She exchanges a knowing glance with a few around the table. "We were thinking how fun would it be to have a bachelor's auction! Really up the energy for the night, engage more of the guests with something fun, less stuffy." When I don't reply, she gets to the real heart of the matter. "And we thought you could ask Cain Landry to donate himself." A few of them giggle.

I wouldn't color myself the type of person to not have anything to say, but here I sit with eight pairs of eyes eagerly devouring the moment, and I can't produce a single word. It takes all my strength to hide my annoyance. The anticipation of my response clings to the air like the cloying sweetness of Geraldine's perfume.

"Well." I eventually find the words. "I certainly can mention it to him." Jesus knows I don't want to, though.

You would have thought there was a contest to hold your breath with the collective sigh of relief. Now I'm wishing they had asked me to donate my services instead.

They prattle on about who else they can include, and some of the older ladies volunteer their friends' college-aged sons. There are a few rascally older bachelors thrown into the mix as well. All this is just one more thing I have to plan.

The meeting eventually breaks up. As I excuse myself, I catch sight of a familiar cartoon bluebird on a flyer in Geraldine's planning folder.

Same bird as on the Toot If You're a Tit bumper sticker on the car of the pink-haired woman Libby rendezvoused with.

"Geraldine," I say to stop her before she heads down the stairwell. "Pardon me for being nosy, but I couldn't help but notice the bluebird flyer you had in your folder." She glances to the leather organizer she's clutching. "Could you tell me what business that logo belongs to?"

She seems a little reluctant to say. Then she does a quick check to make sure the last two ladies aren't headed our way just yet. "Well, it's a senior women's group I belong to." She opens the folder and hands me one of the flyers.

It's a bluebird with a red-and-white polka-dot bathing suit on. The flyer is for an upcoming pool fitness party for an assisted living home from a neighboring town.

"It's the Blue Tits." She whispers the name as if it's a sin to say it out loud. "It's a swim club my cousin over in Camden got me into. A group of us ladies swim to stay fit, but we also fundraise. Katherine." Geraldine stops one of the ladies from the group who passes. "Don't you let them grandbabies boss you around. You let them know Mimi is in charge." Miss Katherine promises to try, then Mrs. Geraldine turns back to me.

"So it's just a swim group named after a bird?"

"Well," she stretches the word, tottering her head. "Sort of. We practice year-round at the Camden YMCA, but our breast cancer awareness fundraiser's in November, and we do a cold-plunge swim in Blue Herring Lake. And let me tell you," she says, stressing her words, "we get our name true enough." She protectively covers her chest and shivers.

"Ah. I see. Sounds like a fun organization," I say as I follow her down the stairs.

"We are one sassy group, sometimes a little rowdy. But, now, look here . . ." She stops abruptly at the bottom—she has a flair for the dramatic. "These local ladies would die before belonging to such a namesake club. If it gets out I'm a card-carrying member, I'll know who spilled the beans." She points a playful finger at me.

I mime zipping my lips. "Not a word from me, I promise." I smile, folding the flyer and tucking it into my purse as I tell her goodbye. Before I leave I swing by the bakery counter that floats in the center of the room. It's a sin to leave Sweet Salvations without taking a sugarboo home with you.

As I place my order, I do a double take at the sight of Cain and Mary Beth Hawthorne seated at one of the small bistro tables on the back patio downstairs, chatting over tea.

I have half a thought that maybe I should say hi. But then maybe I'm just being nosy. Or intruding. Or both. If they were discussing something about the gala, wouldn't they have included me?

My phone buzzes with a text from Nadine. Who's up for wine Friday night?

Calista immediately answers with a raised-hand emoji.

"Here you go." The cashier hands me my change and the sugarboo.

I text the girls back. I'll need an IV.

CHAPTER SEVENTEEN

THE HAWTHORNE GAZETTE has been around for almost a hundred years, but its online archives only go back twelve. There was not a single story about a fire out at Kappy's Campgrounds in those twelve years. But the grave bird I found in the Hawthornes' office has been there at least fifteen years, since the time Uncle Royce took me to the swim party. I dig through all the articles I can find on Kappy's and finally come across one that mentions the owner's death, but it was locked behind a paywall. After an annual sixty-five-dollar subscription to a historical archive and an hour later down a rabbit hole, I eventually hit pay dirt: "Man Saves Town from Potential Disaster." It's a scanned article from *The Hawthorne Gazette* some twenty-five years ago. I've just started reading when there's a knock at my door—it's Nadine and Calista with two bottles of wine for our Friday girls' night. I close my laptop and let them in.

Calista immediately plops down on the sofa while Nadine grabs a few wineglasses from my bar cart. She's started in on her mother and her latest crusade for Nadine to hurry up and get pregnant already, but her smile dwindles when she looks over to me. "What's going on with you? You've been quiet all week."

"Wait, did you guys have sex?" Calista says, raising a snarky brow in question. She was tracking my gaze: Cain was out back, putting away the trash cans.

I roll my eyes at her. "It's nothing to do with him." I scratch a snoozing Sampson behind his ear. "I saw something I can't let go of. Something unnerving." I take the wineglass Nadine passes me. "I think I witnessed a murder." Both women's eyes widen with shock.

Calista sits up all eager. "Like for real? Or is this the I-see-dead-people thing?"

I laugh lightly. "I don't see dead people."

"Just dead birds What?" she says after Nadine wallops her with a pillow. "I'm not being rude. I swear! I just don't remember the particulars of how these ghost encounters work." Calista stuffs the pillow behind her back. "I'm sorry. Please continue with the murder." She fans a casual hand. Nadine glares at her.

So I proceed to tell them what the crow showed me out at Kappy's Campgrounds.

"I looked it up earlier," I tell them, opening up my laptop on the coffee table. "I had to get an archive subscription to find the article. The only fire mentioned out at Kappy's Campgrounds was a couple of decades ago. The main lodge burned down, but no one was killed. It just doesn't make sense why I'd see the boy there if he didn't die there." I turn my computer to show them the article.

Nadine picks up my computer. "It says, 'Mechanic Frank Kilroy with Johnson's Autobody was doing a late-night tow when he witnessed the blaze from the highway and called it in to the authorities,'" she reads aloud. "'Even though the campgrounds have been closed for a few years, there were several propane tanks still on the property that would have caused a major disaster for the county had they exploded.'" She reads silently for a moment. "They go on to say they believe damaged power lines from the previous night's storm were responsible for the fire. They call this Kilroy guy a hero for saving the county and mention some hot dog celebration fundraiser for the Fire Fighters' Association that weekend. But there's no mention of a body being found. So maybe the boy got out," Nadine offers, letting Calista look at the article.

Johnson's Autobody, I think silently. Something about it sounds familiar, but I can't understand why because there's not a shop around here with that name.

"Like, are you sure what you saw?" Nadine asks, drawing me from my thoughts. "Like, did you *see* the boy die?"

"I mean, I felt the heat. The pain. Am I a hundred percent certain? No." I chew on the tip of my thumbnail, trying to recall. "There was a storm," I say, remembering the crack of thunder and the flash of lightning. "Maybe it was a fire caused by the storm like the article says."

"Wait. What were you even doing way out there?" Nadine asks.

To explain what took me out there means I'd have to tell them about the ghost woman in the Hawthornes' home and what she showed me, her murder. I have a career to think about and a future in this town. And as much as I trust my best friends, a murder at the Hawthorne mansion is too scandalous to keep quiet about. One innocent question to the wrong person could jeopardize everything.

"Oh, Dylan asked me if I wanted to ride out there with him. He and Denny are trying to put together a camping retreat for the men's church group and thought it might be a salvageable option, but it's too overgrown to use. Anyway," I say, shaking the melancholy away, "you're probably right, Nadine. He probably got out." Though, the article didn't mention anyone who was rescued either.

"Did I tell you ladies," I say, eager to change the subject, "Ada Grace asked me to ask Cain to donate himself in their bachelor auction for the gala?"

"You gotta be kidding me!" Nadine says as Calista says, "Did you tell her to eff off?"

"It's not like there's anything *official* happening between us," I remind them. Though, I feel like we are on the cusp of taking it to the next level.

My phone beeps, and I glance down at a text from Cain. **Are your friends still there?**

Nadine leans over and sees it's from him. "Speak of the devil." And he shall appear.

"You need to get naked with him," Calista says. A smirk hangs off the side of her mouth.

"You just hush." I mock offense and then text him back. **They're leaving soon, Peeping Tom.**

"Just saying," she says, still smirking. "Because those auction ladies are smart. They're going to make bank on that man alone." Calista fans her shirt like she has to cool herself off just thinking about him. I toss the wine cork at her.

Another text comes through. **Then maybe you should come over so I don't have to peep.** A thrill shoots through me. I shield my phone as Nadine tries to steal another peek. "You just keep your nose out of this," I tell her.

Before I can reply I get another. **I have the good wine.**

Followed by **Paloma is out of town, and I'm alone for the night.**

"Okay, ladies," I say, hopping up off the couch. Sampson yowls in protest from suddenly being jarred awake. "I'm calling it for tonight."

"Good night, Hollis," Louisa whistles.

"Thank you, good girl." I blow her a kiss.

"Babe," Calista says and scowls. "You're just gonna throw us out over some fresh meat? What are we, chopped liver?" A grin hides under her scowl.

I take her almost empty glass. "Yep. Nighty night." I shoo them both toward the door.

Louisa helps me clear them out. "Good night, Hollis."

"I expect details in the morning." Nadine points a finger as she leaves.

"Not on your life," I tell her and close the door, giving them a buh-bye wave from the other side of the glass.

I shoot Cain a quick text. I'll be there in five. I wonder if I should show up in my pajamas or stay dressed in what I have on. I opt for something in between: a spaghetti-strap tank, comfy but fitting joggers, and bare feet.

Fifteen minutes later and out of breath from rushing, I find myself knocking on the back door. It lightly eases open from the touch.

"Hello," I call into the house, but no one replies. The dark inside drinks up the room. Only a single glowing light whispers from upstairs. His bedroom? I swallow hard and let my feet take me before my head can talk me out of some potential fun.

My excitement is a little dashed once I'm halfway up the stairs and realize it's his office light. Just as I'm about to reach the door I hear a small voice, like a child's. Cain sits in his office chair, elbows on his knees as he smiles at the nothing next to his desk.

"Hey," I say because that's all my brain can come up with. My eyes search the room for the other voice I was certain I heard.

He straightens, the concern on his face gone before it can fully register. "That was fast." I don't bother to say it took me longer than the five minutes I originally estimated. His eyes skim over my bare shoulders then back to my face.

"Where's Paloma?"

"In California. She has a meeting with a lawyer about her late husband's estate. Thirsty?" He holds up his own glass of brandy.

"Sure, thanks. Wow, the office looks great," I say, scanning the room in surprise. I'm used to seeing him operate out of moving boxes, but now it's all finally unpacked and put together.

It's interesting to see the mix of modern and vintage. A chunky brown leather chair paired with a modern burl wood desk with chrome legs. The black carved credenza looks majestic under the sputnik light fixture with bare Edison bulbs that hangs from the ceiling.

I walk the long wall of his bookshelves checking out his collectibles. Uncle Royce always had it stuffed full of first edition books he had never read but said made him look smart. And tons of framed photos of friends and family and famous people he had met. (I still have the picture of me and the elderly prince who disappointed my young heart.)

Cain has his shelves filled with entrepreneurial books and objects from his travels. Not things you pick up at a tourist shop but art. A handmade clay desert quail. An acrylic box filled with exotic butterflies. A bust of the Madonna carved from teak. Unique items that seem to speak to the flavor of Cain.

"You like it?" He's poured me a brandy from his bar station.

"It's like I'm seeing pieces of you." I smile and touch the spines of a porcupine resting in a sterling silver 1908 horse race trophy cup.

"Those were a pain in my ass," Cain says. "Literally." He steps closer and hands me the snifter glass. Close enough I can't tell if the sweet brandy scent is from his lips or the glass.

He stays there, watching me as I dare a delicate sip. A smooth maple oak flavor, the spice warms my throat as I swallow.

"Memories," he declares, stepping away, fanning his brandy glass at the bookshelves. "Where I was. Who I knew. I don't want to forget." A quiet note softens his words. "It happens, time passes, and things just slip loose." He gestures toward his head.

We do forget. As precious as my grandaddy was, only a few memories still hold on, already dulled by time. Uncle Royce, this house, those shelves—even after a year, they've started to fade.

"What's this?" I point to a small piece of dull red wood. It's so nondescript compared to all the other objects in the room.

"That," he says and picks it up, "is a puzzle piece. It went to a square board about this big." He holds his hands out, brandy glass in one hand, red piece in the other. "There was a blue jay and a toucan. Some brown bird and this red bird." He holds it out so now I can clearly see it.

A cardinal.

I tell myself it's just a cardinal, it doesn't mean anything. Yet all I can hear is the crashing of birds against the glass windows at the Hawthornes back in May. Their spots of blood smeared on the window. And Mary Beth, acting so strange.

"Paloma said after my parents . . ." He tries to find the words. "After they went on their trip, one I was too sick to go on, I became attached to this silly little piece." He gives it a shake, his smile wide. "Kept it in my pocket and took it everywhere I went, like a good luck charm. Even slept with it like a blankie, she said. I guess I just never grew out of my fondness for it." You can hear the nostalgia in his voice. He looks at it thoughtfully. His thumb rubbing the shallow divot where the paint is worn away.

"Earlier today I saw you having lunch with Mary Beth." I watch him as I say her name to see how he reacts.

"And you didn't say hi?" His eyes search me for what I'm really wanting to know.

"Well . . . I had to rush out. Other errands to run and all that." It sounds as flimsy as it is untrue.

"Hmm" is all he says and doesn't offer more.

Great. Now I'll have to pry it out of him or spend the rest of my night trying to decide if I need to worry about their little meeting.

"You know," I say, "if there's anything about the gala you want to discuss, you can come to me." I fiddle with brass kaleidoscope on his shelf.

A sly smile spreads across his lips. "You have nothing to worry about." He grabs my hand, massaging his thumb on the back of it. "I wanted to get to know her, get a sense of who she is. And see if she's anything like her family."

"And?"

"I think she loathes them." He sits back on the corner of his desk, still drawing circles on my hand with his thumb.

"Oh?"

He sets his drink down. His other hand finds a home on my hip. "Nothing she said. Just a general feeling I picked up from her." He watches me, thoughtful for a moment. "Are you hungry?" There's intensity in his gaze, and those light steel eyes of his glint then deepen to a stormy gray. I feel my pulse kick in response.

But then my stomach gurgles, reminding me I haven't eaten dinner yet.

He chuckles. "Come on. Let's get you something to eat," he says in an assured way and heads straight out of his office.

I obediently follow, feeling my foot slip slightly in my step. I glance back over my shoulder and see a small puddle of water on the floor next to Cain's desk.

Exactly where he was smiling when I came in.

End of July can be damn hot during the day and sticky by night. Still, we opt to sit on the rear balcony patio sofas under the navy night sky and the song of the cicadas.

The large balcony covers the entire width of the back of the house. This is where the gala's VIP guests will dine. It's a commanding deck with its place of prominence and exquisite view of the gardens, the twinkling lights of the subdivision off in the distance. The twenty-foot hedge wall at edge of the property will be the perfect backdrop for a stage.

Cain and I sit on the plush deep-seated patio sectional he had ordered for the space. We lightly discuss the last of the remodeling coming up. Only three more weeks of work, which puts us ahead of my original schedule (because he has the money to pay for things to move faster than I do).

Somehow the conversation about what's left on the remodeling list gravitates into our pasts. Eventually I find myself curled up next to him, head on his shoulder, glass of wine in my hand, and my feet between his legs. His thumb works soft circles on my knee as he talks about his college roommate. Jonathon Radcliff who was an emancipated minor without a high school diploma but who got a full scholarship to the University of California and went on to get a degree in bioengineering.

"Wow, that's an incredible story."

"Right?" His eyes are a little glazed from the effects of the brandy. "That was his entire life focus. Now he has a wife. Little boy who is about two. He just . . . he took his own path. Do you sometimes wonder if you're on the right path?"

Bit of an insecure question coming from a man who seems to have everything under control at all times. But I like that he's showing me a more vulnerable side, something I didn't expect.

"I thought I was. I'm getting there now, I'd like to think."

"Before I came in and ruined everything?"

I lightly chuckle. "Sort of." I dig an elbow in his side. "Life works itself out." And I truly believe that. "If there's one thing I've learned from my granny after losing Grandaddy and half the farm, we all find a way to survive. I just need to create a new vision past owning Uncle Royce's house. It's out there. I just don't see it yet."

He grins, squeezing my knee in appreciation. "Yeah, Jonathon found a way. His moral compass was so clear. Sometimes I wonder if I have the same clarity."

I burst out with a laugh. "Are you serious? You're a consultant for philanthropic causes. You provided a water system for villages in Guyana. You've harvested grain in Panama as part of hurricane relief. You're getting sustainable soybean crops to provide food for people in South America. Like how much more *moral* does your compass need to be?" I look at him, almost incredulous.

He stares at me like he's searching for himself in my eyes. I wonder what broke him so, that makes him think what he's offering the world isn't good enough.

"Well, if you're looking for brownie points with the man upstairs, I have a proposition for you," I say to him.

Cain pulls me more firmly into his lap, his smile hanging a little more loosely. "And what might that be?"

Heat spreads over my body, flushing my cheeks. "Oh, the auction ladies asked me to convince you to be in their bachelor auction."

"You don't say?" He puffs up his chest all proud like a prize rooster. "I wonder which one will pay the most for me?" he says with a gloating smile on his face.

This needles me. "So that's a *yes*?" I don't mean for the bitterness in my voice to be so pronounced.

"Hell, yes," he says with more enthusiasm than I care to hear. I feel myself withdrawing. "Only one stipulation." He squeezes tighter so I can't get away. "You outbid everyone, and I'll pay the bill."

"You're assuming I want to bid on you?" I hold back a grin.

"Something tells me you do." And before I can respond, he leans in, taking my mouth with his own. Lush, full kissing that promises a lot more to come.

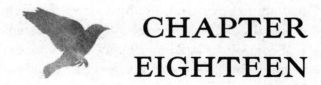

CHAPTER EIGHTEEN

I SLUMP DOWN in the seat of my car in the Camden YMCA parking lot, peering out over the dashboard like an amateur sleuth. After one quick phone call, I found out the Blue Tits senior swim group has a standing reservation for their pool every Monday, Wednesday, and Friday at eleven in the morning. And sure enough, one beat-up, blue PT Cruiser with leopard-print seat covers and a TOOT IF YOU'RE A TIT bumper sticker sits in the parking lot.

I felt pretty proud of myself to have come this far, but then I had no idea how I plan to approach the pink-haired woman. I contemplated going inside, but Mrs. Geraldine Thurmond is here, too, and I don't know how that would look. I'm not even sure what I want to ask her—or why I think she'll tell me anything. It's just there's . . . something going on. I just can't quite put my finger on it yet.

The group of senior ladies trickle out of the YMCA finally, but it takes another forty-five minutes for the pink-haired woman to appear. What in the hell am I going to say? *Excuse me, ma'am, have you been up to anything underhanded or nefarious with Libby Hawthorne lately?*

I follow her around Camden for another hour and watch her pick up her dry cleaning, hit a drive-through for lunch, and eventually park at a construction site where Dunkirk's Construction company is building a three-story office space. It's been ten minutes since she tottered across the gravel parking lot in her hot-pink stilettos and skintight leather leggings, and she hasn't come out yet. I'm beginning to believe this is her job.

If so, then maybe whatever she and Libby were discussing—arguing about?—at the construction site behind Uncle Royce's house wasn't so nefarious after all. Maybe it was just business. I try to search up on my phone the Greater Good subdivision to see who the builder is, but I can't find anything. So I text Nadine to see if she knows, but she doesn't.

Here I am tracking this woman down, and Libby was probably just paying her bill for what she owes them.

There's only so long you can sit in your car before you start to look suspect. I decide I need to at least pop my head in, ask a few questions. I'm barely across the street when my phone rings. I jump, then fumble to answer it.

"Hello?" I whisper into the phone and slow up my pace so I don't get to the office trailer too fast.

"Everything all right?" Bren Dawson asks me.

"Oh yes, all good. I was about to step into a meeting. What's up?"

"Did you know Ada Grace tripled her cupcake order today?"

"Wait, what?" I freeze. "Her daughter's party is tomorrow." I don't mean to shriek, but this woman keeps throwing me curveballs, and she has already upped her guest list once. How many people do you need to celebrate an eight-year-old's birthday?

A front loader passes with a forklift full of drainage pipes. The driver gives me a lurid smile.

"Yep. We are at one hundred cupcakes and triple-tier ice castle princess cake. I just wanted to call and confirm the new total and that there won't be any more additions."

"Are you able to handle the extra order so last minute?" I ask.

"For you, yes."

I sigh with relief.

The construction trailer door swings open, and I flinch in panic, but it's just one of the workers coming out.

"Thank you, Bren. Just update the bill, and I'll make sure you get paid." After I hang up the phone, I head up the steps to the trailer with my fake story at the ready.

I'm greeted with an empty desk with papers stacked a mile high. Filing cabinets run the length of the wall. At one end is a bathroom, at the other it looks like a door to a private office where I hear a man and a woman talking.

This is pink-hair lady's desk, all right. A blue zebra-striped lumbar pillow sits in the office chair. A rhinestone stapler and tape dispenser on the desk. Quite a few pictures of children litter the back wall, the frames equal in bling and flair. There's even a picture of her and Dolly Parton, though it's an old image as she looks much younger.

A bark of laughter erupts as she walks out of the office. Her smile quickly dries up as she lays eyes on me.

"Can I help you, sugar?" Her acrylic nails, long and bright pink like her shoes, grip a manila folder. She walks over to the desk and puts it in a stack with more of the same. She gives me a quick once-over, sizing up my outfit I'm guessing—a vintage Neil Diamond T-shirt with an emerald-green satin pencil skirt, and snakeskin ankle booties—my *edgy but professional look*, Nadine calls it.

"Hi, I'm—" I reach out my hand to introduce myself and pause, realizing maybe I don't want to give my real name. "Holly," I land on.

She shakes my hand because decorum calls for it, but I can tell she's not crazy about it. "Betsy."

Betsy is probably in her sixties and dresses like she's twenty-five: too tight, too loud, and doesn't give a flip what you think. So far I like her.

"I was happening through the neighborhood when I saw the construction going on here and thought I would pop in to see if maybe I can get a business card? We're doing some remodeling on our home, and I'm trying to find a contractor." I name off a few projects we've been working on at Cain's house to make it sound more legit.

She's clearly annoyed I've interrupted her workday with my petty residential remodeling project.

"Unfortunately we only do commercial projects." She fans a hand to the giant corkboard behind her covered in design concepts and blueprints. "Office buildings. Subdivisions. From the ground up–type projects."

"Oh, I see." I scan the wall hoping one of the neighborhood design concepts will look familiar. Nothing. "You guys wouldn't happen to also be building those houses over in Hawthorne, are you? I think it's called the Greater Good subdivision?"

Betsy's eyes narrow slightly. "Where did you say you're from, honey?"

My pulse kicks. I stutter as I say, "I—I was just driving through the neighborhood." I thumb over my shoulder as if that answers her question. Suddenly I feel hot. The tiny air conditioner unit in the window isn't pumping enough cold air in here.

"No, we're not doing any construction there." Now she's coming around from behind her desk, and I feel myself stepping back toward the door.

"Like, recently stopped doing construction on it or were never involved in the project?" The heel of my bootie catches on the cheap Berber carpet, and I fumble to catch myself and knock over a stack of paperwork piled next to a filing cabinet.

"Never. Now, what's it to you?"

Quickly I bend over to straighten the pile. "Oh, nothing, just curious," I say, and my words puff white. Frost spreads from my fingertips over the manila folder, chalking it with a crystalline film. I drop the file I'm holding like it's a hot potato.

Betsy is right in my face once I straighten. I pinch my lips closed. My eyes dart around the room, looking for the thing I cannot see, but I know it's here with us. A pen canister on her desk rattles lightly. The little snow globe from Las Vegas on her desk vibrates and shimmies like it's being disturbed.

Betsy casts a confused look around the room, as if sensing it, too. She shivers at the cold, unsure where it's coming from, then quickly shakes her head a bit. Remembering her ire, she parks her hands on her hips and blinks her feather-thick lashes at me. "You're the second person *today* to ask us about those houses."

"Oh?" I say, twisting to try to get out of her way. "What a coincidence." I realize she's backed me into a corner, and there's a line of file cabinets between me and the door. She's a petite woman, but damn if she's not mighty in stature.

"I don't think so," she says matter-of-factly. "So I'll tell you the same thing I told the other person. If you've got questions about the Grady Owens estate, send them to our lawyer."

All those tense nerves disappear, and my shoulders slacken. "Did you say Grady Owens?" I say, my tone every bit of unexpected shock.

The color washes from her face—which is pretty hard to do with all that makeup. Her eyes dart to the office, then back to me.

Suddenly the front door rips opens and noise fills the small, cramped space.

"Excuse me, Ms.—" the young man in a construction hat says but stops once he sees us oddly huddled in the corner.

"What do you want, Jimmy?" she snaps at him.

"I'll get out of y'all's hair." I push past while her guard is down. "Thank you for your help." I dart past Jimmy and dash down the short stairs.

"Sorry to interrupt, Ms. Kilroy," I hear him say as the door claps shut behind me.

MY HANDS ARE shaking as I drive away, my head whirring with new information. Who else was in her office earlier today asking questions? Cain? But he wouldn't know who Grady Owens was, would he? And what did she mean *estate*?

That wasn't the crux of it, though. Her name is Betsy Kilroy.

As soon as I'm a safe distance away—like she's going to chase after me or something—I pull over into the parking lot of a Dollar General and search up the Kappy's Campgrounds newspaper archive. I zoom in to reread it.

Mechanic Frank Kilroy with Johnson's Autobody was doing a late-night tow when he witnessed the blaze from the highway and called it in to the authorities.

Now, what are the chances Frank and Betsy just happen to have the same last name?

CHAPTER NINETEEN

THERE ARE THREE things I've learned from the dead. One, they always have something to say. Two, you can almost guarantee what they're going to show you won't be pretty.

And three, the dead don't like being ignored.

What I need to be doing is picking up a check for the gala from Jeremiah. *Or* going over my final checklist for the birthday party tomorrow. Instead, I find myself driving across town to the edge of Camden, to Johnson's Autobody.

The phone number I found for the place was disconnected, so I'm not too surprised to find it boarded up. But I am surprised to find myself climbing over the top of the chain-link fence in a skirt to get a peek inside.

Oh shit. I jump down to the ground and duck behind a row of rusted oil barrels as a man at the house next door drags his trash cans to the curb. My heart hammers in my chest. There's a jagged scratch across my palm, but thankfully it's not bleeding too bad.

"How did you get arrested, Hollis?" I whisper to myself as I wait for the coast to be clear. "Oh, just a little trespassing." *What am I doing?*

My phone rings, and I swear trying to turn the ringer off. I hope like hell that man is gone back to his house already. I hold my breath, waiting for movement, but don't hear anything. I glance at my phone and see a missed call from Cain. Then a text from him follows right after. What are we doing for dinner?

I'll text him after breaking and entering, I tell myself.

It looks like this place was converted into a mini junkyard: there's nothing but rotted vehicles lined up in three rows in the parking lot. I jump as something scurries across my path, hopefully just some kind of squirrel with a hairless tail.

No clue what I expect to find in here, surely not Frank Kilroy. When I searched the internet on my phone, all I found was an old NFL player who died at the age of eighty-six back in 2007. Surprisingly, there were quite a few Betsy Kilroys, but none of them fit mine's description. So here I am, rubbing the thick layer of dirt off the grubby windows, peeking inside to what looks like it could have been the front office. Now it's packed full of boxes, a clear sign of hoarding. Next to it is the first car bay, more boxes collapsed on themselves, stacks of old tires, and more junk. The second bay hosts a rusted old truck and a huge engine half-taken apart. The third bay has a skeleton of a car hanging from a hydraulic press.

Nothing out of the ordinary, really.

Except for a pathetic grave bird, lying on its side on the bare, oil-stained concrete floor.

I stare at the small gray bird; it's seemingly unaware of my presence. I wonder if I'm about to meet Frank Kilroy.

This is what I came for. This is what that itching was all about.

The glass front door is locked tight. None of the garage bay doors will budge. Through the windows, I see a shaft of light coming from the right rear of the building.

Sandwiched between the building and a cinderblock wall are a pile of old gas station signs and shelves full of rusty parts. From over the concrete wall I hear the chatter of a television and the occasional laughter of a man from the property next door. I stifle a scream as another critter, which I'm hoping is a cat, scurries behind the signage.

The thick metal door is wedged open by an acid-corroded battery. When I shoulder against it, the hinges cry out with a shriek.

Shit.

I freeze and listen for any indication I've been discovered. And after a long silent nothing, I squeeze myself through, into the garage.

It reeks of oil and dust and loneliness. There's a wall of boxes and junk I have to navigate around, but I finally get to the grave bird.

I glance up at the corroded car hovering above my head on the lift. From the cobwebs alone, it's clearly been there a very long time. And it'll be there a long time more, I tell myself.

I crouch low to the ground. The gray mockingbird doesn't even wake to my presence.

"Hello, love," I say and make little kissy noises.

Its shoulder wing flinches, finding life. Then its head twists around to see me. As if the moment he's been waiting for has finally arrived, he jumps to his feet.

"There you go, sweet boy." I hold out my hand for him. He hops over to me then jumps into my open palm.

I am thrown back in time.

I still my breathing as I hide in the closet. It smells of mothballs and musty old magazines. A rich beam of sunlight pours in from the gap under the door. Her shadow passes back and forth a few times as she searches the room for me. I grip my coin jar tight. I know she stole my Christmas money from the library fireplace. She tore my room apart on more than one occasion, so I knew better than to hide it in there again.

But my coin collection, I wasn't going to let her take it.

"I know you're in here, you brat." Her voice full of venom. She doesn't play fair. She isn't kind. And she's a thief.

Her shadow stops in front of the door, and I bury myself deeper into the coats and pray she doesn't find me.

The bright morning light shoves itself into the closet. A hand thrusts inside and grabs me by my hair and drags me out into the hallway. She rips the light blue mason jar from my hands as I stumble forward . . .

And decades later I step into the mechanic shop. I do not fear her like I did when we were younger.

Rain slants against the night, running off the roof in sheets. The thunder rolls in the sky until it splits it open with a zipper of lightning.

The flash gives me a glance of the dark room. Sitting on the oil-stained concrete floor, the light blue mason jar from twenty years ago. Empty.

She's toying with me. Up to her old tricks.

I don't trust her.

She wouldn't have asked me to meet her here unless she wanted money. If our parents didn't want her to have a dime, then I won't give her any either.

I reach down to pick up the jar, and a loud groan yawns from above. I look up as a car on the hydraulics crashes down on me.

I scream. A shower of coins rains down on my head. Their metal clatters violently in the empty garage. Crouched near the floor, my arms poised above my head. My breaths hard and panting. Fear sharp as iron on my tongue.

I press my palm to a faint brown stain on the floor around me, wondering if this was where the man's blood pooled. Coins—actual coins—scatter around my feet, seeming to fall from the air. I shake, and a few more fall on me. I pick them up: old buffalo nickels and wheat pennies. Coins from different countries. Tons of them.

Outside a gate rattles. A man commands his dog, "Go find 'em, boy."

Quickly I scoop up as many coins as I can into the bottom of my T-shirt.

A dog barks at the garage bay door, his nose taking in loud sniffs.

Shit. I scramble to the side door where I entered, glancing back over my shoulder to see the man peering through the filmy glass. I hide just outside the door and freeze, my heart thundering in my ears.

A moment later the chain lever to the bay door rattles and clanks as it's yanked. A loud groan follows as the metal door protests being opened.

I use the cover of the noise to climb the wire rack against the cinder block wall and scale over the top. Roaring barks echo in the garage. I can hear the dog's nails on the concrete as it chases after me.

Tightly I grip my makeshift T-shirt pouch and jump to the ground, into the man's yard. My skirt rips as I do.

Down the street I find safety in my car. I glance over my shoulder, out the window as my tires squeal, trying to gain traction, and I take off toward the highway. I catch sight of my sweaty face in the mirror. I bust out laughing, feeling fifteen again when Valerie Cole and I got caught smoking in back of the Lucky's Quick Stop and had to run from Mrs. Wanda Dewberry.

My lap is full of coins, and I hold one up as I drive: a bicentennial quarter. A fifty-cent piece. I'm not sure what compelled me to take them. I wanted to protect them for the boy, I guess. The fog of his memory clings to the dark corners of my thoughts as I try to recall the girl, but it fades faster than I can catch hold of it.

A car killed a man. Dropped straight on him. Whoever this woman was that he was so wary of, she killed him. I'm sure of it.

In as many months, I've seen four dead souls and their grave birds. The little girl, who stays near my studio and Uncle Royce's house. The woman, terrified for her life and her children's, who died at Hawthorne Manor. The boy who burned in a fire at Kappy's Campgrounds. And now this man, whose coins were stolen by a mysterious woman.

Are they connected? They have to be, right? I just need to figure out how.

And, more importantly, what they want with me now.

CHAPTER TWENTY

LATER I SWING by the Hawthorne church to pick up a late
gala payment from Jeremiah. Even as I drive over there, my
nerves are still rattled. The drop of that car was horrific. But
the coins—coins that fell from the sky? I've never come away
from a grave bird encounter with a souvenir before, never anything tangible.

In the sanctuary, the women's choir is practicing for Sunday's
service. The long hall to the left hosts an assortment of offices,
and Jeremiah Hawthorne's is the one at the end. He sits in a big
old leather chair, laughing loudly on the phone. I dart my head
in the doorway and wave, to let him know I'm here.

He gives me the wait-a-minute finger with his burned hand
and arm. The bandage now gone, it seems to be healing okay,
but the skin has a ruddy puffiness to it still, a remnant of the
day the fire almost ate him.

I sit in one of the hallway's chairs, catching up on texts I
missed while gallivanting around Camden. I text Cain back.

Italian sounds good. I send Nadine a picture of the tear in my satin green skirt and ask her where I should take it.

"Is that right?" I hear Jeremiah say. When I glance up, he lowers his voice. "New investor is asking questions he shouldn't . . . Don't worry about her. Mother already asked me to take care of it . . . Mm-hmm . . . Yeah, I'll head over tomorrow, see if I can't get that done." He turns in his chair and says something lower, but I can't make it out.

The choir has begun to exit the sanctuary and out walks Paloma. She sees me as she leaves, and I meet her halfway to say hello.

"Hey, Paloma. I didn't realize you were back from California today." I try not to sound disappointed. I've liked staying in Cain's bed the last two nights.

"Things wrapped up quicker than I expected. Are you going home after this? That will save me the trouble of calling Cain." She gestures to her phone.

"I can give you a ride home, if you don't mind waiting? I have some business with Jeremiah," I say and thumb over my shoulder.

Sunlight jumps into the front entry hall as a ruckus tumbles into the church from the side door. Mary Beth and her three children in tow.

"Hey, Mary Beth. How are you?" I say.

"You're just the person I'm looking for," Mary Beth says.

Paloma kneels down in front of Eve, asking about her dolly. Sweet little Ruth, who has her momma's strawberry hair, is only two and a permanent fixture on Mary Beth's hip. She introduces her children to Paloma.

"And my boy," she says pointing to the six-year-old who's flying a cop car down the hall, "is Elijah."

"Biblical names," Paloma says, smiling. "How beautiful."

"Thank you," Mary Beth says, a little bit surprised. "Most people don't notice. But it's a Hawthorne tradition that goes all the way back to my great-great-grandaddy Constantine Hawthorne," she says. I didn't realize it myself, but now I remember she mentioned being named after Mary of Bethany, the woman who anointed Jesus's feet.

I glance over to Jeremiah, whose son is named Roy Wayne.

"Well," Mary Beth adds, following my eyes, "Jeremiah doesn't care for tradition. But I'm glad we ran into each other. I was dropping this off with him, but it's actually for you. Mother said you needed a write-up of one of our missionary families, something for the emcee to read the night of." She hands me a manila folder and a USB drive.

I flip open the file. It's pictures of a man, woman, and two children, in some desert location, smiling widely in their pristine clothes. Some biography typed up. I had hoped the family themselves or at least the pastor missionary could come and speak; instead I get a press kit on a family.

"Mother said this is all you needed, right? A mock-up for a missionary. Some backstory. Images of a family. Et cetera."

"Uh, yeah." I flip through a few of the pictures. It is the most perfect family I've ever seen. Bright-eyed, wide smiles, smooth and shiny hair, even in the photos where they've been supposedly building houses. They're too perfect. "Was there a photo shoot for this or something?"

"Yes . . . I believe so. There was a wonderful story done on them for the website. The Henley family, they're our Mary of Bethany Award recipients this year. Since they are unable to come back for the gala, I've put together a slideshow of their life. Something I'll narrate live."

"Henley? I thought Libby said the family was the Wattermans?"

"Oh, yeah . . ." she fumbles. "That family was nominated, but the Henley family won. So . . ." Her smile wobbles, setting off my internal alarm.

"Sounds good, Bill," Jeremiah says at full volume again. "Tell the missus we will get dinner on the books soon. Later, buddy." He hangs up and waves me in.

"This is great, Mary Beth. Thank you. I'll be just a moment," I say to Paloma.

You would think a church office would have a picture of Jesus. Maybe some framed Bible verses. Or a cross, even. Instead, the wall behind Jeremiah's desk is covered with pictures of him and various rock stars from the eighties. Autographed albums of Def Leppard and Judas Priest.

"Sorry I'm late," I say.

"It's fine," he says but sounds irritated anyway. He searches around his desk a moment, then opens a drawer and pulls out an envelope with my name on it. "Here you go."

I check to make sure it's made out to my company and not me. I look at the amount, and it's half of what it should be. "Wait a second, Jeremiah. This isn't the full payment."

"Uncle Jer!" Mary Beth's boy runs into the office and tackles him with a hug. I look back toward the hall to see Paloma and Mary Beth having a very intense conversation.

"Don't know what to tell ya." Jeremiah shrugs. "That's what Mother told me to write it for. Take it up with her." He fake-jabs with his nephew.

"I'm taking it up with you," I say, not accepting the answer. "You wrote the check. I'd appreciate it if you would void it and write a new one. Our contract states I'm to be paid in four installments, including vendor invoices. They'll be expecting their final payments soon, so this isn't just about me."

"You tell your vendors payment is coming. The church will get them the funds, just be patient."

"It's not about patience, this is business. And the church didn't hire the vendors, I did. I have my own contracts with them that I would be held responsible for." I don't understand how he doesn't comprehend this. "I suggest you give your mother a call so she can give you *permission* to write a new check."

Oh, that hits a nerve. His brow knits tight. "My mother doesn't run the show."

"And yet here you are, not writing me a new check without her consent. I guess I will have to take this up with Libby," I say as I leave.

"That's what I told you to do in the first place," Jeremiah says to my back. I feel my teeth grind as I tell myself to save my energy for Libby.

"You don't know what you're talking about," Mary Beth snips at Paloma. Mary Beth's eyes are watery. She cuts a look toward me, not realizing I was there. "If y'all will excuse me, I need to speak with my brother." She grabs Eve by the hand, and they go into Jeremiah's office. "I told you I wanted nothing to do with this," I hear her snap at him before she closes the door behind her.

"Shall we?" Paloma pushes a smile onto her face, acting as if nothing just happened.

It's not until we leave the church parking lot that I ask Paloma, "Everything okay back there?"

"Of course. Just a misunderstanding." She smiles but keeps her eyes on the road ahead.

"Well, I know Mary Beth. She's got her hands full right now with the kids, and that can take its toll, but she has a good heart. I'm sure whatever she did, she didn't have any ill intentions."

"You think she's innocent because she's a mother?" Paloma's irritation is electric in the car.

I don't know how the conversation twisted so quick, but I look at Paloma and ask, "What exactly is she guilty of?"

It's a quiet moment before she says, "They're refusing to give you the money they owe?"

I'm a little embarrassed she overheard the conversation. And I surely don't want her to regret Cain offering his home. "I'll clear it up with Libby."

"For those who do not know God, he will take his vengeance with fire . . ."

"Excuse me?"

"God will punish those who wrong us," she says as though it's a fact. "Perhaps he already got a taste of that punishment with the burn on his arm."

"Oh that. That was from the fire tornado."

"Yes, so I hear. I wonder what he must have done to invoke such anger from God."

I don't say anything for a moment. I grew up in a religious family, hell most of the town is downright fanatical, but there's something in her voice, almost like she *knows* what he did.

I turn left off the highway onto the road toward home. "I don't know if he did anything. It was just an accident." I notice a small wren flying at pace with us along the side of the road.

Paloma hmms a note of disagreement. "I've been attending that church a month now. I wanted to get a better sense of who these Hawthorne people are. Why they are so revered by the community. Why they're viewed as fine stock, good breeding. As if they are somehow better than the rest. But I think they are wrong. I think you are all wrong. The Hawthornes, they do not know God. People of God are not liars." Paloma sharply turns my way. "And the Libby Hawthorne you know is a liar. The sooner you see that, the sooner you will separate yourself from these people. For good."

"Paloma, I . . . I don't know what to say. I'm not sure what you think they've done." I pull into our driveway, my hands shaking. The little wren darts across the driveway in front of us. "Look, I know they're not perfect, but who is, right? And I'm really only in business with them, with Libby. This gala is a great opportunity not just for me but for the town and the church, but if you just tell me what's happened to upset you, then I can help clear things up. Just tell me how to make it right." I feel myself getting sweaty; a clammy cold spreads over my hands. My tongue is dry.

Paloma releases a calming breath before turning to me and laying a gentle hand on mine. "I'm sorry. I didn't mean to upset you. There is nothing you need to fix. Everything will be made right." She opens the car door and pauses. "What is done in the dark always comes to light," she says over her shoulder before getting out, the conviction in her voice extra sharp. It's a side of her I've never seen.

When I scan the yard for the wren it's gone, but I'm pretty sure it was Grady Owens's grave bird.

CHAPTER TWENTY-ONE

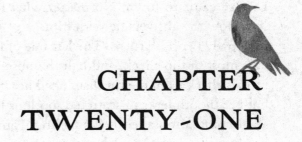

Saturday morning when I wake, there's a dead woman sitting on the edge of my bed. A familiar cold creeps over me as I stir. Puffs of white smoke from my mouth with every fearful breath. A beam of early morning sunlight pierces through the branches of the oak tree, through my glass ceiling, and through the dead woman.

She sits with her back to me, her face toward the sky like she's trying her best to feel the sun on her skin again. I don't have to guess who she is; I know. I know from her gorgeous long cascading copper hair. From the dated green palm-frond dress she wears. She's the ghost woman from the office at Hawthorne Manor. I feel myself longing for her as if she's my mother. Or she is someone's mother that I am meant to find.

Or maybe the dead are just fixtures in my life now, like the vase on my coffee table or the art on my wall. A part of my environment I must learn to live with.

One thing is for certain, though: it all started the day Cain

Landry came to town. No matter what I need to do, I know somehow the answers lie with him.

Slowly her head turns. The left side of her face—around the eye, most of the cheek, and half the nose—concaved from the brutal whack from the bat that ended her life. She tries to speak, but her mouth jerks in stuttered motions like a fish gasping for air. I could almost recall the feeling from the moment of her death as she choked on her own tongue.

I hear a sudden squawk from a bird—a crow?—and my head whips around, searching for it. When I turn back, she's gone. But the sadness she leaves lingers, like a stain on my sheets.

THE DAY OF the birthday party has finally arrived. My head is still reeling from my encounter with the dead woman as I make my way to the other side of town.

Ada Grace's home is in Blessed Oaks Estates. It's the second tier of the higher-end developments that were built on Grady Owens's property. The homes are all slight variations of the same: built in one of three shades of brick and paired with your choice of white, tan, or mocha-colored siding. The lawns are sprawling and unfenced. There's a community pool and tennis courts, and HOA restrictions maintain a level of uniformity that's apparently pleasing to some.

It's a gorgeous place to live, no doubt, but there's a pretentious quality to the whole idea, founded on being separate from everyone else. Unlike Uncle Royce's seasoned neighborhood, whose homes are full of character and feeling.

I arrive hours before the party to make sure the bouncy houses are set up in the right area, the live princesses know their positions, and the petting zoo is far enough away from dining tables.

We are well into the party by two o'clock, and thankfully everything is going smoothly. All the mothers are dressed like it's a fine garden party. Sundresses of chaste coloring and *en vogue* florals. It's unimaginable one eight-year-old has this many friends.

As I walk over to remind one of the waitstaff to keep the trash cleared, I catch the wisp of a palm-frond dress disappearing behind the hedge. It stops me in my tracks. I watch for a moment longer and wonder if I'm imagining things. There's a crash behind me, and I turn. Mary Beth has knocked over her champagne glass, taking down a few other glasses with it. Her gaze is locked on the tall hedge. Fear washes the color from her face.

Did she see it, too?

"Maybe Ada Grace shouldn't have had a mimosa bar," a lady at the buffet says in a hushed tone to the woman beside her.

I snag a towel from the waitstaff. "Not to worry," I tell Mary Beth as I blot the excess from the tablecloth. "Happens all the time." But I can tell from the way she's swaying on the spot she's had a bit too much to drink. "Let me get you a water."

As I fetch her a bottled water from the ice bin, a few more ladies scowl in her direction. Judgmental old biddies.

When I turn back around, Mary Beth is over by one of the bouncy houses, trying to get Eve, her oldest child, out of it. Her attention is split between talking to someone on the phone and yelling for her daughter to hurry up. My first thought is the embarrassment of being caught drunk in front of everyone was too much, but the sense of panic in the way she's pleading with her daughter tells me something else might be going on.

Little Eve finally crawls out of the bouncy house. Mary Beth, with her purse under her arm, snags her by the hand and drags her protesting daughter toward the house.

There's no way she should be driving, though. I head after her to stop her, when two ladies step in front of her, imploring her to stay. A few tears slip down Mary Beth's cheek.

"I have to go," I hear her say in desperation.

Both of the women relay a look of concern to me as I join the conversation. "Everything all right?" I ask.

"I have to go, but apparently there's concern I've had too much to drink." Mary Beth throws out a sloppy, dismissing hand, the thick roll of her words giving her away.

"Oh, Mary Beth, we didn't say that. It's just . . ." The blonde, who I think is Kayla, looks to me for help.

"It's my fault," I quickly say. "I'm liable for guests whenever I plan an event, so no one who's had two drinks or more is allowed to drive. Let me call you someone, if you wait here—"

"I have to go to the hospital," Mary Beth's voice breaks, and the tears start to flow. "Mother called. Father has had a stroke."

Her words sends a cold chill over me, like fingers crawling up my spine.

The little girl now looks terrified. Kayla places a hand on Mary Beth's shoulder, trying to comfort her in light of the revelation.

"How about I drive you?" I offer, handing her the bottle of water to drink. "Kayla, why don't you take Eve back to the party. Then we can call Landon to come get her, they can meet you there—"

"We don't have time. I need to get to the hospital." She tries to step around us, determined to leave.

"We can help. Right, Kayla?" Kayla nods emphatically. "Don't worry, we'll take care of you," I say. After a quick call to Landon to update him on the situation and confirm that Kayla will drop Eve off to him shortly, Mary Beth and I are on the road to the hospital.

"I knew this would happen," she says quietly to herself through a sob. She holds on to her cell phone for dear life, rocking slightly in the passenger seat.

"It's going to be all right," I try to reassure her. "They're at the hospital. I'm sure the doctors are doing everything they can."

Her phone rings, and Libby's loud voice pushes through. They were walking into a meeting when Noah swung around in a circle and timbered forward. There was some question if it was a heart attack or a stroke: further testing was needed.

"I knew this day would come," Mary Beth says after she hangs up the phone. "A day of reckoning. You can't sell your soul to the devil and not think he won't come collect," she says to the windshield, eyes lost to the road ahead.

Her eyes are glazed like the day of her birthday when she was staring at all the dead cardinals. I don't want to push her to silence. I need her to keep talking. What did she get in return for her soul?

"They think I'm crazy. All of them." She yanks her head my way. "I'm not crazy. And it wasn't a dream," she says. Her eyes are filled with tears.

As if the heavens themselves are grieving with her, it starts to rain. A light pattering on the window. The forecast was clear for today: I checked several times to make sure we didn't need a tent for the party. Then a tiny tink hits the windshield. Followed by another. It picks up in pace as the rain continues.

And coins.

Hundreds of them splatter and plunk against the hood of the car. The dead connecting the dots for me. *She knows something,* I think.

Mary Beth's brow furrows as she stares, perplexed at the rain and coins hitting the car. Can she see the coins? But then the coins subside and it turns to hail, making me wonder as well if it was real like before at the mechanic's garage.

"Mary Beth, I think this worry and the champagne has got your thoughts a little jumbled up right now. Let's just get you to the hospital and get an update on Noah. Then you'll know what to do." I encourage her to drink more water. "Is there anyone I can call for you?" I ask her. "I'm sure Libby has been busy talking to the doctors. But is there anyone else who needs to know?" I pause, then cautiously suggest, "Maybe . . . his sister?" The words land flat in the silence of the car.

Discontent slithers on Mary Beth's face as her red-rimmed eyes pan over to me. "Sarah Hawthorne is a loathsome human being." Shockingly, she spits on my floorboard to hammer her point home. "I hope she burns in hell for all she's done." Then her numb, hollow gaze focuses on the rain-soaked road again.

I don't think I've put enough stock in the long-lost sister. Whatever her crime, so to speak, Sarah Hawthorne has shamed this family something fierce. Enough to get her erased from the history books. But you can't erase someone completely, no matter how deep your pockets go.

"It wasn't a dream," Mary Beth says again, absent-mindedly to the windshield.

I don't ask her what dream she's referring to. I don't want to piss her off any further. I need her willing to talk again later.

The temperature in the car drops significantly, and the windows begin to fog over. Even Mary Beth shivers at the change, clueless to what it is. But I've felt this eeriness before. The hairs on the back of my neck prickle. Movement eclipses my review mirror—something in the back seat—but I refuse to look. Instead I jack up the heat in the car and turn on the defrost.

CAMDEN HOSPITAL IS about twenty minutes outside of Hawthorne. I drop Mary Beth off at the front entrance. I implored her to let me at least walk her up, but she was insistent she go alone. The intensity of the situation and two bottles of water seemed to have sobered her up a bit. It's not until I pull out of the parking lot do I notice she has left her purse on the seat. I return and park the car. The front desk nurse directs me to the second-floor waiting room. I'm coming down the hallway almost to the waiting room when I hear a smack.

"Mother," Mary Beth hisses.

"You're drunk," Libby growls. I round the corner to find Mary Beth cupping her cheek. Shame wells across her face. Quietly I draw back against the wall.

My heart races in my throat.

Libby straightens her shoulders in an attempt to compose

herself as a nurse comes down the hallway, followed by what looks to be a doctor. They both head directly to Libby and Mary Beth, who's still pressing her hand to her cheek. I stay glued to the wall but just beyond their view.

"Hi, I'm Dr. Warner. We got the X-rays back. Is there any chance Noah hit his head when he fell?" she asks Libby.

"I tried to catch him, and then we kind of slumped to the floor together. But no, he didn't hit his head, I don't think," Libby says.

"Well, the X-rays are showing a fracture to the orbital bone around the left eye."

"I thought he had a stroke?" Mary Beth says.

"That's one possibility, but until we complete all the tests we won't know for certain. And given the skull fracture, we may need to look at alternate explanations. The fracture looks like a result of blunt force trauma."

Libby thanks them for the update, and the doctor and nurse head past me down the hall. I use this as an opportunity to make my presence known. Libby's face immediately sours as she sees me approach.

"Hi, Mrs. Hawthorne, Mary Beth." I hold up the purse, my face composed in a look of apology. "I'm so sorry to interrupt, but Mary Beth left her purse in my car." I offer it to her. The left side of her face is still a touch too red, and her eyes are watery.

"Thank you, but if you could now leave us be?" Libby's bark calls my attention to her. "We're obviously dealing with a family matter right now."

"Of course. I'm so sorry. If there's anything you need, please let me know." I turn to leave, mulling over the doctor's words: *blunt force trauma.* From the triage room they wheel out Noah on a gurney. Surrounding his left eye and over his cheek is purplish-red bruising. The markings are eerily familiar. Not only that, the spasmatic way he opens his mouth, like he's choking on his tongue, just like the ghost woman.

I press the Down button for the elevator. As the doors open and I push the button for the lower level, I hear, "Hollis, hold up." A hand is thrown out to stop the doors from closing, and Mary Beth appears.

"Is everything all right?" I step out of the elevator and let it go down without me.

She swipes a hand through her hair to cover the shakiness of her movements. "Look, Mother didn't mean to snap, it's just . . . it's a lot."

"Oh my gosh, don't even sweat it. It's understandable." Though, Libby is testy even at the best of times.

"That's generous of you to say. Listen, can you do me a favor?"

"Of course. Anything."

"Wonderful. Landon will have his hands full with the kids. And Mother's house staff have the weekends off. Could you go by their house and grab her a change of clothes and maybe some pajamas? Just something for the night. I wouldn't ask you this if we weren't in such a pinch. I don't want to leave her here alone, when we still don't know how Father is."

I'm almost stunned at the opportunity, unfettered time in the house to snoop around. I school my face so my eager thoughts don't shine through. "Um, sure, I can help out." Though, the request does make me a little uncomfortable, but I don't let it show. "I won't be able to get over there until after Ada Grace's party is finished."

"That's fine," she says with a breathy appreciation. Her smile is one of delight, and it's something I'm not sure how to read. She tells me where I can find a overnight bag and some of her mother's clothes. "You can leave it at the nurse's station when you come back." She removes a house key from her key ring and hands it to me.

"Yeah, no problem," I say as I go to take it from her, but she captures my hands in her grasp.

"There's one more thing I need you to grab." She takes a quick glance down the hall, then back to me. Her eyes glint. "I think we might need Father's Living Will Directive. It's in Mother's desk, in the office, in a locked drawer, bottom right. You can find the key underneath the brass inkwell on top."

The thudding of my heart pounds in my ears with a loud whooshing. A wave of uncertainty flushes up my neck and over my ears. This feels like a bridge too far. Like maybe I'm not the one for the task. And I'm about to say as much when Mary Beth grips my hand, keeping me from slipping away.

"I hope I'm being overly cautious. I wouldn't want Mother to know I asked you to grab it. It's just that we need to be prepared. You understand, right?"

I swallow my nerves and nod my head. "I'll grab it, too." I wax on a smile that I hope says *No problem at all.*

Inside the elevator I stare at the small piece of brass in the palm of my hand.

I've been given a key to a kingdom I'm not certain I want to enter alone.

CHAPTER TWENTY-TWO

EVEN THOUGH I have been given permission, I feel like a thief inside the Hawthorne mansion. It doesn't help that the sun has already started to set and the streetlights are coming on.

There's an eeriness that accompanies an empty house. Dust particles float in the fading sunlight as it slips in for one last peek. Somewhere down the hall a refrigerator snoozes with a light buzz. My footsteps echo with hollow, dooming beats. The quiet murmur of my heart thrums inside my chest.

At the top of the stairs, the hallway splits off into two directions. Just as Mary Beth said, the master bedroom is to the left, in the east wing of the home. A gorgeous view overlooks the pool. The master bedroom closet—holy hell!—is almost the size of my entire studio. She owns more silk pajamas than I do socks. Going through Libby's underwear drawer is humiliating. As I head over to her bathroom to grab toiletries, a loud metal ping sounds throughout the house.

I freeze, thinking I've set off an alarm I didn't realize was on. I stick my head out into the hallway.

"Hello?" My voice is flat against the silence. "Is someone down there?"

But the quiet eats away at the house again, and nothing else comes.

This house was built over a hundred years ago, I remind myself. All kinds of creaks and noises and things that go bump in the night can be heard in a house this old.

After I grab a few toiletries and stuff everything inside a black Chanel overnight bag, I head downstairs to Libby's office. A metallic ping echoes throughout the home again, like a hammer hitting an anvil.

It has a natural quality to it, and something about it is familiar. *Do what you have to do and leave*, I tell myself.

Anticipation courses through my veins as I take the long hallway past the billiards room to Libby's office. I lightly glance into the room as I pass—a half-naked man, standing in nothing but a loincloth, stares back at me.

I just about jump out of my skin, then I realize he's not moving. I look again: it's a life-size portrait of Saint Constantine Hawthorne, our town's namesake. The rich brown of his skin leathered and creviced like a dried desert. A bushy white beard puffs around his face. His layered, white hair skims his shoulders where a bird is perched. Bright white feathers with a bare blue face and throat.

Saint Constantine's family took root here in South Carolina sometime at the beginning of the nineteenth century. This painting has to be at least a hundred and fifty years old. Nikki said the painting unnerved her. I lean to one side, then the other. Sure enough, Saint Constantine's steel-gray eyes follow me. There's something familiar about him, too. Maybe it's because I've seen the fountain made in his likeness at the center of town a thousand times. But seeing him in color makes him come alive.

Something about him . . .

"Get what you need and get out," I say aloud to myself and

head straight to Libby's office, convinced Saint Constantine is staring at my back.

The door is at the far end of the hall, and my heart flips as I push it open.

But there's nothing. The absence of the mourning dove has made this room ordinary again. Good.

The day's fading light filters through the partially open wood shutters. It makes my presence here feel even more criminal. Just as Mary Beth promised, a key hides underneath the vintage brass inkwell. It's absolutely silly my hand is shaking as I unlock the drawer. I guess I expected to find hanging file folders with all their important paperwork, but instead this drawer is just stuff.

There's a jewelry dish with a gold charm bracelet. A pair of cheap, matching gold rings dangling from a white ribbon. A small linen box holds a tiny round frame of a baby's foot imprint. A Zippo lighter with YOU LIGHT MY FIRE engraved on one side and a date below it from more than thirty years ago. And other random keepsakes. But no documents at all.

This is the only locked drawer in the entire desk. Maybe Libby moved the files, and Mary Beth didn't know it. I go to set the box back inside the drawer and see an envelope had been underneath it. I pick up the envelope and open it, just to make sure it's the will.

But it's photos.

My heart stops at the first image.

A family. On vacation.

Immediately I recognize what they are: the blackmail photos Libby mistakenly confronted me with back in May.

The woman—the ghost from the Hawthornes' office. And what looks like her husband and a young boy I don't recognize. And a little girl, the ghost who has been visiting me. A happy family at a lake. Given their dated clothing, this happened a long time ago.

My mind races through who this family might be and what happened to them.

A thought stops me up short. Could they be Grady Owens's heirs?

Grady Owens had at least one heir: his grave bird showed me a pregnant woman who wouldn't marry him. Could this be their child? If so, and if they were still alive, the land should have gone to them. The Hawthornes bought the property through the church for dirt cheap years ago in an auction. If they knew there were heirs but covered it up, it means they obtained the property illegally. They'd have to give the property back. It was acres of woods back then. Now it has several subdivisions built on it; it would have to be worth a fortune today. If they had to give back the property, it would wipe them out financially. Wipe the church out since they used it to purchase the property. *Holy Moses.*

I flip through the rest of the photos. A Thanksgiving dinner. A little girl's birthday. Snippets of their lives. I pause when I see the mother standing next to a young woman. I can't say one hundred percent, but this looks like a skinnier, tanner, and longer-haired Paloma. Fear prickles over me.

Quickly I shove the photos back in the envelope, save the one of Paloma that I stuff in my purse. I need Nadine to see this, to tell me if I'm right in thinking this is Paloma—though, I have no idea what that would mean. I put everything back in the drawer exactly how it was and decide to tell Mary Beth I totally forgot to get the living will.

As I head back down the hallway, it's like I've walked into a void and all the subtle sounds of outside have been blocked out. I slow up in my step, and the world around me stretches and pulls at the edges, like I'm walking through muddy molasses. The air around me feels pressurized. For a glimmer of a second, the white walls and marble floors return to the brown wainscoting and wood floors from all those years ago when I walked these halls with Uncle Royce. Or maybe long before. I feel I've stepped into a time and place where I have never lived.

I look around for the grave bird that must surely be here, that must have brought me to this place, but I don't see it. Which means there mustn't be one. I trudge ahead, pushing against this alternate reality, hoping the world outside will right itself. Just as I almost make it to the front door, I hear a whisper over my shoulder. *Come find me.*

I tell myself not to turn around. But my feet are already pivoting.

I'm in front of the portrait wall. There's a hazy orange glow upon the massive collection, amassed over the last hundred years. Five generations hang on this wall. One in particular stands out from the rest: Libby and Noah, some decades ago, with their two children. A young Jeremiah, in his early teens. But Mary Beth isn't there this time. Her face has been melted away. Like the heat of the sun has penetrated the oil on the canvas, causing the paint to slide down like drooping old skin. And there, where Mary Beth's face should be, the face of a different young girl.

One I've seen before.

One that haunts me.

The drowned little girl.

I stumble backward over the threshold. I don't know if what I'm seeing is real or if the ghosts within these halls are showing me what they want me to see. I grab my phone from my purse and snap a fast picture. Then I hustle out of the house and lock the door tight behind me, hoping I never have to return here again.

CHAPTER TWENTY-THREE

TWO NIGHTS AND I still haven't slept a wink. Over and over I dream of the grave birds or, rather, what they've shown me. Visions from the past play on loop in my mind, a forced connection I'm unable to break free from. But I need to, *have* to. The gala is only a few days away, the biggest event of my career so far. It's all coming together, but I can't shake the feeling there's something going on here, something I need to piece together.

This feels so much bigger than me.

"What do you mean a whole family was murdered?" Nadine asks as she closes the double doors to her office library.

I need somebody to purge my soul to, and Nadine is the only one who truly understands me and this . . . gift? Ability? Maybe she can help me figure it all out.

"I don't know, maybe. I think so. No, I'm pretty sure." I feel itchy in my own skin. I'm going to wear a hole in her plush carpet pacing back and forth.

"You know the little boy's grave bird I found out by Kappy's Campgrounds?" I figured that's as good a place to start as any. "Well, I lied. I didn't go out there with my brother. I went because I found a grave bird on the floor in the Hawthorne mansion. It showed me a woman who was murdered there." I purge it like a sinner to a priest.

Nadine's jaw drops. "I think we're going to need a drink."

"Agreed," I say as she goes to grab a bottle of wine and two glasses.

I tell Nadine about the woman in the Hawthornes' office and the plastic trout key chain. How it led me to the little boy at Kappy's and the fire that burned it all down. Then the article with Frank Kilroy took me to the mechanic shop and the grave bird I found there. "Not to mention the dead little girl who loves to visit me and leaves a puddle of water behind each time."

"Oh geesh." Nadine sits on her reading sofa, taking a stiff sip of her prosecco.

My phone dings with a text from Cain. Tie or no tie?

I huff a laugh. It's dinner with my grandmother, for crying out loud. Absolutely no tie. Just dress casual, I text him back.

"Sorry," I say and put away my phone. "Granny invited Cain and me over for dinner Saturday night—apparently she heard we were dating, so now she expects to meet my *boyfriend*. And he's stressing over how to dress."

"He wants to impress your family. That should tell you something." She bobs an eyebrow. I smile.

It does feel nice to have someone to introduce. Someone to distract me from . . . whatever this all is.

"So these grave birds," Nadine says. "You found them all in different places, right? They could be just people who died, not all related or connected."

"That's what I thought at first, too . . . until I found their family photo." I tell her about the pictures in Libby's drawer. "Weeks ago Libby accused me of blackmailing her, and she had some pictures. I didn't know what to make of it at the time. I'd never seen the pictures before, and she wasn't making sense. The next day I saw her giving money to this Betsy Kilroy woman." I explain about the Blue Tits senior women's swim group.

"Wait. You stalked this little old lady at the YMCA?"

"Well, when you put it like that it sounds bad . . . Okay, yes, I did. But I had good reason."

"Do you have any idea who the family is?"

"I think they might be Grady Owens's heirs."

A confused look crawls across Nadine's face until she processes the name. "The cranky old man who died in the woods when we were kids?"

"Yep." I take a seat next to her, exhaling a huge breath. "Twelve years ago, I found Grady Owens's grave bird in those woods. I never told anyone." I tell her about the moment in the past the grave bird showed me. About the woman he loved, pregnant with his child but who chose to marry another man. "Charlotte was her name. It took two years before anyone found him after he died, as he kept to himself almost entirely. With no one there to claim his house or his land, there was eventually an auction, and they sold it all off." I'm staring off toward the bookshelves, knowing there will be no taking back what I propose next. You can't accuse the most influential family in the town and not catch heat over it. I turn to Nadine. "The Hawthornes bought the land. And Betsy said—"

"The pink-haired older lady?" Nadine asks.

"Yeah, her. She said I was the second person in there that day asking questions. And if I was there to ask about Grady Owens's estate, then I needed to speak with their lawyer."

"Oh wow."

"I think this woman, the one in the photo, is Grady and Charlotte's daughter. I think the Hawthornes found her and had the whole family murdered so they could keep the land and money they've made off it. Because why would she mention Grady Owens's estate, like it's an unresolved affair? What if they know he had an heir?"

Nadine collapses back against the sofa. "This is huge."

"Right?" I lean back, too.

An antique clock on her library shelf ticks away with our thoughts.

"Surely Libby and Noah wouldn't pay for someone to take them out, right?" Nadine asks.

I want to believe that, too. They create the appearance of being good stewards in the world, but my gut knows they aren't as righteous as they pretend to be either. It doesn't make them bad people, just means I wouldn't be surprised if they'd gotten their hands dirty more than once.

"So you think this Frank Kilroy is involved?" Nadine asks. "He's obviously not just some innocent bystander who called about a fire if he's also associated with this Betsy woman and she's blackmailing Libby. It's not a coincidence."

"I agree. When I searched the internet, all I found was a deceased NFL player. What if Frank's the one who started the fire?" There was an older boy in the memory; maybe he killed him?

Nadine looks over at me. "Why call the fire department if you're out there murdering people?"

I shrug. "Unless you got caught where you shouldn't be and tried to twist the narrative."

"Ooof. Maybe. He worked at that mechanics' shop. What if he's the man who died there?" Nadine hops up, going over to her desk to her computer.

"I don't know. Maybe. He could be the dad I saw in the family picture. I never saw the dead man's face." When the grave birds take me back in time, they show me everything through the eyes of the deceased. The little girl and her mom came to me separately.

She searches for a death at the Johnson's garage, but nothing comes up.

"If you killed someone there, you'd cover it up. So I doubt we'll find anything," I say.

"True." Nadine turns to me. "The woman said there was a second person in there that day? Who was the first?" she asks.

"She didn't say. But I wonder if it was Paloma." When Nadine looks at me with surprise, I pull out my final puzzle piece. "I didn't show you what else I found." I grab the photo from my purse, the one I stole from the envelope in Libby's drawer, and lay it down for her to see. "This is the woman I saw murdered in the Hawthorne house. And this woman next to her . . ."

Nadine picks the picture up and scrutinizes it a moment. Then she turns to me with shock on her face. "Is that Paloma?"

"I *think* so. I can't imagine how she would know Grady Owens's family, though. But I don't think she's here now by coincidence." Then something occurs to me. "Those family pictures, Libby found them in the boxes I brought out to the country club. I thought maybe someone from the country club snuck them in there. But they came from my greenhouse. What if it was Paloma who put them in there? What if Paloma's the one trying to blackmail her?"

"Hold on. You're letting yourself get tangled up in a wild tale, and you don't even have all the answers yet. It could simply be she's trying to track down an old friend," Nadine tries, but I give her a *Come on* stare.

"She and Libby have had some tense moments, though. I thought it was one strong woman in the presence of another type of thing. But now? I don't know. The whole thing leaves a bad taste in my mouth."

And what would this mean for Cain? Does he know about Paloma's connection to this family? If it was him asking Betsy about Grady Owens's estate, then he knows something. But what? He wouldn't be a part of anything like this, right? He moved here for business—but he didn't just pick Hawthorne, South Carolina, from a spin of a globe and the touch of a finger. Paloma must have guided him here.

"Everything started happening when Cain and Paloma arrived," I say to her. "The ghost visits. Hundreds of cardinals crashing into the Hawthornes' windows. The fire tornadoes. Heck, I have a cup full of old coins at my place that fell out of the sky. Plus something has been bugging me ever since last Saturday when Noah had his stroke—well, that's what they are saying. The doctors don't know what actually happened to him. But the morning of Ada Grace's party, she—" I point to the woman in the picture with Paloma "—was there when I woke up, sitting on my bed. When she looked at me, half her face was smashed in—left eye and cheek and half her nose. That's how she died, a blow to the face. The doctor said Noah's eye socket was fractured, said it was blunt force trauma. But Libby said he didn't hit his head on the way down when he fell over."

"What are you saying, Hollis?"

"I'm not sure I'm ready to say anything. But what if these ghosts are getting their revenge?"

"Honestly, Hollis. I think you're exhausted from all the remodeling. And you're so stressed about making this gala perfect you're conjuring up actual ghosts. I know you try to do right by these birds, but whatever it is they need from you, it can wait one more week. The dead aren't going anywhere, sadly. The gala is going to be *incredible*! Don't let this other stuff take away the joy of what you're doing. Focus on the excitement of what you've accomplished, and we can sort out the rest later."

I hear what she's saying. I do. And she's not wrong: I've had a lot on my plate the last few weeks. My mind's been all over the place with the gala. But there's a sick feeling in the pit of my stomach.

Nadine doesn't know the grave birds like I do. They won't leave me alone until I've helped them.

CHAPTER TWENTY-FOUR

CAIN'S RANGE ROVER smells of leather and his musky sandal-wood and citrus–scented cologne. It's a great anchor in this moment, because my thoughts keep slipping. What are he and Paloma doing here? Is it really to source soybeans for a non-profit? Is there another reason? And why would he be hiding it from me?

"You all good?" Cain asks. He reaches out and puts a hand on my leg and gives it a light squeeze. I nod. His touch warms me. It's a soothing sensation that makes me think building something with him could be a good thing.

"I'm sorry I was running late," he says. "My meeting with a new prospect ran longer than I expected."

"Farmers giving you a hard time?"

"No. Some people want me to invest in their development, so I was getting to know them a bit better, seeing if it's something I might be interested in. You look beautiful, by the way." He brings my hand to his lips for a kiss.

I chuckle. "I'm literally wearing a will-work-for-sugarboos T-shirt and cutoff jean shorts."

He laughs. "Those sugarboos are like crack! What do they put in them?"

"Mr. I Don't Eat Sweets got himself a little addiction, huh?"

Cain eyes me up and down. "Oh, you have no idea." I almost purr in response.

He's dressed in a long-sleeve lavender linen shirt—that complements his tanned skin perfectly—gray chino shorts, and white leather sneakers. His hair, still slightly wet from the shower, is perfectly tousled. I forget all about the Hawthornes for just a moment.

"Please tell me there won't be gizzards or mountain oysters or pickled pigs' feet for dinner tonight?" Cain says, driving past the Baptist missionary church.

I laugh. "Who have you been conferring with about Southern meals?"

"The men out at the co-op really paint a gruesome picture of what constitutes a Southern delicacy."

"I promise you, whatever Granny cooks you'll love. As her only granddaughter I should know how to cook better, but it's Dylan who got the cooking gene. His peach cobbler might be better than Granny's. But don't tell her that."

Long about dusk we turn down the dirt road that leads to Granny's house. Dust clouds billow in our wake. We pull up in front of the simple farmhouse, white clapboard siding with hunter-green shutters and a porch swing to boot. I remember sitting on the swing as a little girl, drawing a picture of Grandaddy on a piece of paper. He paid me twenty-five cents for it, a fortune to me at the time.

Granny stands on the porch in her apron with a big ole smile on her face.

And sitting on the porch railing right next to her is a brown little house sparrow. I will myself not to look at it. To pretend it doesn't exist.

"I hope you brought your appetite with you" is the first thing she says to Cain.

"Yes, Mrs. Wade, I sure did."

"Oh hush with all that fancy talk. Call me Gladys." He's taken by surprise when she hugs his neck but doesn't seem to mind. "Y'all come on in and eat. It's ready."

A part of my heart wonders if Grandaddy would have liked Cain. I try not to let my thoughts dwell there too long.

Inside, Cain pauses to scrutinize an extra-large sixth-grade photo of me hanging on the wall. A tank top over a fitted T-shirt, my hair helmet round and long. Braces rack across my teeth like a metal grille of a car. He raises a brow as if to ask if it's me. I simply grumble then pull him on along to the kitchen, which earns me a light chuckle.

Granny's prepared a buffet of food. You'd have thought there were twenty of us coming to supper. Cornbread, black beans, cream-style corn, fried pork chops, mashed potatoes, fried green tomatoes, and a pie that I believe is lemon meringue.

"You got yourself a strong biblical name there, don't ya?" Granny says as she passes the plate of green tomatoes to Cain.

"Yes, ma'am. I do."

"Well," she says, "I don't know if I would've named my child after the first murderer, but who am I to judge?"

I mouth an *I'm sorry* to Cain.

"If it's any consolation," he says, "I'm named after my mother's grandfather. Or so I'm told." He dollops a mountain of mash potatoes onto his plate.

"Well, I guess that counts for something." She releases a big sigh, like now we've got that out of the way. I stifle a laugh.

The conversation flows in even waves about her farm, his company looking to buy the local soybean crops for organizations that work primarily in South America, her church, my brothers and nephews, what I plan to wear to the gala—she does not lecture me about the Hawthornes, thank God.

"What's your momma and daddy think about you turning into a Southern boy?" Granny says, finishing up the last of her dinner.

"I'm not sure. They've been gone a long time."

"Oh dear," Granny says. "I'm sorry. I didn't know they had passed." She pats a wrinkled hand on top of his.

"I didn't realize that either," I say. We only talked about his parents the one time in the kitchen with Paloma. I thought he said they were absent from his life, as in no longer active.

His smile wobbles as he grabs a second piece of cornbread. "Well, technically we're not sure if they're dead. They've been missing since I was a child." He reaches for the butter. "They went on a trip and never came back. Haven't seen or heard from them since," he says matter-of-factly, and he shifts in his seat, staying focused on buttering his bread.

After a long stretch of silence where Cain takes a mouthful of bread, he finally says, "Gladys," his voice shifting to jovial again, "this cornbread is the best I've ever had. Is there cheese in here?"

"It's my secret ingredient. I only cook it in a cast-iron skillet. No sugar. I like my cornbread savory, not sweet." Granny tries to grab his empty plate the second he's finished to carry to the sink, but he protests and helps her clear the table for dessert.

It feels a little strange that I didn't know his parents were missing. But we've only known each other three months, and we have both been busy: it's not something you can toss casually into a conversation.

But pulling at the edges of my thoughts is a snippet of what his grave bird showed me the first time. There was a sadness that he wasn't going on a trip with his family. The second time, his grave bird showed me the young girl, and he knew they'd leave without him since he was sick. I wonder if that's the trip he's referring to?

"Did you have a sister?" I ask as he returns to the table to grab more food to bring to Granny to put away.

Cain stiffens. "I did," he says cautiously, then walks away, not adding anything more. I hear Granny tell him where he can find the dessert plates, and then she goes into explaining how she whips her meringue to make it so fluffy.

I pick up my plate and the butter dish and join them in the kitchen. "Were you really close?" I ask him, setting my dish in the sink to wash.

He swallows hard. "Yes."

Granny parks her hands on her hips. "What are you pestering this boy about?"

There's a strained look in Cain's eyes, as if this conversation is too private to be had just anywhere. So I let it go, for now anyway.

"Nothing, Granny," I say, pushing up my lips into a smile. "I hope I get some of those leftovers to take home." I nod toward the dishes of food. The tension in Cain's shoulders loosens.

Granny turns to him with an exaggerated exhaustion. "If you're looking for a wife who can cook, you won't find one here." She sours a look of disappointment at me, shaking her head.

"Oh my word," I say and cover my face. "Please stop, Granny. Just . . . no."

Cain chuckles.

Even as we make small talk over dessert, my head keeps swimming back to Cain's family. Could his family be Grady Owens's heirs? Cain spent most of his life in California. I guess Charlotte could have moved there. But Grady died when he was an old man. In his memory, they were both young, in their twenties if I had to guess. It would have been sixty years ago at least, maybe longer. That could make Cain Grady Owens's grandson? Even I know I'm stretching for answers here.

After a cup of coffee and another slice of pie, Granny loads me up with enough leftovers to last a month. Cain thanks her a thousand times for everything and gushes over her cooking—which is exactly the way to win her over. She makes him promise to come back soon.

"Will you be there for the dedication?" Granny asks before I get in his car. I stiffen. Every year on my grandfather's birthday the family goes down to the riverbank where he died to pay their respects. As a kid I had to go, but once I left home I didn't go back. I can't face that day again. "It's been fifteen years. We thought it would be nice to set out a memorial stone on his birthday, down by the river. Preacher's going to say a few words on his behalf. Denny and Dylan are coming. It'd be nice if you join us. It's after your big fancy party, so you'll be freed up by then."

I feel myself hollow as what she's asking me is impossible. To stand on the shore where they pulled his body from the river . . .

"I can't," I say without looking at her. "Just have too much going on with work and all," I offer as a pathetic excuse. Hurriedly, I get in Cain's SUV and close the door, shutting out the pain of disappointing her again.

I don't mean to be as quiet as I am on the ride home, but so much is cycling through my thoughts.

"I think she was pretty sad when you said you couldn't be there," Cain says. Shame of him noticing wells over me.

"I know." It's more of a whisper as I stare out the window into the darkness huddling against the side of the road.

"If you want me to go with you . . ." he says. The invitation lingers in the air.

I wouldn't know what to do with myself out there, much less with him. But I smile, letting him know I appreciate the offer.

I want to ask more about his family. When did they go missing? Where? What do the cops think? He had a sister? What if the drowned little girl is his sister? I was sure he said he was an only child. Or maybe he was just raised as an only child.

"Are you thinking about calculus over there?" Cain says, knocking me from my thoughts.

"Huh?" I turn to him, realizing we're almost home.

"You must be thinking about differentials or integrals or contemplating Einstein's theory of relativity with that stern, crinkled brow."

It's been such a lovely night it feels wrong to start grilling him. And it's not like he owes me that information anyway.

Instead I lightly laugh and hope it doesn't sound forced. "No, just going over all the last little things I have left to finalize for the gala."

"You've done an incredible job," he says as we turn into the curved driveway.

The landscape lighting puts the front lawn on full display for the evening, giving the home a whispered glow. The beautifully trimmed weeping oaks drip with perfect clusters of Spanish moss. The lawn is lush and green. The azalea bushes have filled out so nicely over the last few months, they will be gorgeous with blooms come the spring.

My arms are stacked full of leftovers and a spider plant Granny said I needed in my already plant-full greenhouse.

Cain jogs around to open the door for me.

"I swear I don't need another plant," I say as he takes the plant and closes the door behind me. I keep walking toward the house. "But my granny can't bear to send me home with just food. She always has to—oh shoot." My purse slips out from underneath my elbow and spills out onto the driveway.

"I've got it," he says.

"Good, because if I drop this pie, I'm going to be mad for the rest of—" Fear jolts through my body as I realize Paloma's picture is in my purse. "I've got it!" I hurriedly say and spin on my heels.

But he's already kneeling on the driveway, scooping the contents back into my purse.

"It's okay. I don't mind." His demeanor has shifted, though. It's nothing I see, but the ground quivers under my feet, and heat ripples in waves. He looks ashen. My heart stutters. I have no idea how I'm going to explain why I have that picture of Paloma in my purse. A thousand lies race through my brain, all of them thin as glass.

Then he stands with a chipper hop. "You know your grandmother loves me," he says as if facts are facts. Then he takes the stack of Tupperware from me and hands me my purse. "I will put these in your fridge."

I stand there a quiet second; a cricket chirps to let me know we're not alone. The sweet scent of honeysuckle vine laces the night. The front porch light glows with a sweet comfort of home. Whatever it was I thought I felt isn't there anymore.

I sigh and tell myself to quit being so paranoid. *Jesus.*

"Go grab us a good bottle of wine, and I'll meet you on the balcony in two minutes." He leans forward and dots a kiss on my lips. The loose grin and hooded eyes send a shiver through me. He lowers his voice. "And when *Madrina* goes to sleep, we will slip into my bed. Sound like a plan?"

My thighs tighten at the thought. "Yes, sir. But I can't stay late," I whisper back, kissing him deeper than a peck. "I have an early morning."

He pulls away with a light growl. "*Yes, sir?* I love it when you talk Southern to me."

I playfully kick him in the butt as he walks away. "That's not Southern. That's just regular talk."

He turns around, walking backward. "No? But it's sounds so amenable. So submissive."

He disappears into the dark, down the side of the house toward the studio.

The lights inside the house are off except for the lamp in the entry. I slip off my sandals so I don't disturb Paloma. Then a familiar creak, as her bedroom door opens.

Too late.

She comes out in a robe holding an empty teacup. "Oh, you're home." It's a flat observation. Her eyes dart around for Cain. "You had a good time?"

"Yes, ma'am." I say. "We're just going to grab some wine and sit on the balcony for a bit." I disappear into the wine vault, not extending her an invitation.

I wonder when she plans on going back to California?

Or maybe she's taking her sweet time going home to keep us apart? I can never get a read on whether she's okay with Cain and me dating or not.

Quickly I select a wine and two glasses, then pad up the stairs. As I pass Cain's office I see someone dart across the room.

Short and small.

I should let it go. Dismiss the movement as my eyes playing tricks on me. Shadows shifting in the moonlit room, simply the swaying branches of a tree.

And yet the air upstairs shouldn't be this cold here at the end of summer. I step into his office.

The quiet is so flat it rings in my ears. Even the night outside seems to have shut off: there's not a single sound. My eyes dart around the room, looking for a shift in the shadows. I stand in the silence long enough I've convinced myself I saw nothing at all, but just before I turn to leave, I see the familiar Hawthorne Missionary Baptist Church logo, the steepled red silhouette of the church, on his desk. I slide away the manila folder—

At the murmuring of voices downstairs, the air rights itself. I put the folder back and step into the hallway as Cain comes up the stairs.

He watches me curiously for a stilled moment at the top of the stairs. My heart leaps into my throat. Slowly he stalks down the short hallway toward me. His eyes darken with that devilish stare he's mastered so well. What would I say if he asks why I was in his office? He's almost upon me when I finally manage a "Silly me" with a gassed sigh.

"Yeah?" He stops right in front of me, quirking his head.

"I forgot the corkscrew." I hold out my arms to show the wine bottle in one hand and the glasses in the other as proof.

"Hmm" is all he says in reply. He loops a possessive arm around my waist and leads us in the direction of his bedroom.

"I thought we were having wine on the balcony?" I say, though he clearly has other plans on his mind.

"You said you can't stay long, so we're skipping to the good part."

"What about Paloma?" I whisper then moan as he kisses my neck.

He simply grunts, and then his hands find the button of my shorts. Nothing more is said for the rest of the night.

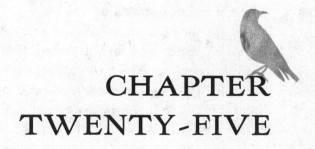

CHAPTER TWENTY-FIVE

Hours later, I pull free from his sleep-heavy arms and kiss him good-night. He grumbles a complaint but rolls back over almost instantly. I tiptoe down the hall, wincing when a floor-board squeaks underfoot. I'm sure Paloma heard it.

As I near the darkness of Cain's office doorway, I feel myself tense. Even before I realize it, my steps have slowed, and I will myself not to glance into the room as I walk past, but a cold breeze brushes over me.

Come find me, whispers the dark.

Soft and childlike.

The hairs on my arms prickle. Without even looking I feel something . . . or someone lurking in the shadows. As I step into the office, the energy shifts, as if scurrying from one side of the room to the other.

Instinct tells me to leave, but it's the second time tonight something is trying to speak to me. It's called me in here for a reason. I just need to find out why.

I steel myself and walk over to his desk. Only a kiss of moon-
light drifts through the window. I have no idea what I should
be looking for, but I scan Cain's desk for clues. It's mostly paperwork: farm reports, invoices from the remodel, MLS house
listings for Paloma, and the Hawthorne church folder I found
earlier. I'm reaching for it before I can stop myself. It's a profes-
sionally printed folder with a sketch of the Greater Good planned
community on the front. A Post-it note attached to the bottom
reads *Our new investor packet, Jeremiah*.

It looks like any pitch deck one might put together to sway
investors. Paper-clipped inside is a handwritten note from a Jay
Haywood:

Looked into the property's background. It's as you
expected. Emailed full prospectus of the Owens estate
for your review. Legal action suggested against the
Kilroys . . . unless you want to handle yourself.

His business card is attached: Haywood Private Investigations.
So Cain knows. Whatever game Paloma is playing, Cain
knows. Or at the very least he's not oblivious she has roots here,
whatever those might be.

Maybe this is something he discovered after coming here.
But he's kept it from me. Of course, he's not required to relin-
quish all his private business to me. Still.

This means we've both been on the same investigative path,
though, haven't we? Cain's car at the gas station out near Kappy's
Campgrounds. Then his meeting with Mary Beth at the bakery,
which he says was simply about getting to know her but now
I'm wondering if there wasn't something more he was trying to
glean from her. And now the person who was poking around at
the construction site, asking Betsy Kilroy questions.

A soft clunk knocks on his desk, and I flinch. Next to a picture of Cain and Paloma, the little cardinal puzzle piece he favors has fallen over.

As I reach for it, it feels as if I'm stretching through a dense layer of cold, like I'm pushing my arm through a ghost. The small piece of wood feels like ice in my palm.

Come find me I hear from one corner. The sound of shuffling fabric darts across the room behind his desk.

Come find me. The whisper jumps from another corner.

"I don't know how," I say backing up, my heart thumping in my chest. A rush of wind passes behind me, and I spin. My bare foot steps in something cold and wet.

From the shadows behind the office door, the drowned little girl steps forward, sopping wet in her dress, just like that very first night she came to me. Dirty water burbles from her mouth. Slowly her arm lifts, and she points a gray-skinned hand at me, to the piece of puzzle I'm holding.

Frost crystals split from my palm and encompass my hand. Feathery veins race up my arm, around my neck, and force themselves down my mouth. I gasp as my breath is snatched away. I drop the wood piece, clawing at my throat, trying to escape the icy hand.

Needles from the cold sting my lungs. The clog in my chest tightens. My head starts to lighten from the loss of air. This is how it felt the day I died.

The day I drowned.

Then the water expels from my mouth onto the floor with a loud splatter. As I gasp for air, the cold fades from the room. My lungs still burning, I'm wondering how I'm going to explain all this water—except the floor is bone-dry.

Not a drop anywhere.

And the little girl is gone.

I don't think, I simply run out of the office, down the stairs, and skid to a halt in the long dark hall that leads to my escape out back.

Paloma stands there in her silk patterned robe. Cup of tea in her hand. Lightly stirring it with a dainty spoon, like she was waiting for me.

"I was just leaving," I say, breathless from my rush down the stairs.

"Oh?" Her eyes narrow. "Because you look as if you've seen a ghost."

A chill ripples up my spine, and I suppress a shiver. I huff a small laugh and manage to find a tiny smile.

"Did you enjoy the wine?" Paloma says, but her flat tone and sharp glare do not match the friendly ask. She takes a delicate sip of her tea. Her eyes not leaving me. Her brow stitched tight.

"It was a lovely Bordeaux." I push up the corners of my lips more then quietly bid her good-night as I continue past her to my studio out back.

A hot breeze blows through the gardens, the moon casts a pale glow over the grounds, the insects singing all together.

"Good night, Hollis," Louisa greets me when I enter the studio.

"Good night, my sweet girl." I lean near her cage to peck her kisses.

A loud yowl rips at my feet. "Sampson!" I yelp and almost trip. "Goddang it, cat!" He darts past me and out the door.

I don't know what's unnerved me more, the little ghost or Paloma.

Feeling too vulnerable to be alone, I flip on the small TV in the corner. I strip off my clothes to take a quick shower. The late-night news chatters in the background about sunny skies for the next week's forecast. Which is good, because I'd rather not have to tent the gala.

Even as I close my eyes to wash my hair, all I can see is the drowned little girl pointing at me.

Her little voice whispering *Come find me. Come find me. Come find me.*

But how am I supposed to find her? I towel-dry my hair and

throw on some pj's. This is no longer something that can wait
a week but something dire, if what happened tonight is an indication of what I can expect from her. I massage my left hand,
the frost burn still ghosting on my skin.

I'm brushing my teeth when I hear from the other room
". . . woman dies today at one of Dunkirk's Construction sites."
I poke my head out of the bathroom and look at the news. The
reporter is standing in front of a construction site with yellow
police tape roping off the area behind her. "A local woman fell
to her death today from this third-story framed building in what
the contractor is calling a freak accident." The camera points
upward, and when it pans back to the reporter, I catch sight of
a small bird latched to the ground behind the yellow tape.

My blood pressure whooshes in my ears as I watch the grave
bird flop and flutter.

"The woman identified was Camden resident Betsy Kilroy,"
the reporter goes on. "She was also the company's beloved sec-
retary. Authorities say a concerned friend called them because
Kilroy had not picked her up for bingo yet." The video switches
to a woman being interviewed. "Betsy never missed a bingo
night," the woman sobs before the reporter's voice-over continues. "She was found after hours with her car still parked at
work. While police are still investigating, currently they don't
suspect foul play. Back to you, John."

I return to the bathroom and rinse the toothpaste out of my
mouth.

Numb, that's how I feel right now. I just saw her this past
Saturday. After her fight with Libby. After someone else was
asking about the Owens estate. After . . .

*Legal action suggested against the Kilroys . . . unless you want to
handle yourself.*

. . . unless you want to handle yourself.

. . . handle yourself.

Cain?

I cover Louisa's cage and leave the TV on for company as I slide into bed—

My thigh meets with something cold and wet, and I rip back the covers to find a dead cardinal lying in my bed.

I'm breathless, half-stuck between shock and fear.

"Leave me alone." It's a pathetic sob drowned out by the television.

I snatch up a small bag and pick the bird up. Tying off the end, I carry it to the outside trash cans on the other side of the house by the garage.

As I storm back across the rear porch, I catch sight of Paloma sitting in the ballroom on the dark-green velvet sofa, drinking her tea . . . in the dark.

CHAPTER TWENTY-SIX

WHAT I SHOULD be doing is tucking myself into bed like a good girl because there's so much left to do this final week before the gala. But I toss and turn in the bed, thinking about the news this evening, announcing Betsy Kilroy's death. Did she fall? Or was she murdered? A sinking feeling niggles inside me.

Damn it to hell, I have to know.

I throw back the bedcovers and put on some sweats. Five minutes later I'm sneaking out of my studio and driving over to Camden to Dunkirk's Construction. It's been hours since the news reporters were there. Police officers still might be staking out the place to preserve the crime scene, though.

To my surprise, it's empty; there isn't a soul monitoring the place.

I shouldn't be here—trespassing, creeping around on private property in the middle of the night. But the roads in this business park area are invitingly deserted. A lone streetlight interrogates the construction trailer with a static buzz. Beyond the yellow police tape I pan my cell phone's glow over the ground.

Betsy's blood stains the concrete. A faint, rusty color as if someone tried to wash it away but it refused to be erased. Forgotten.

Then, there it is. What I came looking for.

A fat little chickadee: black-capped head, gray wings, and a
full white belly.

And feisty. It fights against the invisible rope tying it to the
ground.

"Hold on, little fellow," I softly say as I kneel. My hand is
still opening when he leaps into my palm. I am shoved from the
here and now and fall back through time.

*"Fuck 'em!" my sister-in-law yells, followed by a wild shush of papers,
as if flung across the room.*

*I pause in my step; they obviously didn't hear me announce I was
here.*

*"They didn't even mention me or the kids," she says. "They think
they can cut me out forever? They have another thing coming."*

*"They're dead now," my brother says dryly. "Seems like they al-
ready got theirs." The sharp silence is an electric bite to the air, a warning
that he's playing with fire for being so blunt.*

*I edge forward and peek through the crack in the doorway, unsure
what my brother and his wife are going on about, but it sounds tan-
talizing enough to keep listening. A cloud of cigarette smoke hangs in
the dimly lit kitchen. She's pacing while he casually sits at the lopsided
table, more interested in his microwave dinner than another one of her
tantrums.*

*"You don't get it. You've always lived without." She collapses into
the dining chair and stubs out her cigarette on a dirty plate. "I'm sick
and tired of unpaid bills, roach-infested apartments, and rubbery food."
She shoves away her own lukewarm meal.*

"We could fight it," he suggests.

*"And how in the hell are we going to pay for a lawyer? You can't
even keep a job more than a week. Jesus." He shrivels back into his
chair, his eyes returning to the plate in front of him.*

I told my brother she'd be a mess of trouble. She was trying to live a champagne life on a beer budget. Constantly racking up bills to keep up with the Joneses, only to end up broke and bankrupt without so much as car to get them from A to B.

Wait till she finds out I'm here to tell them my boyfriend is evicting them—they're overdue three months' rent. To hell if they think they're going to move in with me again. I feel sorry for the kids, but this mess isn't mine to clean up. I inhale a silent breath, readying myself for a fight.

"What's the difference between his family and ours?" she asks him. It's her tone that has him sitting up straighter and causes me to pause.

"Nothing." He shrugs, not seeing her point.

"Exactly." A wry smile twitches at the edge of her mouth. "Why should they be the ones to get it all? I'm the oldest. It should be me." She nibbles on the end of her thumbnail. I don't know what she's going on about, but if there's one thing my sister-in-law is good at, it's fucking over other people for the benefit of herself. "Maybe I could have it all . . ." she starts. I whip out my phone and hit Record as she proceeds to detail out exactly what she plans to do.

My heart is racing as they leave the house. What she's suggesting might actually work. If there's anything she and I have in common, we're opportunists.

What benefits her can benefit me. I close my cell phone.

I walk over to the newspaper lying limply on the floor. The Hawthorne Gazette. *It's not until I flip through the crumpled pages and find the obituary section that I realize more fully what's at stake here.*

It's insane. It's absurd. But what if it works?

A cold wind fills my lungs, jolting me from the past. Not what I expected to see at all. I was prepared to see the moments before her death, but this was different—something unresolved, something Betsy regretted. Whatever plan her brother and sister-in-law had, she regrets being a part of it. Maybe deeply.

But whose obituary was in that paper? Grady Owens's? Could Betsy Kilroy's sister-in-law have been related to Grady?

But what this all has to do with Libby Hawthorne I'm not sure. Betsy knew something that Libby didn't want the world knowing, something she could use against Libby or her family—why else do you meet someone at an abandoned construction site, with no one else around? Does Betsy know something about the land? Because what that land is worth now with all those houses versus what the Hawthornes paid for it in auction—ten-fold the value, if not more. Certainly something worth fighting over.

MONDAY MORNING THERE is no time to contemplate the dead cardinal in my bed, Betsy, or Paloma because the very next day a ruptured pipe causes a portion of the ceiling in the ballroom to collapse. We are six days away from the gala, I've got my hands full, and now I have this disaster to deal with?

Fixing the pipe is easy, to an extent. Through an act of God the contractor has been able to get it done double-quick but he never does come up with a good explanation for the initial rupture. Burst pipes you expect in the winter, sure, but late summer? He says it is all a bit odd.

All this extra work has minimized my time with Cain, which is good and bad. Good because I haven't quite figured out how to shuffle these new feelings now I know for sure he's on to the same investigative path the grave birds are leading me. Bad because I would love to lose myself in him and forget all the chaos.

Part of me wonders if these ghosts aren't playing a role in all this, because by Tuesday the reflecting pool in the gardens inexplicably has drained itself. Which isn't the end of the world because once refilled, everything seems peachy keen. Surely that's enough mishaps for one week.

Then the unthinkable happens.

Or maybe not unthinkable, but I wake up Thursday morning to the nightmare of all nightmares.

Faint plink tink clinks hit my glass roof. Soft tiny sounds. I open my eyes.

Spiders.

Thousands of them.

Overnight they have rained down and set up camp over my greenhouse studio. Fibrous sticky strands, like angel hair, encase me inside. Through the windows I see that every last flower, shrub, and tree we have delicately fostered and grown over the last three months is completely covered in snowy-white cobwebs, like some apocalyptic arachnophobia hell.

The exterminator thinks the waterlogged ground from the drained pool caused the spiders to the leave their burrows for higher ground and escape drowning—but he also says spiders are rare this time of year, and he honestly can't even guess where they're coming from. As he continues to survey the property he keeps shaking his head and mumbling about how odd it all is. We have to pay the landscapers extra to clear the remaining webs without damaging the gardens. Paloma watches from the balcony with a bland expression like she doesn't even care.

It's after five on Friday when I flop into Calista's salon chair, exhausted from the week. She closes up the shop so it's only us, and I've brought us a bottle of wine to share, as I lay all my problems at her feet. Isn't that the secondary duty of every hair stylist?

"How are you holding up?" Calista asks as she drapes the cape over me. She wants to do a quick run-through of my hair before tomorrow night's big event.

I all but start bawling on the spot. I purge my soul about the horrible week I've had. My disconnect from Cain. My concern about Paloma and what she might be up to. And the dead that have haunted me for three exhausting months. The worst of it is I still have not been able to confirm who this family is for certain but they are absolutely connected to Cain and Paloma and Betsy Kilroy.

"How do you know Betsy was pushed?" Calista asks, tucking and pinning the last curls of my messy bun updo.

"Because . . . well, I really don't know for sure. But I believe she was blackmailing Libby Hawthorne. If that's true, then maybe they shut her up for good. If I'm right and Libby finds out I know . . ."

She swivels me around in the chair, sharp-like, and grips my chin.

"Fuck it all," she says, looking me square in the eye. "You walk into that ballroom tomorrow, kicking ass and taking names. You don't let some crazy woman's side agenda or dead ghost birds or Libby's stick up her ass stop you from giving Hawthornians a night they will *never* forget. Is that understood? I won't take anything less from you."

She's right. Tomorrow is my night to shine; it should be the best night of my career. But what these ghosts are showing me I can't shrug off so easily. I tell myself the other stuff I can deal with Sunday.

Calista's *White Wedding* tattoo of a skeleton bride glares at me from her inner bicep, giving the world the middle finger. It makes me smile.

"There's my girl." She nods smartly, then she lets go of my chin and turns me toward the mirror.

"Damn, I look gorgeous."

"Uh, duh." Calista smiles, her hooked lip pulling up on the one side. She waves off my credit card when I try to pay her.

"Okay," I say affirmatively, finding new vigor. "Gala only, from here until Sunday." I leave her cash on the salon's receptionist counter next to the gorgeous bouquet of flowers. A small tag hangs from a piece of twine; it reads FARM FRESH. My brain gets caught on the words. *Farm Fresh*. I roll it around in my thoughts, trying to pick free why it sounds so familiar.

"Tomorrow at noon, right?" Calista asks, pulling me from my thoughts, looking at her appointment calendar on the computer.

"Yes, I'll be at Nadine's at noon tomorrow. Do my hair first because I need to get back to the house to direct the servers and caterers and whatnot. I won't get into my gown until closer to five. It's a zipper dress so all I have to do is step into it," I say to her.

"Good. And if the little girl comes knocking on your door again tonight, you tell her to fuck off."

"Ghosts don't seem to respect boundaries, but I'll try."

Calista frowns at the cash I left, but I'm already pushing out the door before she can give it back.

My car is parked out front, and I get inside. Then I realize I have a picture of this little girl. I rip out my phone and pull up the photo I took last Saturday at the Hawthornes' house of Mary Beth's melting face and the little girl appearing beneath. I pull it up—except it's just a young Mary Beth in the family portrait. I was certain the photo would have captured it, but there's nothing out of place whatsoever.

At the sound of happy squeals I look up to see Mary Beth and her three children exiting Boucher's Real Estate. The littlest one giggling as her father Landon pretends to toss her up in the air. A smile always seems to spread on Mary Beth's face when she looks at her children or her husband; it's the only time she looks truly happy.

A bird lands in the dogwood tree out front of the building. A cardinal. A living, breathing, bright red cardinal. It twitters there in the branch a moment then flies away.

Mary Beth notices me sitting in my car and smiles. She lifts her hand to wave hello—and it hits me.

The day of the gala presentation, Mary Beth's birthday, and her lifting her hand to the window touching the spot of blood from the dead cardinals outside.

Flowers were delivered on her birthday. Mary Beth said she loved farm fresh flowers.

Fresh flowers, like the bouquet that now lay rotten out at Kappy's Campgrounds, near cabin 14.

MY FOOT FEELS heavy on the gas pedal as I drive the winding, dark roads to Kappy's. I almost miss the overgrown turn to the lake. My headlights beam over the metal X-bar gate that closes off the road. From my roadside kit Denny bought me for Christmas, I grab a flashlight that will reach farther into the night than my phone.

A late summer sunset still glows faint purple across the sky, the day about ready to put itself to bed. A murder of crows settles in the trees; it's the hour when the day has almost ended and the night is not quite here. Their cawing and cries slowly dissipate as I near. I feel them watching me as I walk.

Deeper into the woods I step, the dark eating away at the light until only a thin beam of leftover sun breaks through the trees. Bellowing croaks burp all around me as the bullfrogs begin their nightly routine. Lightning bugs wink and bob, only to disappear farther up ahead. Off in the distance the tremulous honking croon of a night loon mourns its loneliness.

And here I am, traipsing through the trees and the mosquitoes and anything else that might want to take a bite of me.

A heaviness weighs on me, like gravity is pushing me down. The density of it causes my breaths to strain and the sound of the woods to hollow. I know I'm there before I see the cabin.

I train my flashlight to the top of the door and find the *14*. Then I pan it over to the coordinating dock. Wooded rib bones stretch out across the small pooling of water.

I swallow hard.

One more step forward and I know there will be no turning back.

But I have to know if my gut is right.

On the sludgy embankment to the dock, the flashlight beam finds the rotted flower bouquet, now covered in a fur of black mold. I nudge it with my toe and find the Farm Fresh tag.

Then I skim the light over the water's edge.

A short trickling of bubbles to the surface.

A small feathering of the water as something moves beneath.

A grave bird.

A cardinal, if I had to guess.

It's just a guess, though. It could very well be a gator. There's really only one way to know for sure.

Walking into the lake, the muck beneath my feet becomes murky water around my ankles until half my calves are submerged. Sweat stipples on my forehead. My breath rasps with a short, weighted pace. Even my heart is trying to punch itself free from my chest.

"You can do this," I try to tell myself, but my head isn't listening. I try to shake the anxiousness from my hands.

"It's just water," I say a little more calmly, letting my body get used to the cool temperature, the lapping against my legs.

I exhale.

I'm not scared of water. I can swim just fine.

It's the idea of drowning that I don't like.

But if there's a grave bird at the bottom, I need to see what it has to show me.

Water ripples a few feet away from me. The stagnant smell of sulfur and rot wafts from the surface, reminding me of boiled eggs and wet dog.

The flashlight struggles to illuminate beneath the surface, dulled thinned by the watery brown.

But something stirs at my presence.

I stretch my arm in farther, deeper, and I lose the light to the depth.

"It's just water," I whisper, then take deep a breath and sink beneath the surface.

The light beam only stretches inches from my face. The held breath strains against my lungs to get free; instinct tells me to return to the dock. I pan the light around quickly, and then it catches on something: a cardinal. Its brilliant red feathers a splash of color in the muddy brown. Bubbles trickle upward from its beak. Its beady black eyes stare at me.

It leaps onto my face and shoves me back in time.

Something is wrong with my head. The world sways with each step. Trees blur, split, and double. I think it was the Coca-Cola the man gave us: it tasted funny. Fingered branches reach for me like scary hands. I stumble and fall to evade their grasp. Be quiet, I tell myself. Be quiet. My brother told me to run. If I can get to the cabin, I can hide there. Maybe they won't find me. It feels too far away. Maybe I passed it? I spin to see where I am; they call for me. Desperate. Angry. A dangerous warning echoes into the night. I run. They promise they won't hurt me. Liars. I saw what they did to my big brother.

Every glance backward the fire grows. Flames eat away at the huge building I snuck free from. Starved like wolves, they leap. Their prey the old wood.

Where is Mother? Where is Father? Why have they not come for us yet?

Sobs grow in my chest too big to push down or keep quiet. All I want is to lie down. Curl onto the ground and make myself small. So small they won't see me. Maybe I can. It sounds inviting enough. I slow up my steps and consider doing just that. I tell myself it's not giving up if you need a rest. My limbs grow heavy. My eyes, like slamming doors, too hard to keep open. A small break is all I need.

A twig snaps to my right, and a little girl cowers in the bushes. Her eyes full of fear just like mine. Quietly we stare at each other with only my ragged breath and the fear of the dark to keep us company. I blink through my woozy Coca-Cola haze, wondering if I'm staring at a mirror. I would have thought her to be my sister if I had one.

A woman leaps out from behind a tree, startling me half to death. The little girl burrows deeper into the shadows. But I run—the wrong direction as the lake quickly approaches. Surface so black and still, it reflects the moonlit sky. It splashes up around my feet—maybe I can swim free.

The woman's weight falls upon me, and under the water I go. I fight. I try. But she is too strong. Too heavy.

"Mother, please." The young girl's voice is shaky. I try to tell her to run. To go get help. With every watery scream, my mouth inhales more of the lake. It feels like vomiting in reverse. My body loses the fight, and I succumb to the water.

Then I feel nothing. Darkness seeps in.

I am no longer sad.

Or scared.

I hear my father's voice. Warm and surrounding, wrapping me in his light. Mother has come. Brother, too.

They call me to join them in the light, so I do.

I rip myself from the water and the grave bird's grasp, scrabbling backward through the muck, and claw my way back onto the safety of the wood dock. I gasp and choke and vomit up a stomach full of putrid water.

Desperately, I try to catch my breath, but the violence I witnessed is too great for my soul to bear. I cradle my legs, cycling through the images over and over. Succumbing to the grief, I shake with great, heaving sobs for the dead little girl. For her mother. Her father and the brother. For the family I am certain Libby Hawthorne killed. It was her who jumped from behind the tree. A younger version of herself, but it was Libby.

The worst part, come tomorrow—I will be helping a murderer fundraise millions of dollars.

EVEN ONCE I'M home, safely in bed, I don't feel safe, nor do I feel whole. I stare up through my glass ceiling at the black sky and wonder how in the world I am going to make it through this gala. How am I going to show the world what I've seen? Libby Hawthorne is a murderer. And Mary Beth witnessed it all.

I'm not crazy. It wasn't a dream Mary Beth kept saying on the way to the hospital. This is what she meant. She couldn't have been more than ten years old when she watched her mother murder the girl. She said a day of reckoning was coming; now I know for what.

But by who? And to what end?

I cycle through the same thought over and over and over.

Libby Hawthorne is a murderer.

This is all I can think as I try to fall asleep.

Late in the night I wake to find myself standing in the street in front of Uncle Royce's house. I don't know how I got here.

The summer night is suffocating and sticky. The crickets long since put themselves to bed. The sky is purple and deep blue; it tastes like blackberries on my tongue. Someone takes my hand.

By my side, the drowned little girl's ghost. She looks up at me with her watery-gray skin and wet hair. She pulls me forward, forcing me to come with her. We dissipate into a tunnel of twinkling lights. An infinite, blinding white pulls us through to another place. Where is she taking me?

We're on the balcony now. A soft, sweet melody drifts up from the backyard, luring me to peer over the railing, into the garden where flowers bloom and fragrant vines grow. Eden.

But this is not Eden as it should be.

A sea of thin, colored birds jump and flutter. Desperate for the sky they can never reach. All attached to the lifeless, elegantly dressed bodies piled in the gardens. Hundreds of them. All paying for the sins of the Hawthornes.

Death, she waits on the stage below. Darkness shrouds her eyes. Her hatred like smoke in my mouth. Revenge tastes sweet, like peaches and cinnamon on my tongue.

Death is coming, the little girl whispers in my ear. *Tomorrow.* She points down below.

"Hollis?" Cain's confused, sleep-filled voice calls from behind me. I look down at my pajamas, the dream clinging to the edges of my mind.

The gardens below are neat and trimmed; gone are the bodies and Death. For now.

CHAPTER
TWENTY-SEVEN

AT THE CRACK of dawn I drag myself out of bed, my brain tortured from a sleepless night. I go over my list for the day, making sure everything is ready to go, but I can't shake the dream I had. Or what I know. Dread nibbles at me.

I'm going over the final version of the missionary presentation when I notice something I didn't see when Mary Beth handed this to me at the church that day.

A faint watermark over the missionary family's photo.

It's a stock photo.

Something in my stomach drops.

I whip open my laptop. My hands shake as I pull up the stock photo website. I type *missionary family* in the search bar. Sure enough, the second page of photos in, this family pops up. When I click the full portfolio, it's a photo shoot of a family on a camping trip in New Mexico. "What the hell?" They used a fake photo, but why? Why not just get an actual photo of the family?

Unless . . . Granny was right. There are no missionaries.

There's no one out on a mission to feature a photo of. So why lie to the town? Why make such a fuss about all the good work they're doing for the Lord, the trips they're funding, the charities they're propping up? And why host a fundraiser aimed at raising funds that are going . . .

The Hawthornes are broke. They've shorted me with partial payments. The Greater Good construction site shut down, and the going rumor is they weren't paying their employees. Now they're looking for more investors. That's why they reached out to Cain.

This whole fundraiser is a fraud—and the last twenty-five years of galas? Have they been a fraud, too?

Sweat prickles over my skin. I feel myself get dizzy. I will be ruined once the town finds out. Who would believe I didn't know? Especially if I'm the one who gets Libby arrested for murder, I can't imagine she wouldn't try to take me down with her.

"Hollis?" I hear my brother Denny call from my doorway.

"Yeah?"

He gives me a queer look for a half second, then says, "You okay, Holls?"

If what I think I know about this fundraiser and Libby being a murderer is true, he can't know anything. It's bad enough I've involved Nadine. I'm going to need to prove what I know. And I don't want anyone else involved in the meantime. If Libby was willing to kill once to keep secrets buried . . .

I clap my computer shut. "Just want everything perfect is all," I tell him.

"Okay," he says, not sounding like he's buying it, though. "We're going to double-check the lights and test the system one more time to make sure we're good for tonight."

I hired Denny and Dylan to string up the lights for the party. Their crew has been working for four days straight to get everything set up. It will look incredible once it gets dark.

"Awesome. I can't thank you enough."

"You're paying me. That's thanks enough."

"Got him!" Dylan says, thrusting inside the greenhouse. Sampson, yowling his certain death, has finally been caught. "Peanut butter," Dylan says. "I knew he couldn't resist." He beams with pride.

"If you could drop him and Louisa over at Nadine's I would be forever grateful." Tonight will be too much noise for Louisa to handle. And out of extra precaution, Sampson will be crated over there as well. I don't trust that furball not to ruin this evening if given the chance.

"No problem." Dylan glances outside toward the gardens. "She asked if she could stop by," he says, shrinking with his words. And I'm about to ask him who he's talking about when Granny walks past the wall of windows. I scowl at Dylan. "She loves you," he quickly adds. "Hey, Granny," he says, then steps out of the way for her to enter.

"Oh my, what a pretty dress," Granny says, spying my ball gown hanging on my armoire. My brothers hug her neck and then make their exit.

Quickly I glance around, looking for that torturous grave bird of mine who likes to tag along with Granny any chance it gets. But the feral thing is nowhere in sight.

"Your dress makes what I brought even better." Out of her purse Granny pulls a small square jewelry box with a foreign character marked on the front. I know immediately what it is.

"Are you serious?" I take the box from her and open the lid. Her wedding pearls.

It's a gorgeous strand of gray pearls with matching dangle earrings. Simple but stunning. I've sneaked peeks of these pearls in the dresser drawer where Granny keeps them along with her costume jewelry. But these, these are real.

"Your Grandaddy got them when he was stationed in Japan. They're freshwater so not the super fancy kind. But I thought they might look nice with your gown."

My heart melts into itself. I stroke a single pearl with the tip of my finger, cool and smooth and everything dreams are made of. When I was eight, I tried on her pearls and stood on her bed, staring at myself in her dresser mirror, pretending I was royalty. I'll never forget the fear I felt when she caught me. She wasn't mad so much as she wanted me to ask permission first.

"When you told me your gown was dark gray, I thought these would be perfect," she says, and her smile wobbles unsure. "I'm an old lady now. I don't have need for fancy things. But you . . . you're about to make the world shine."

I feel a little bit of my heart's pain bend right then. Like the weight of her love is more powerful than the wall of guilt I have built. I want to bask in her words and let them soak me through, enough that they could heal me.

Maybe if I'd let them.

"Thank you, Granny," I say, my words crispy and frail and almost to breaking.

"There you go," Granny says and opens her arms, pulling me into her warm embrace like she knew she finally had me.

"Now, I may despise those people," she says, "but I love you and want every success for you. Those people, on the other hand, are rotten. You, however, are not." Granny has no idea how right she is. "Those Hawthornes are in good keep with the devil, but he'll turn on them eventually. Devil always does. Besides," she says and pulls out *The Hawthorne Gazette*, "tonight is more about you than those no-goods." She hands me the paper. It comes out twice a week, Fridays and Mondays.

Front page news: "25th Hawthorne Missionary Gala to Get a Full Facelift." The large picture of me from the photo shoot. I had thought it was going to be a quick mention in the events section of the paper about the Hawthornes and their missionary work. Instead of the write-up being about the Hawthornes, they wrote it about me. The article talks about how a fresh pair of eyes may prove to be just the thing the gala needs. It goes on to speak of the previous events with the Richardsons and the *tired and dated* Serendipity Country Club. He contributes the decline in enthusiasm, and fundraising dollars, to lack of luster and a feeling of sameness of the last ten events. "'But with fresh blood injected into the mix this year at the hands of Hollis Sutherland of event planning business Sutherland & Co., this may just be the jolt of caffeine this town needed.' This is incredible."

"I believe in you and all that you're capable of." She squeezes me with one long hug goodbye before she leaves.

I pore over the article again. I owe this man a thank-you: this kind of publicity alone should pull in enough work to keep me busy the rest of the year. I'd be able to save up enough money to find a new apartment, maybe even set my sights on buying an alternate venue. Everything is falling into place, except . . . the Hawthornes.

Libby Hawthorne drowned a little girl in a lake over two decades ago. A young boy burned to death in the campground's main building. A woman was struck in the head and killed in the Hawthornes' own home. A car fell on and crushed a man to death at an autobody shop. And Betsy Kilroy was possibly pushed from a height on the construction site.

The Hawthornes have been siphoning money from the people of this town for years, maybe decades. They've assumed a holier-than-thou persona that's fueled their lies and their thievery. What else have they done? What else might they do?

And what will people say when they find out—and that I was in business with them?

But what if I could expose them for everything they are—frauds, thieves . . . murderers? What if, instead, I could help save the town from any more death, any more corruption?

I glance down at the missionary write-up and thumb drive Mary Beth gave me. Maybe Granny is right, the devil will turn on them eventually, and I'm going to help him out.

I grab my keys and tell my brothers I'll be right back.

As soon as I make it to my car I hear a small cheep and look over my shoulder. There, sitting on the tree branch, is my grave bird. The little house sparrow quirks its head, antsy and anxious. She's right, this is something I need to finally take care of.

"Okay, little bird, I'm ready," and I open my palm. It flies down and lands in my hand.

I fall back in time, to the day I stole the peacock haircomb.

CHAPTER TWENTY-EIGHT

HELL HATH NO fury like a woman who has to write a huge check yet doesn't have the funds to back it up. I should have collected a final check from Libby weeks ago, but I allowed her pathetic excuses, "I'll get to it you this afternoon" or "I thought Jeremiah already paid" or whatever delay tactic she tried to employ. Then, of course, Noah's stroke last week made it impossible to ask again. But here we are, me standing over her, and her sitting at her desk, about to write the final check for six figures.

"I've explained to the vendors you guys were strapped for cash," I say, as she pulls out the checkbook. She glares up with a displeased stare.

"A tad exaggerated, don't you think?" she sneers. "We *are* the Hawthornes. If anyone's good for it, we are."

"Huh," I say, with every bit of frown in my tone. "With the Greater Good housing development on an indefinite hold, and the constant delays in payment to me, I just assumed . . ."

She cuts me with a look. "Well, that was your first mistake, then, wasn't it?"

"I see," I say with every attempt to sound genuine. Then I tack on the *one* piece that's been eating away at me ever since my grave bird showed me the day I died. "Well, I was going through some boxes of my things last week, old Christmas presents and knickknacks and such. And I came across this beautiful comb. My grandfather left it for me as a present his last Christmas with us—you remember him, don't you?"

She gives the slightest nod to indicate she's heard me but nothing more. So I press on.

"I know he was the preacher at a neighboring church—a rival church, you could say, I suppose. So I'm not sure how much you two knew of one another." I pause a moment, in case she wants to help fill in the details but see I'm going to have to do all the work myself. "But I know you must have been in touch a little bit back then. See, I remember this one time, we were at Roy's Drugstore, it was the day he died, actually, never will forget that day. And you were there."

She looks at me full in the face now, clearly I've earned her attention.

"You and he were in a such fuss about money. Seemed you wanted him to agree to something he wasn't comfortable with. Preachers can be like that, you know. Moral, *honest*."

She continues to stare at me, searching my face for clues about just how much I recall.

I was in the back office of Roy's Drugstore. Shame hung around my neck like an anchor. There was a narrow view down the cold-and-flu aisle where I could see the manager, Mr. Allen Pattinson, explaining to my grandfather what I'd done.

After Grandaddy heard his piece and turned to come collect me, he was stopped by Libby Hawthorne. She was animated, agitated even. They were talking in hushed tones, but I could still hear them. He said something about money and paying folks off. When he tried to walk away she snagged him by the elbow.

Almost seeming desperate. But grandaddy refused to back down. Whatever she was offering, he wasn't taking it.

When we got to the truck I was still so focused on Grandaddy and how mad he was. But my petty thievery wasn't the only thing on his mind. He was scared.

His eyes kept darting to the rearview mirror. His fear growing like a heavy fog. It filled the cab of the truck. Something was creeping up behind us. When I went to get a look for myself, he barked for me to duck down.

The moment before the other truck rammed into us felt worse than getting caught for stealing. Grandaddy was able to right the truck after the first blow. But the second one, the other driver was determined to make it count. And they did, slamming into us as we crossed the bridge, shoving us into the cold depths of the river.

It wasn't an accident.

It was intentional.

And I'd spent years believing it was all my fault. That if I hadn't stolen that comb, none of this would have happened. But there was more at play than I ever knew, much more.

I think my grandaddy was onto the Hawthornes. Whether it was Grady Owens's stolen property or their fake missionaries, he knew something, and I believe it cost him his life.

And now I know.

I release an exaggerated sigh. "Anyway, no clue what made me think of that," I say, not sharing how much of that day I truly remembered. But it's enough to make her nervous.

My eyes dart to the key hidden underneath the vintage brass inkwell. My plan, as dumb as it may be, is to ask to use the restroom on my way out so I can sneak back into her office.

Thirty seconds is all I need.

"Hey, Mother." Mary Beth interrupts us, baby on one hip, another child running over to Libby. She finally breaks eye contact with me as she picks up her granddaughter. "Oh hi, Hollis. I didn't expect to see you this morning."

"She was just leaving," Libby says, tearing off the check and handing it to me. "Don't take it to the bank until Monday." Venom laces her voice.

"Momma, do you mind helping me bring in Ruthie's play-pen? It's too heavy for me by myself."

Thirty seconds is what I got.

CHAPTER
TWENTY-NINE

A LINE OF expensive cars stretch around the corner as the valet boys hustle to park vehicles. Most of the guests are simply wealthy in their own right, but there are several somewhat-famous guests as well. Among the invited: a lawyer and author of a bestselling crime novel; an up-and-coming country music star from Nashville; an heir to a Kentucky whiskey distillery; a retired pitcher from the Atlanta Braves; and an actress who starred in a popular Western in the late nineties. The power of the Hawthornes to draw such a cast of celebrities is quite impressive.

As excited I should be to host this evening, my thoughts are flooded with what my grave bird showed me about that fateful day fifteen years ago. I wonder how in the world I could have misremembered it all. Those details my brain overlooked simply because I was focused on punishing myself for what had happened instead of who was truly at fault.

"Wow," Cain says from over my shoulder. Then he places a light kiss on my neck. Nadine helped me pick the gown, and damn if she didn't nail it. The upper half, black lace and V-shaped, is broad at my shoulders, then narrows at the waist, the bottom half a gunmetal gray satin A-line skirt that barely grazes the floor. Tasteful and professional, but I still feel like a princess.

His arm slides around my waist, and I spin to face him. His tuxedo is a deep shade of midnight like he freshly stepped out of the darkness. His silk tie is the same shade. His cuff links wink and look to be real sapphires.

"Not bad yourself," I say and smooth out the gray silk handkerchief in his pocket. Pinned to his lapel, a wild game-bird feather boutonniere with a velvet gray ribbon around it, the only real source of color besides the pocket square. It's the same one he wore the day he strolled into town.

"It was my grandfather's, from his wedding day," Cain says as he notices me admiring it. "Or that's what Paloma tells me . . . God I miss you," he says into my hair. I have been so busy this week, we've barely had any alone time. A few glances dart our way, so he pushes me out of view of prying eyes. Then he presses his body against me, stealing a kiss.

"I have to work." I smile against his mouth then pull away. "Later. Okay?" I say, and his hand slides off my hip as I slip away.

All the guests mingle in the ballroom for cocktails until we open the rear garden doors for the dining and events portion of the evening. I am abuzz with energy: everything could not be more perfect.

Guests are entering through the Art Deco double doors on each side, more like gates, the flat brass forming a geometric pattern, something straight out of the 1920s. Spoonflower wallpaper, of black and teal and blush, is scalloped up the walls, the lines accented in hand-painted, twenty-four-karat gold. Dark green velvet curtains ripple from the top of the windows like someone has poured liquid emeralds down the walls. We had the original parquet flooring sanded down and stained then inlaid with thin lines of brass sporadically in the thatch-and-weave pattern.

But it's the three crystal chandeliers Uncle Royce bought the Christmas before he died that steal the show. Folded waves of gold metal with black crystal-quartz fringe drips from the ceiling like fine jewelry. The quartz strands cast inky purple prisms on the floor. Coordinating sconces, ten feet high, frame both sides of the fireplace in the middle of the ballroom.

Several guests try to steal a glance behind the curtains to get a sneak peek into the rear gardens, but the windows are coated with a temporary black tissue paper. The lighting coordinators—aka my brothers—know to not turn on a single light until we open for the dinner.

The evening has only begun, but so far Libby has done everything she can to avoid me. I'm walking along the perimeter of the room, mostly surveying to see how things are going, but every time I get near she pivots and finds someone new to absorb in conversation. She wasn't happy about me stopping by earlier, demanding final payment, and clearly her mood hasn't improved much since.

I was shocked to see Noah with her: he just got home from the hospital two days ago, and it's hard to believe he's really up for a night like tonight. And he's a pretty pathetic sight. Slumped in a wheelchair, not seeming quite aware of his surroundings, they have him parked off to the side. His face is still purpled from ruptured blood vessels, his mouth like a gasping fish, almost like he's trying to say something. If I stare at his lips long enough, it looks like *I'm leaving. I'm leaving. I'm leaving.* He should be home resting, but instead Libby brought him here, setting him up in the corner like a prop to gain sympathy—and more money.

I make my way to the kitchen, which is in full swing for the party, something I haven't seen in years, and it warms my heart. Chef Roberts has the room mastered and working like a well-oiled machine. He's currently having an intense conversation with Paloma, and she seems irritated with his response. By the time I get over there, she's already back among the crowd.

Chef Roberts comes over to the door when he sees me lingering. "Was there a problem for Mrs. Cabrera?" I ask.

He looks past my shoulder, as if making sure she isn't near. "She wanted to make a menu change for the Hawthornes to lobster bisque soup instead of tomato bisque. But I told her Noah and Jeremiah are allergic to shellfish. She tried to tell me I had incorrect information about their allergies, but I've cooked for them before, and I never forget if there's something that might kill a guest."

A knot of fear tightens in my stomach. The soups look similar enough that one might not realize if they received the wrong dish. I put on a pleasant smile. "Oh. Well, I wonder if maybe she was referring to the . . . the Haywoods? They asked about a menu change. Let me confirm, and I'll get back to you." I'm about to walk away to find Paloma, but I turn back. "And just to make sure there are no allergy risks, any menu changes should go through me."

"Of course." He nods and goes back to the kitchen.

I'm halfway down the hallway when my brother finds me.

"We're ready to turn on the lights whenever you are," Denny says to me.

I lightly smile, about to respond when I notice a puddle of liquid on the ballroom floor. A cold chill runs up my spine.

One of the waitstaff carrying a water pitcher stoops down to clean the spill. *It wasn't her, then*, I think.

"Awesome. Let me do a once-through real quick, and I'll meet you on the rear patio out back."

As I dash upstairs to the VIP balcony, I see Cain trapped at the bar by old Mrs. Vickie Garrett who's chatting his ear off, pawing at him every chance she gets. I chuckle at the sight.

Upstairs the long table is perfection. The VIP balcony overlooks the gardens and the stage at the far end of the lawn, backdropped with tall privacy shrubs—then the nightmare engulfs my vision. Dead guests piled on top of each other. I try to shake away the thought, but I can't. There's something else still at play here, something that I can't see yet. I know enough about Libby, about the Owens estate, about her fight with Grandaddy. But I can't figure out how Paloma fits into all of this. Or Cain. And the thought gnaws at me as I try and pull my focus back to the evening at hand.

I've selected my best waitstaff to focus on the VIP table. There are large throne-like chairs where the Hawthornes will sit, along with Cain and Paloma. This was Libby's idea, to be on the balcony overlooking the gardens like a queen overlooking her kingdom. She scoffed when I suggested they eat with the other guests, since she was hoping to drain their wallets by the end of the night.

"Miss Sutherland!" Jaqueline, my head waitstaff, urgently races onto the balcony.

"What's wrong?"

"The champagne," she says, half out of breath. "The Dom or whatever it's called—the good stuff. It's gone. We looked in the subzero fridge. I checked with the bartender. We can't find it anywhere."

"Take a breath," I tell her. "A case of expensive champagne didn't just disappear. We'll find it. Try the fridge in the kitchen. It could be there." Halfway down the stairs I run into Paloma coming up.

"What are you doing?" I say, not hiding my accusation.

"Using the restroom." She tries to blow me off and pass, but I snag her by her elbow.

"Why were you trying to change the Hawthornes' order with the chef?"

She straightens to her full height, unashamed. "I don't know what you're talking about," she says, almost indignant.

"You know exactly what I'm talking about," I say.

Paloma is a steel frame, unwilling to bend to a single emotion.

"You're the one who put those family photos in my box at the country club, aren't you? Why are you trying to scare Libby?"

"I don't know what you mean," Paloma growls.

From the bottom of the stairs, my brother Dylan calls my name. He raises his arm, tapping his watch. It's past time to let the guests enter the rear gardens for the dinner to begin. I give him the one-minute finger.

"I do know, Paloma. *Spirit eyes.* Remember?" I say. "I know what Libby has done. What she is capable of."

Paloma stares at me with heartbreak in her eyes. "You can't imagine what she took from me, what she's done."

"Paloma, please, trust me. I know enough. I saw the paperwork on Cain's desk about Grady Owens's estate. After tonight, we can go to the police. Together. If Cain is Grady Owens's heir, we can prove it, and all the land the Hawthornes stole will go back to him."

Paloma quirks her head. "Who is Grady Owens?"

Suddenly it feels like I'm on unsteady ground. "Grady Owens. He owned the land the Hawthornes bought, but it wasn't supposed to go to them—he and Charlotte had a child, the family in those photos are his heirs. You tried to blackmail Libby with them. They should have inherited the property. The Hawthornes saw to it they wouldn't get the land."

"The woman in those pictures, she was my friend, but I do not know a Charlotte or Grady Owens. Why don't you ask that greedy impostor down there who my friend is?" She nods to Libby, then turns sharply, continuing up the stairs.

What Paloma's saying doesn't make sense. "What are you saying? Why are you trying to blackmail Libby, then?"

She glares over her shoulder at me. "I'm not. Libby Hawthorne has been dead a very long time."

"Hollis?" Dylan calls from the base of the stairs. "We ready?"

he asks. I can hear the urgency in his voice. I turn back to see Paloma has disappeared down the hallway.

"Yes, coming now." I hurry down the stairs, unsure what in the hell Paloma is talking about. What does she mean, Libby has been dead a long time? Dead to her, to Paloma?

I position myself at the rear garden doors and give a slight nod to my brothers. The lights in the ballroom dim, and only the purple glow of the black crystal chandeliers remains. The chattering guests rile from a moment of excitement then hush quiet.

Ethereal music pipes through the hidden speakers and fills the room. With a flick of a button, I remotely open the curtains to the ballroom like a grand movie theater. Staff are positioned at the three double doors, leading to the rear gardens. I nod to Denny, then a gentle synthesized voice speaks. "Welcome to the Empyrean Gala."

The staff open the rear doors to the gardens, and a canopy of lights ignites. Over one thousand strands, more than fifty thousand tiny, twinkling lights. Billowing smoke, like heavenly clouds, rolls throughout the gardens. It slowly recedes, revealing richly dressed tables.

Hushed *oohs* and *aahs* murmur through the crowd as they descend into the rear gardens.

The reflecting pool is dotted with rose petals and tea lights. Dining tables dressed in midnight-blue linens and gold flat-ware are scattered throughout the gardens. Floral arrangements of crimson cockscomb, eggplant-colored succulents, and blue passion-fruit flowers drape gold bowls like fruits for the gods. Name cards for each guest are attached to their custom gifts, the constellation necklaces and wristwatches I outlined in my initial presentation.

At the far end of the lawn sits a stage with a large screen, which currently plays the rolling clouds of a nebula, deep in space.

Everything is perfect, exactly as I imagined it would be. And yet there's a trail of sweat forming on my spine that has nothing to do with the weather.

"Well," Libby says, coming up behind me during the second course, "I didn't think you could do it." A backhanded compliment if I've ever heard one.

I survey Libby Hawthorne as though I'm seeing her for the first time. She no longer looks powerful or in command. She looks guilty.

There's no unknowing the truth now. Libby Hawthorne has this entire town fooled. I look her dead in the eyes and silently vow I'll do everything in my power to get actual evidence to prove everything to the police. But for this evening, public exposure and humiliation will have to do. I can't let her get away with all of this.

"Well, *Libby.*" I uncharacteristically use her first name, and her eyebrow spikes annoyed. "The best is yet to come." I let the smirk hang on my face for a moment, then walk away and let her marinate in that.

I'm halfway down the stairs when a staff member stops me.

"The emcee says he doesn't have his prepared copy for what he's supposed to say about the missionaries."

My heart skips a beat. The moment is fast approaching.

"It's in my greenhouse. Let me grab it." I slip away to the back side of the building and down the side path to my studio. Upon entering my room, I am immediately met with the sense that something's not right. The greenhouse is eerily quiet despite the chattering noise from the gala guests outside. I glance around the room to make sure nothing is out of place. Except my purse has been spilled out onto my bed. I can't remember whether I tossed it there in my rush back from the Hawthornes' this morning—or has someone been pilfering through it?

Suddenly something darts in my left peripheral vision, but when I turn to look, there's no one there.

A thin band of light outlines the double doors of my armoire. I don't remember leaving the light on.

Fear flushes over my body, the instinct to run too tempting. All I can hear are my steadied breaths as I realize what might be waiting for me on the other side. I push myself to go over. The handle is ice-cold in my palm. With a forceful pull, I rip open the door.

Nothing.

Just a pile of clothes waiting to be worn and a top shelf of shoes crammed together like a stack of logs. Everything exactly how it ought to be.

I tug the light's chain to turn it off and move to close the doors when I see it. A patch of wet on my hanging dresses. My eyes trail downward.

Lying on the bottom is the wooden cardinal puzzle piece from Cain's room. It sits in a small pool of water.

Outside, the emcee is announcing the beginning of the bachelor auction. *Shit.* Quickly I grab the USB drive with the missionary family's presentation I made.

Gala music fans into the room as the door opens behind me. "Sorry, Jaqueline, I just had to grab the—" I turn to address her and freeze.

The noise from outside hushes. Only the soft gritty sound of Jeremiah's shoes whispers on the tile floor as he steps into the room. Menace knits his brows.

"What do you want?" My voice is even-keeled, but terror races at the edge.

"Mother wants to know why you came by the house today."

"I came by to pick up my final check." I stand strong on my half-truth.

"You need to mind your business." He tosses something at me. I fumble to catch it. It's the crumpled photo of Paloma and her friend. My eyes slide to my disheveled purse, realizing where he got it from, and I swallow hard and find my nerve.

"Mind my business? You mean instead of your family's? Like the business of faking mission trips? Or the business of stealing property out from under people?"

Jeremiah points his finger at me. "If we go down, you go down. You understand me?"

His threat is punctuated by his burned, scarred hand from the day the fire tornadoes chased him down.

Fire.

"You set fire to a little boy," I say before I can stop the words from slipping out.

Shock and fear scramble on Jeremiah's face.

"After you beat him near to death, you set fire to the cabin out at the lake and let the flames finish the job." There's power in putting all the pieces together. "I bet you killed Betsy Kilroy, too." The phone call with his buddy at the church after the day I visited Betsy: *Mother already asked me to take care of it.*

"Was it you who ran my grandfather and me off the road?"

Jeremiah's eyes grow bold, knowing exactly what I'm talking about.

"My grandaddy would still be alive today if it wasn't for you."

Out of nowhere Jeremiah's fist flies through the air and cracks against my jaw. My neck cranks so fast, I hear something pop. His brutal hands give me a hefty shove, and I fall back into the open armoire, fumbling to catch myself. Clothes and shoes tumble down on top of me as I do.

Jeremiah slams the armoire doors shut. Dazed and in the dark, my head swims. I tell myself to move, but my thoughts feel like they've been dragged through mud. I will my eyes to stay open, but they have other plans. The volume on my television rises to an abnormally high level. Through the crack between the doors I watch his shadowed movement as he rifles through my room. My eyes are too blurred to focus or stay awake. Sounds from the gala flood through room once again as he opens the door to leave.

"The final bachelor up for auction," the emcee says. "Cain Landry."

And I feel myself slip into the darkness.

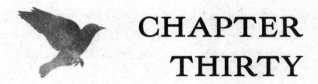

CHAPTER THIRTY

GET UP, A little voice whispers in my head.

But my blurry thoughts bob in a sea of uncertainty and fog. Smarting off to Libby with my just-wait-and-see tone made her paranoid. So much so she sent her attack dog after me.

A thundering pain grows in my jaw. Slowly I cradle my cheek, the pounding so fierce it causes my left eye to twitch.

Get up! Something loud whacks the outside of the armoire, startling me awake.

I shuffle in the dark box of the armoire, trying to gain my bearings. I need to get out of here, but when I try to push on the doors they don't budge. Jeremiah has wedged something between the handles, trapping me inside. I find my way to my feet.

"Help," I try to scream but wince. My jaw clicks a disjointed movement when I try to open it. So I pound my fist on the armoire. The muffled clumsy noise doesn't stretch past the loud television and frenzied auction chatter. I can't just wait here for someone to find me.

Or for Jeremiah to come back and finish what he started.

"Think, Hollis." Swinging right next to my head, a coat hanger. I grab it and feed it through the thin slice between the doors. It looks like he jammed my curling iron in between the handles, the cord wrapped through. I shove the hanger underneath the rod portion, but the curling iron only slides farther in place.

"Shit." I bend the hook of the hanger to get a more snug grip, then I slide-joggle it to the left. Again and again, until the curling iron falls out with a swinging smack against the door. I push on the doors, and the space widens enough I can get my fingers through and unthread the cord, pulling it toward me and loosening it until it's open enough that I can squeeze myself out.

I stumble into my living room, almost losing my footing. The bottom of my gown snags on something and tears. Damn.

Covered in sweat, I smooth a hand over my hair, tucking a wild tendril behind my ear.

I have to get to the sound guy.

The auctioneer calls out bids in thousand-dollar increments as I step out of the greenhouse. I pat my pocket to make sure the USB drive is still safely there.

The world tips sideways as I sway in my steps. I pause behind the wall of shrubs blocking the greenhouse and blink past the spots in my sight. *You've gotta stay upright.* Just get the drive to the sound guy and let the truth play out for everyone to see.

I make an effort to straighten and walk with smoother strides down the side of the gardens, past the guests' dining tables. I keep to the shadows, scanning everywhere for Jeremiah. Adrenaline is waking me up with every step.

Bidder paddles shoot up all over the crowd, trying their luck to win Cain the Bachelor. He stands onstage, beaming and looking charming as the devil while his eyes search the audience.

"We found the champagne," Jaqueline says, cutting me off,

her smile full of relief. "It was in the— Miss Sutherland, are you all right?" She frowns at my appearance.

"Not now, Jackie." I move her out of my way and race toward the sound guy as I hear, "Sold! For fifty thousand dollars to bidder number seven-seven-two."

"Randy," I say to get the sound guy's attention. "As soon as Mary Beth is done speaking about the twenty-fifth anniversary, she will announce the Mary of Bethany Award," I say to him slightly breathless. "Use this for the slide." I shove the USB drive into his hand.

"And Parker knows what to say?" He looks over at the emcee on the stage.

"I'll narrate, just give me the remote to the slideshow."

"Mary Beth has it. Get it from her once she's done." He sticks the drive into his computer, and I sigh with relief. When I glance back up at the balcony to see if Jeremiah is there, it's Mary Beth who's staring back.

I freeze, wondering if she knows what Jeremiah has just done to me. To that little boy. To Betsy Kilroy.

What he did to my grandfather all those years ago.

Her shoulders soften, and she simply smiles, giving me a grateful nod.

Then the emcee introduces Mary Beth, and the lights on the stage dim, and the spotlight shines on her.

"Thank you all for coming," she says into the microphone.

All of the Hawthornes are up there alongside her except for Jeremiah. At the end of the long VIP table, Paloma, is seated still.

Next to her sits a pathetic Noah as he stares off into nothing with his broken mouth still agape.

Suddenly Paloma straightens. Her eyes are sharp and keen, as she watches Jeremiah slip onto the balcony. Whatever he whispers into his mother's ear alarms her from the surprise on her face.

They'll both be really surprised when they find I'm not still in the armoire. It's not enough to watch it unfold from down here. I want to see them, look them in the eye when I expose them.

Quietly, I skim along the perimeter of the gala and into the house. I hike up my skirts and take the steps two at a time.

Paloma's words keep nibbling at me, like someone else is replaying them in my head, willing me to understand. *Libby Hawthorne has been dead a very long time.*

When I reach the balcony, I stay in the shadows of the doorway, just out of the reach of the light.

Mary Beth speaks about the importance of the evening. "And my mother is especially grateful," Mary Beth says, "as she has her heart set on a shopping spree in Paris." The crowd laughs, assuming it's a joke.

"Congratulations, sir," a staff member behind me says to someone. I turn back to find Cain, coming up the stairs.

He pins me with a humorous, exaggerated glare. "You, young lady," he points to me, "are in a heap of trouble." He's eat-up with a grinning smile as he nears. "Mrs. Garrett is going have her way with me, and it's all your fault—" But his smile fades as he picks up on the fact that something is wrong. "What happened?" he says, looking me over, noticing I'm a little worse for wear. Then he snags my chin and turns my head to the side. "Who did this?" he growls.

"But first," Mary Beth's voice punches through our conversation, "let's thank our gracious host, *the* bachelor of the evening, Cain Landry!" Mary Beth says, startling us both. She waves for him to come out there and join her in the spotlight. The guests applaud their appreciation.

"I'm okay," I whisper to him. "Go." I nudge him to go out on the balcony, but he's reluctant. "Trust me. What is done in the dark always comes to light," I say to him—exactly what

Paloma said to me recently. Something in his eyes softens. He squeezes my hand, then joins the others on the balcony.

I don't escape Jeremiah's and Libby's notice, neither of them happy to see me.

"Thank you so much for donating yourself, Cain," Mary Beth says to him with a smile. "Though, I think Mrs. Garrett overpaid." She winks at the crowd, and they laugh. "Mrs. Garrett," she calls out down below, "be careful with Cain. You know what happened to Abel."

Oh, the crowd eats that up. A couple of others heckle. Mary Beth fans an arm for Cain to take a seat. He obliges, but his eyes dart back to me, still unsure of what's happening.

"All kidding aside, tonight's evening has a deeper meaning for our family. While our cause may appear noble, our gala's origin started from dark beginnings." The lights go out completely as the screen flickers to life with the memorial wall on the side of the Hawthorne church.

Mary Beth explains how the birth of the gala started twenty-five years ago, after the tragic loss of Jedidiah and Patsy Hawthorne when a drunk driver hit and killed them. She talks about her grandparents' life in the service of God. The screen plays out pictures of young Jedidiah growing up in the church and how he met Patsy when they were barely twenty.

"It all started with their marriage. Grandpa Jedidiah was as strong-willed as his biblical name," Mary Beth says, continuing to read off her note cards. "As the schoolbooks have taught us, after only two months of courting Patsy, he told her, 'Put on your Sunday best. We're going to the courthouse to get hitched.'" The audience laughs.

The screen flashes to a picture of their wedding, out at the old, smaller Baptist church. Torn down when Noah and Libby took over and built the new, bigger church that stands there now. They were a simple couple, modestly dressed despite their wealth, her in a white knee-length dress and him in a dove-gray suit with a game-bird feather boutonniere.

My heart stutters, and I glance toward Cain. The same boutonniere adorns his lapel. He walked into town wearing it that fateful day months ago. It was his grandfather's, Cain said earlier tonight. From his wedding day is what Paloma had told him.

Cain watches the screen thoughtfully as Mary Beth tells us the Hawthorne family history. The expression on his face does not change. Not so much as a recognition of the boutonniere or a curious tilt of the head that it looks exactly like his.

He saw it, though. You can't miss it on the huge theater screen. Maybe most might not place it or associate it with Cain and what he's wearing tonight, but I did.

He must have, too, even if his face gave nothing away.

Which tells me he already knows his grandfather is Jedidiah Hawthorne.

The images transition through Jedidiah and Patsy's life as Mary Beth continues their story as missionaries. But I'm still swimming in this newfound knowledge. Cain Landry is Jedidiah Hawthorne's grandson?

Cain, a biblical name, a tradition in the Hawthorne family.

Not Grady Owens's heir.

Libby Hawthorne has been dead a very long time.

Greedy impostor.

When I turn back to Noah, his eyes land dead on me. The ruddy bruise stains half his face, almost screaming at me. The exact same as the dead woman who sat on the foot of my bed one morning a week ago. Her mouth gawping just like his. Not choking or gasping for air but trying to tell me something.

I watch his lips carefully as they shape the words.

I'm Libby.

I'm Libby.

I'm Libby.

"The dead woman is Libby Hawthorne," I whisper to myself. The realization sends a chill across my skin. So if the dead woman is Libby, then who are these people posing as the Hawthornes? And if they're impostors, it means Jeremiah and Mary Beth are, too.

"My grandparents were married for forty-six years when tragedy struck," Mary Beth says. Then the couple's memorial mosaic on the side of the church is brought back up on the screen again.

The memorial mosaic was based on the oil painting at Hawthorne Manor. Quickly I pull out my phone from my skirt pocket and scroll through my images to find the one I took the day Noah went into the hospital. The day I thought I saw a melted face of the drowned little girl in the painting. Something my phone didn't capture at the time, but on the same wall is the oil painting of Jedidiah and Patsy and their two children.

I find the picture and zoom in on the older portrait, the young girl in particular. The Hawthornes' daughter . . . Sarah Hawthorne.

I glance at Libby, sitting at her table, guzzling her cocktail, sending wary glances my way. Then I relook at my phone, at Jedidiah's young daughter, then back to Libby. Reality seems to have flipped upside down, and I feel dizzy. Because even though Libby is now a grown woman, it's her.

She's Jedidiah and Patsy's daughter.

She's Sarah Hawthorne, Noah's estranged sister. But is he . . .

I glance at the oil painting again, but the young Noah in the portrait does not look like the man sitting here now. He's larger-boned, has a thicker nose. Even the eyebrows arc differently.

Noah and Libby are both impostors.

Something small darts through the air in front of the screen. Gone before I can identify it. Far off, the rumble of a coming storm.

"But from dark beginnings, we can find the light," Mary Beth says, her voice rising to a definitive tone that sets me at unease.

Something swoops low across the balcony past the Hawthornes, but none of them notice. The hairs on my neck prickle.

Sitting on Mary Beth's shoulder, something not there a moment before, is a grave bird.

A cardinal.

My eyes dart around, searching the dark corners for more movement.

"And for the last twenty-five years," Mary Beth continues, completely unaware of what sits on her shoulder, "tragedy has been turned into something none of us could have imagined was possible."

Mary Beth finds me in the dark of the doorway. Her faux smile drops from her face.

She knows.

Of course she knows. She's the one who told me where the key to Libby's locked drawer was hidden. She even made it possible this morning when she distracted her mother long enough for me to take the rest of those photos from her drawer.

Of course she knows. She witnessed her mother murder a little girl.

"We have a very special family whose sacrifice in the service of God has impacted us all. Eight years they stayed in Paraguay spreading His good word when God called them back to the States for the funeral of my grandparents. You see, this family were the sole heirs to their parents' fortune. A wealth grown for over a hundred years, and it all started with my great-great-grandfather, Saint Constantine Hawthorne. Tonight," she says with inflection, "we honor the missionaries Noah and Libby Hawthorne."

Surprised, the gala guests erupt in applause. Libby postures herself as if pleased, but her eyes dart back and forth from me to Mary Beth.

Then an image of the dead family appears on the screen.

Libby's face ashens.

Cain stiffens in his chair.

And a wry smile tugs at the side of Paloma's mouth.

Paraguay? So that's how Paloma knows them. The pieces of who the Hawthornes truly are and how they fooled everyone start to fall into place.

"Hollis," Mary Beth calls my name, and it causes me to straighten. "Please do us the honor of coming out here and telling us what you've learned about this beautiful family."

She holds out the microphone and projector remote for me to take. Barely a breath of hesitation passes before I'm marching out of the shadows and into the spotlight, more than happy to expose this fraud.

"Thank you, Mary Beth," I say into the microphone.

Libby mumbles, "Don't do this."

"Sit down, Mother." Mary Beth pins a hand on her mother's shoulder, keeping her in her seat.

I try to find the right words as I'm still piecing the whole thing together. It doesn't even feel like my story, but something in the way the grave birds have spoken to me over the past few weeks assures me they've chosen me to tell it.

"I wasn't born yet when the Hawthornes left for their mission trip. Many of you were, though, but I doubt you remember what the family and their two young children looked like before they left. Eight years is a long time to be away. Young children grow and change so fast."

A crow flies in front of the screen and lands on Jeremiah's shoulder. Not any crow but the dead boy's grave bird. Jeremiah doesn't notice. Another rumble shakes the sky as the clouds roll in and eat up the stars.

"I think most of you probably didn't recognize them when they—" I pause as Cain's grave bird flies onto the balcony rail. Then he does a little short hop and flies over to his shoulder. I look at the three grave birds. A cardinal for the real Mary Beth. A crow for the real Jeremiah. A robin for Cain.

Twice now his grave bird showed me he was sick. His family had to go on a vacation without him. But they didn't go on vacation. They came to the States for a funeral—that's the obituary Betsy Kilroy found in the kitchen the day she heard her brother and sister-in-law plan everything.

"Enough of this," Libby hisses, bringing me back to the present. She shrugs Mary Beth's hand off her shoulder.

"But they had a third child." I look to Paloma. She nods, very pleased I've figured this out. "A child no one knew existed because he was born abroad."

A soft smile rests on Cain's face.

"I said stop this." Libby stands. Droplets of rain hit the stage. A ripple of lightning ignites behind the clouds.

"One could never truly fathom what a person would do for wealth—"

"Stop this! Stop this right now!" Libby stomps my way.

"That's why Sarah Hawthorne and her husband Frank Kilroy murdered Noah and Libby's entire family."

The crowd gasps. Jeremiah gets to me faster than Libby and yanks the microphone from my hand.

Cain flies out of his chair, pinning Jeremiah to the wall. A low chatter shuffles among the guests.

Libby picks up the dropped microphone. "This is obviously a cruel, sick joke orchestrated by Hollis Sutherland to humiliate our family." Droplets of rain drizzle faster as she points an angry finger my way.

"It's the truth," Mary Beth shouts.

A pop jumps from the cascading strands of lights. Sparks fly over the audience as a section fizzles out. Guests cry out and scatter.

Libby covers the microphone and turns on her own daughter. "What have you done? You'll ruin this family. We will all go to jail, Mary Beth." The cardinal on Mary Beth's shoulder flaps its wings in irritation.

Mary Beth snatches the microphone from her mother. "My name is not Mary Beth Hawthorne," she shouts to the crowd below. "I am Candace Kilroy, the daughter of Sarah Hawthorne and Frank Kilroy." She turns and points to her mother.

When Libby tries to go after her, Paloma steps in her way.

"I was a child when I watched my mother drown my eleven-year-old cousin." Mary Beth's shoulders slacken, seemingly free of the burden she's carried so long.

Despite the rain there's a large number of guests who watch as the lies of this family unfold.

"I was forced to live a lie for twenty-five years, for fear I'd receive the same fate as my cousin. But tonight, all that ends."

"You ungrateful little bitch!" Libby shoves past Paloma and raises a hand to slap Mary Beth, when the little grave bird cardinal jumps off her shoulder and claws her face.

Libby swats the air at the invisible attack. She wipes a hand over her cheek. Blood trickles from a scratch.

Something darts from the dark across the balcony. The grave bird from the mechanic shop, the mockingbird, gets a lick of his own in. The cardinal attacks her again. Libby swats the air in various directions. Then the crow joins in, pecking her eyes.

Everyone shrinks back in horror as no one understands why Libby is behaving so erratically.

But I can see them.

They have come for her. Seeking justice. Libby swats and twists until she slams into the balcony rail. Her breath catches, blood streaking down her clawed face. Her footing slips, and momentum yanks her back, and she falls over the rail onto the portico stairs below. She lands with a sharp crack of her neck, and a splash of coins dashes out around her.

Noah slumps in his wheelchair, eyes wide open but the life in them gone. The dead mother's mourning dove grave bird—from the true Libby Hawthorne—sits in Noah's lap, soundly sleeping. Until she fades and disappears. This time for good.

CHAPTER
THIRTY-ONE

You never know if people will turn on you. Small-town folks tend to be very set in their opinions. I'm fortunate enough most of the locals saw my side of things and put every ounce of blame on the impostors. With so many witnesses the night of the gala, "Libby" Hawthorne's death was declared a suicide. It solidified her guilt to the majority of people. Gossip of what happened spread through the town like wildfire. What the family did was a betrayal to all Hawthornians. They had donated their hard-earned money to the church for years, believing they were helping spread the word of God, only to find out the money was funding the family's extravagant lifestyle.

Given the extreme level of fraud, the local authorities brought in the FBI to investigate the murders and the IRS to sort out the last twenty-five years of the church's and family's taxes. Until then, the Hawthorne Missionary Baptist Church has been ordered to shut down and all their funds have been seized by the government. Seems as though the mission trips stopped two decades ago. Even their Greater Good housing development looks like a Ponzi scheme, from what Cain and his detective uncovered. They were taking money from new investors to pay old ones, and no one was ever going to see a dime from it.

It's going to take months, if not the better part of a year, for the DNA testing to sort out the truth of who's who. The real Libby, an only child, had distant family in Ohio. They were able to find the grave of her grandfather, Cain Elijah Landry. Though it's doubtful a corpse in the ground that long will have any DNA to spare, they're still going to try.

Authorities plan to exhume Betsy Kilroy's body to determine if Noah was indeed her brother Frank Kilroy. Court orders to dig up the dead take time. They suspect the Hawthornes had a hand in Betsy's death, though; they just haven't figured out which one is guilty.

But I know.

Apparently Betsy had been receiving large lumps of cash from Sarah Hawthorne to keep her mouth shut about who they really were. Those photos Paloma slipped into my box out at the country club made Sarah paranoid. She sent Jeremiah over to *take care of it*. He enjoyed every second of shoving Betsy right off the third floor of the construction site. Watched her fall the entire way down with glee in his eyes and evil in his heart.

I know because her grave bird showed me the second time I visited it.

Betsy's biggest regret: not blackmailing her brother and sister-in-law for *more* money. Some people are just rotten to the core.

I don't know if they will ever prove Jeremiah Hawthorne ran my grandaddy off the road. The fifteen-year-old memory of an eleven-year-old girl who died and was brought back to life isn't enough to build a case, but at least the police promised me they'd look into it.

On a Saturday afternoon, a few weeks after the gala, Cain and I are settled on the back porch with a glass of iced tea when a knock comes at the front door.

It takes Cain by surprise to see Mary Beth standing there. It's a breath or two before either of them speak, both unsure of what to say.

He's been wrestling with his emotions about what he should feel in regards to her. Eventually he's decided—what I think most of us have—that she was a child of horrific circumstance who lived in fear that what was done to her cousin would be done to her.

"How are you, Mary Beth?" Cain's voice, enveloped in kindness, causes Mary Beth's shoulders to soften.

"I go by Candace now."

Candace Kilroy, barely eleven when it all happened, is not suspected of foul play based on her age alone. Police say she's been a critical witness to the whole case. She's the one who led them to the bodies of two children, her cousins—the real Mary Beth and Jeremiah—buried in the woods near Kappy's Campgrounds. Only bones were left, but they match the age of the two children.

Cain asked his lawyer to find out from the police as much as he could. Candace had been asleep in her parents' car; they told her they were driving to Disney World and when she woke in the morning they'd be there. All she had to do was drink a little cough syrup to help her sleep. But she woke to screams. To flames eating away at the woods. Alone in the car in a place she didn't know, she went looking for parents and found murder.

Cain's mother and father have not been found and might not ever be. Libby and Noah, or rather Sarah and Frank, are both dead, and they might be the only ones who know where the parents were buried. Jeremiah is refusing to cooperate . . . or go by his true birth name, Jason Kilroy, the fourteen-year-old son of Sarah and Frank Kilroy—who burned his younger cousin alive, from what the grave bird showed me. I just hope he doesn't get the same benefit of the doubt on his age back then as Mary Beth has.

"I thought you should have this." Candace reaches into her purse and pulls out a child's charm bracelet. It's the one I saw in the desk drawer the day I found the pictures.

Cain accepts it from her. The gold chain, double looped with an assortment of dangling charms, a mix of gold and silver. His thumb brushes over a little glass cardinal charm, no bigger than my pinkie nail.

"I found it on the dock. I believe it was Mary Beth's." Candace chokes on her words. "I kept it for a long time to remind myself it wasn't a bad dream. That what happened to her was real. I felt it was my duty to remember her. It was the least I could do." She wipes away a loose tear. "Anyway, at some point it went missing from the shoebox I kept hidden in my closet. For years I assumed I had misplaced it. Until we were going through Mother's things. I'm sorry." Her voice breaks. "I'm sorry I never told someone. I'm sorry I lived their lie for so many years. I'm sorry. I'm sorry. I'm sorry." She looks up to Cain, and tears sliver down her cheeks.

Cain's shoulders shudder as he listens to her. I choose to step away to give them the time they need to heal. To grieve. To forgive.

CHAPTER THIRTY-TWO

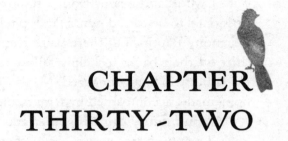

Down by the river, where the wild grass grows and the cool blue water ripples, lies a memorial stone for my grandfather. I stand next to it with my granny, my brothers, and even my mother—who I choose not to be angry with today. There are a little more than a handful of grandaddy's friends who are still alive and have gathered with us.

We listen to Brother Ralph, the preacher who eventually took over Grandaddy's church, talk about how "Waylon Josiah Wade was a fearsome man of God."

He tells us the story of how there were only twenty people who gathered every Sunday to hear my grandaddy preach at the old five-and-dime that had closed down. It was their makeshift church until one could be built. They showed up with their lawn chairs when they didn't have pews. Raggedy Bibles that reached back generations.

"They had Jesus in their hearts and hope for something more for their small church. And God delivered."

Grandaddy and his twenty parishioners built their church

out of wood and beams from a hundred-year-old barn commissioned to be torn down. Hands pitched in that didn't attend Harmony Baptist, but there were plenty who would take the shirt off their backs to help a fellow neighbor. Lemonade by the ladies was hand-squeezed. Meals to feed the workers were homemade, accompanied by fritters and pies.

"A community came together and built something out of love. They used this very river to carry the wood a half mile down where they built it. What a lot of you may already know, but I'm going to tell you again," Brother Ralph continues, "is that I was baptized by Waylon in this river over thirty years ago."

So was my mother. My brothers.

So was I.

"What you might not know is some sixty years back, Waylon was baptized in this very river by his father. You see, the good Lord found it fitting that if he was going to call Waylon Wade home, he would leave this world from the very place he started his journey with God. God was right here that day. Ready to take Waylon on his second journey, where he now resides as a guardian angel. Watching over me. Over you. And over his beautiful family." Brother Ralph looks directly at me.

Granny squeezes my hand.

There are scars you carry around so long you assume they can never heal. Parts of your life permanently missing. The thought of having a wedding some day and the two most important men in my life, my grandfather and Uncle Royce, won't be there in body hurts—bone-deep if you let yourself dwell on it too long.

But they'll be there in spirit. They're always with me.

Sometimes it's just a feeling I get. Their presence simply known, not seen.

Other times it's a little bluebird, full of color and life, that lands on the sidewalk right in front of me, before fluttering off into the trees.

Until a few days after the memorial when another bluebird lands on Granny's porch railing as I go to visit her. Another, a few weeks later, sits on the rosebushes outside my greenhouse. Then days pass before I see another on the dogwood tree outside the bank when I go to sign my new loan in January.

One even perches on the branch right now outside Nadine and Jackson's new nursery.

"You look like you're going to pop, Nadine." Calista sits cross-legged on the carpet with a glass of wine in one hand and the directions to the crib in the other, frowning at Nadine's protruding belly.

Me, I'm stuck with the parts and tools and no clue what the hell I'm doing.

"Isn't this the men's job?" I ask, embracing a slightly sexist notion to get me out of manual labor.

Nadine stretches her back. "No. I thought it would be a good bonding moment for us girls. And, Calista, you hush. I still have three months to go, and I don't need you reminding me of the bikini I might never fit into again. You'll understand someday when you're pregnant."

"Nope." Calista shakes her head. "Not for me."

"Where does this go?" Jackson and Cain carry in an adorable—giant—stuffed elephant made into a rocking horse.

"Over there." Nadine points to a spot near the window.

That's how it goes for the rest of our Friday night. More talk of babies. The men trying to supervise as we put the crib together. Jackson orders pizza from Zamillio's. Cain brings over the good wine, as he calls it. We laugh. We hug.

We never talk about the night of the gala, or the Hawthornes, ever again.

CHARLESTON IS THREE hours away, but I'm buzzing with energy. Sitting in the passenger seat, I glance down at the news article. I

wasn't sure if it was her when I first saw the wedding announce-
ment in *The Post and Courier* newspaper. After Uncle Royce
died, I never canceled the subscription. He was old-school and
believed news should be consumed in pages, not on screens.
Taking up the habit of reading it felt like I was holding on to a
piece of him. I like to read the events section first. That's where
I found her.

Charlotte . . . or rather her daughter who's a spitting image
of her mother.

It's about dusk as I drive through the streets of a modest sub-
urb, something a newlywed couple could afford.

Alongside my car flies a fat grayish-brown wren. Thin, transparent wisp of a bird.

Grady Owens's grave bird.

It lands in the tree of a small brick home with a well-kept
lawn. It took a long time for me get here, but I've finally found
a way to give Grady Owens peace.

I give it a slight nod before I get out of the car. It disappears
on the branch right in front of me.

A soft knock on the door, and a beautiful young woman
answers.

"Hi. Are you the daughter of the late Charlotte Austin?" I ask.

She watches me with a wary look then answers. "Yes. Can
I help you?"

I can't be certain if she knows Grady is her real father. Or if
the man Charlotte married raised her as his own. Either way,
she should know the truth.

"Could I come in, for a minute? I knew your real father,
Grady Owens."

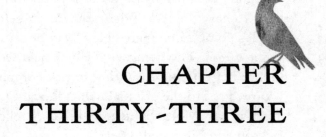

CHAPTER
THIRTY-THREE

IT ISN'T UNTIL early summer when the first phase of construction is done on the Royal Oaks Estates, formally the Serendipity Country Club. It sat half-burned well into last October. The members of the club were all part owners, mostly older couples who weren't very active in the last few years anyway. The idea of remodeling after the fire twisters was more adventuresome than they were willing to take on. It eventually went up for sale, and after two months and no takers, they dropped the price.

That's when I made my offer.

It was a pinch more than I was able to pay, and there's going to be a lot of work that needs to be done. But I found two investors who believe in me.

"Oh my word." Nadine's voice echoes in the empty ballroom. "These wood floors are gorgeous! Is that what was hiding under all the horrid carpet?"

"Yep. But there's so much furniture it needs still. I'll have to open up in phases. West portico with the dining and bar first.

And the grand ballroom in the south before Christmas. And I hope to have the rest of the venue ready before next spring."

"It's going to be incredible," Nadine says, arching her back so she can sit. The twins will be here next week, since they will induce her early, not wanting to risk complications. "I'm glad you reverted to the original name, Royal Oaks Estates. I like it much better. More sophisticated than Serendipity. It looks like Jackson and I invested wisely."

"I can't thank y'all enough." My phone dings with a text. "If it wasn't for you and Cain, Sutherland & Co. event planning would have died last fall. Oh," I say after reading the text. "Cain's here to pick me up. I've gotta go. Are you good here?"

Nadine glances out the large wall of windows, off toward the golf course where Jackson is practicing his swing. "Yes. I'll give him a few more minutes before I make him take me to get barbecue. It's all I crave anymore. I've eaten more pulled pork in the last nine months than I have in my entire life."

I laugh. "You're going to give yourself indigestion again," I say as I hug her goodbye.

She fans a *whatever* hand at me. "The craving is stronger than the consequence."

Out front of the Royal Oaks, Cain waits for me.

"You ready?" Cain asks as he opens the passenger door. The light blue button-up cuffed at his sleeves changes those steel-gray eyes of his to a cool-water blue. Those tan linen pants make him look like he was born to be a Carolina man.

"Ready as I'll ever be." I suppose. Inside my purse is all I need, the two strands of ribbon and the little velvet pouch I grabbed from my jewelry box.

The drive to Meadow Street isn't far, just on the other side of town. We park at the end of the cul-de-sac, next to the giant oak tree Spencer and I kissed behind. Over the years the houses have changed. The adjacent woods have grown and thickened. I don't know exactly where it is, so we head in a vague direction until a hushed whisper hums in my heart. Not anything I can hear with my ears, but something I pick up with my extra senses after dying.

This way, they whisper.

The twinkling sound of an out-of-tune wind chime is what guides me the last of the way there.

The Mourning Tree.

Grave birds litter the ground. Tucked between the branches and the leaves, a baby spoon clanks against an old Coke bottle, a faded rag doll swings next to an antique teacup like she's had more than tea to drink.

There's a reverence that comes with standing in front of the massive oak tree. Words have no place here. Simply silence as you allow your grief to leave your body. It slips into the soil, down deep in the tree's roots. Clumps of Spanish moss weep from the branches.

I hand Cain one of the ribbons. He ties it to his cardinal puzzle piece.

And I the peacock haircomb, the one that's haunted me for sixteen years. I give my guilt back to the universe where it dissipates into nothing.

Healing work, my granny would call it.

By the time we get home, the sun's gone to sleep for the day and the night begins to wake, and Cain walks me back to my greenhouse. High in the moss-covered oaks the cicadas whir their hypnotic buzz. The midnight-blue sky crusted with twinkling stars whispers granted wishes for all of those who ask. It's been almost a year since I walked across this path and my world turned upside down. But here I am, better off than I was then and feeling so blessed for the changes in my life.

"You think Paloma will stay in California?" I ask.

Paloma helped the authorities a ton with her testimony about Cain's parents. They found his birth certificate in Paraguay, listing Noah and Libby as his parents. It's a step to help verify his identity. She stayed through the spring so they could bury Cain's brother and sister after the police released the bodies from evidence. They chose a small plot out at my grandfather's country church cemetery.

"I don't know." Cain takes my hand. "Depends on when I have children."

I glance up at him. "Planning on having them soon?"

"Maybe." He glances up at the house. "It's so sad and lonely living in this huge house all by my lonesome." He tries his best to look forlorn.

"Oh, don't start this again. I'm very happy in my greenhouse."

"Are you? Because you've taken over half my closet already."

"It's a big closet."

"You sleep at the house five nights out of the week."

"I'd miss Sampson too much."

"We eat dinner together every night."

"That's because you have the good wine."

It's almost a year since he moved here. From our rocky start I never would have guessed I'd fall in love with the devil. But here I am, head over heels, and I couldn't be happier.

"I'll think about it."

He grabs my hands, tugging them behind his back to draw me in closer.

"Think faster." Cain leans down to kiss me.

"Pretty bird!" Louisa squawks as she sees us outside the window. "Hot damn. Hello. Pretty bird!" She bobs up and down, dancing across her perch. And she'll keep doing it until he goes over and gives her kisses. "How's my favorite girl?" he says to Louisa once inside, cooing over her cage.

I roll my eyes. "You should move your *other* girlfriend in with you."

"Or how about I move in here?" Cain presses his mouth to mine, backing me toward the bed.

"I prefer your king-size bed," I say between kisses.

"I'll take any bed with you in it," he says across my mouth, tugging at the bottom of my shirt then peeling it off.

This is how I want our nights to always be. Happy. In love. The infinite oneness I felt in the afterlife for those thirty-two minutes is impossible to feel back among the living.

But this with Cain is damn close.

ACKNOWLEDGMENTS

To MY KICK-ASS AGENT, Jill Marr, you freaking rock! You did it again, and we sold another book!!! You are hands down the best partner to work with. Your confidence amazes and reassures me. You always have my back first and foremost. Your insights on the industry and trends are spot-on. I'm just so grateful you chose me as your client. Big thank you!

To Meredith Clark, the murderer of my little darlings, thank you for killing all those unnecessary words. Your editorial magic makes me look talented and smart. And even though you cut most of the "sexy time" in this book, I wouldn't want to work with any other editor but you.

To the MIRA art department, who probably thinks I'm the biggest pain in the ass, thank you so much for putting up with my nitpicky notes and then taking my suggestions and exceeding my expectations. I am truly grateful for your design insight and talent. Thank you for your dedication in championing my book for the highest success. And thank you for another gorgeous cover.

To MIRA, I am so grateful you took a chance on me again. I promise to always deliver, and I cannot wait to work on many more books with you.

To Vanessa Wells, if we had a nickel for every *further* that should have been a *farther*, then we'd have a lot of damn nickels. Thank you for keeping me from looking dumb.

To all those readers who loved and reviewed *In the Hour of Crows*, I am so grateful for your love of my words and your support. You are truly the champions of books. Thank you. Thank you. Thank you. I hope you love *Grave Birds* just as much. Extra thanks to my Street Team: Little May Books, Lindsey the Librarian, Stress Reader, Lexinator Reads, and BecReadz. Your enthusiasm is simply the best.

To Chris, thank you for putting up with the emotional roller coaster as I drafted this book. I know I'm not the easiest to live with when I'm writing, but I appreciate all your support and patience.

To Luke, Reed, and Jackson . . . my boys, my everything . . . it would really be nice if you actually read one of my books someday. Until then, you will NEVER get a single recipe of mine. Never! I will die and take them to my grave. Love you all so very much! XO, Mom.

To Hollis Peterson, for having a cool-ass Southern name and letting me borrow it.

To Ara Hale, thank you for being an awesome friend. You have always been such a huge supporter of my writing. Thank you for accepting the challenge of reading my book in three days and giving me great advice for what to fix. Phew! We did it! You were a big part of helping this book get across the finish line.

To Valerie Cole, my book-nerd bestie, there's not a bookstore in the world I wouldn't want to visit with you. You have always been the best cheerleader of my stories. I am so grateful for your loyalty as a friend. You're the best little sister a woman could have, and I'd go momma bear for you anytime. And jars of human teeth *are* pretty cool, right?

To Tracy Murphy, you are my emotional rock. Thank you for loving me so much and giving me all your sage advice. I am so lucky to call you my friend. You are an amazing woman and mother, and I admire you so much. Love you.

To my Daddy, I'll always sit on the porch with you. My love for nature was fostered from you. Thank you for being the best daddy a girl could have. P.S. I know I'm your favorite, but I won't tell Vince.

To Miss Vickie Kerr Garrett, thank you for giving me a safe and loving home in high school. You are the mother I wish I always had. I hope I make you proud.

To Katie and Stephanie Lewis, I am so grateful for your friendship. Every time I share any book news, you guys are always my number one supporters. Stephanie, you are a sister to me, and I would never have survived high school without your friendship. I love you, girl.

To my Cruise Boat Bitches: Jackie, Cat, Belinda, and Emily . . . There is no sea I wouldn't sail with you ladies. I love you, you badass beautiful bitches. Pirate eye for life!

To Evelyn Skye, there is no way I could navigate this life without your love and support. Your positivity and light is a beacon for me and a reminder of all that is beautiful in this world. I am ever grateful for your love and friendship. Here's to many, many more writing retreats.

To Kellie Elmendorf, from the bottom of my heart, thank you so much for reading those raw first-draft pages. For sitting down with me for hours just so I could talk the story out to you. For giving me the most amazing advice for how to fix the broken parts. And for seeing and loving the story despite its flaws. You were there for me at a chaotic and critical time, and I am ever grateful for all you did to help me finish this manuscript and turn it in on time.